P9-BYS-489

THE WICKED
DUKE

MADELINE HUNTER

JOVE BOOKS, NEW YORK

JOVE

An imprint of Penguin Random House LLC
375 Hudson Street, New York, New York 10014

THE WICKED DUKE

A Jove Book / published by arrangement with the author

ISBN: 9780515155181

PUBLISHING HISTORY
Jove mass-market edition / June 2016

PRINTED IN THE UNITED STATES OF AMERICA

10 9 8 7 6 5 4 3 2 1

Cover photography by Claudio Marinesco.
Cover design by Rita Frangie.
Text design by Kelly Lipovich.
Cover photo: HEVER CASTLE AND GARDENS © IR Stone/Shutterstock.

Penguin
Random
House

THE WICKED
DUKE

CHAPTER 1

The whole world rocked. That was the first thought Lance had while wakefulness slowly came to him— that the whole damned planet bounced through the universe. The violent movement gave him a head fit to burst. Holding on created an exhaustion so deep he yearned to return to blissful oblivion. Only he could not, because of that damned movement.

A bit more consciousness emerged. It was not the whole world. Only his bed. In the next second, an awareness of pleasure slammed into him. *What the hell—?*

He forced one eye open. Skin. Breasts. Plump thighs. Long tendrils of blond hair.

A woman sat astride his hips. She had made use of his morning erection. Since he had neither initiated this, nor agreed to it, it was the closest thing to a woman forcing her pleasure on him he had ever experienced.

Who the hell was she? He closed his eyes, and enjoyed the ride, as it were. His pained, befogged brain tried to remember where he was and how he had gotten here. The last thing he remembered with clarity was tearing off from Merrywood Manor on his horse two days after Christmas, as soon as he sent his brothers and their wives back to London. Something in him had snapped as those carriages rolled away, and he had ridden hard for miles, full of anger at his impossible situation, until near night he entered a town right across the border to Herefordshire.

The woman groaned. She bounced harder. If he'd had the strength to take over, he would, so maybe his head would not thud like this. He might even stop her, because this did not feel nearly as good as it should.

She must have noticed him stirring. She bent forward, even as she continued her thumps against his hips. She kissed him. She tasted of beer.

She straightened again. *Beer.* Now he knew who she was. There had been a tavern, and a young woman delivering beer. He had flirted, because, aside from lots of drinking, that was what he was there for.

She finished with a loud groan. His own climax was more of a whimper.

She did not move. She giggled, and bent to kiss his chest while she caressed it. "Poor thing. All these bruises. Fought like a tiger, you did. Three against one ain't fair, but you held your own, didn't you?"

Each kiss sent a little jab into his head. Bruises. No wonder he felt thrashed. Only he could not remember a single moment of it. All the same his pride stupidly glowed at hearing he had held his own.

Her mouth pressed his lower chest. Then another pressure came, on a spot on his shoulder. His mind pondered that. It felt as though—

"For a man who took all those blows, he did not disappoint." The voice that spoke those words sounded deeper than the blonde. Older.

One half of his brain snapped alert. It painfully sorted through the last five minutes. He opened his eyes to see just what was what. The blonde smiled up at him from where her chin rested on his torso. Another smile beamed at him from his shoulder.

There were two of them.

He took in his surroundings. The walls showed the half-timbering and rough plaster common to ancient inns. The bed would barely fit two, let alone three. Yet here they all were.

He paid attention to his body. Oh, yes, lots of blows. That was clear now. He stretched his right hand. The knuckles did not want to straighten completely. Damnation, it must have been one hell of a fight.

The blonde reached down and caressed him. She grinned. "I think, if I am not mistaken, that you are ready again." She began that lowering descent of kisses.

"No." His voice sounded strangled. His face hurt. He raised his hand and felt it, gingerly. The aches said that but for his beard, he probably looked half dead.

"No?" the older voice asked, teasing. "Such a gentleman he is, Joan. Not that you'd have known it two hours ago. I've not seen the likes of it, Jamie."

Jamie? He had used a fictitious name. Shrewd. It would not do for the Duke of Aylesbury to be here, with two women. Not when he was supposed to be living the most boring, tedious, and disheartening life imagined, to prove how very good he could be. If on occasion he went up to London or rode to Herefordshire to pretend for a few hours, or a few days, that his life had not become so insufferable, he could be excused.

He sat, which meant both women had to move. He gestured for the blonde to get out of the way, so he could swing his legs off the side of the bed. He reached for his clothes.

"Ladies, I need to leave. I thank you for your company."

Peals of laughter greeted that. "Oh, no, sir we thank *you*," the older woman said. "Pity no one will believe us when we tell about it."

"Such a gentleman he is too. Did you hear that? *Ladies, I thank you for your company.*" The blonde sighed. "You must promise to come back."

He might, if he had any idea where he was. Since he didn't, he just smiled. Which hurt his face. "How much do I owe you?"

The older woman tucked her head against his neck while she pressed against his back with her breasts. "You already paid all you owe. We did not mind all those extras. Did we, Joan?"

"Not at all. It was a magnificent night."

It was deucedly annoying to be the only one who did not know what the hell they referred to. When a man was magnificent, he wanted to savor the memory, damn it.

He began pulling on his clothes. Still they did not leave. He ignored them, and the bruises, and his cramped hand, and the way the top of his head carried a leaden weight.

Finally dressed, he bowed and left them giggling. He found his way down some stairs and into a blinding December sun and abrasively crisp cold air. Both made him groan.

From all evidence, he had enjoyed quite a night. A good fight, a good drunken party, and a good rut—that was just what he wanted when he went looking for trouble. Normally a night like this could sustain him for a month or so.

It irritated the hell out of him that he could not remember any of it. Not a single thing.

CHAPTER 2

The flower had noticed him.

That was what Lance first thought he saw through the branches—a flower abloom in the graveyard despite the January cold. Impossible of course, unless someone bought a bouquet from a hothouse to lay on Percy's grave. He could not imagine anyone doing that. It would be a very belated sentiment after nine months, squandered on a man who left no positive legacy.

It was not a flower, but a vision just as pretty, as it turned out. A woman had ridden here, on a horse the same dappled gray as the barren branches. The horse ate grass near the low wall surrounding the graveyard. She must have used the wall to dismount. Now she examined Percy's grave without emotion. She might be viewing a new painting.

The deep rose hue of her riding habit contrasted starkly with the dull trees. Even the steel-toned stones of the chapel appeared designed to make her more obvious. Her copper hair, shot through with gold, drew attention to her deep blue eyes.

It had been some time since he had enjoyed the sight of a lovely female at Merrywood Manor who was not a relative. His blood stirred. He might be one of these old oaks, and spring had arrived.

She had noticed him now, and to lurk in the woods would make him a fool. He stepped forward, to the edge of the clearing.

She arched one eyebrow. Whatever she saw in him did not impress her much. He could see the conclusions she drew about the musket and hares that he carried. He stepped over the wall, then set the gun and the day's kill down on the ground.

"Are you paying your respects?" he asked as he walked closer to her. He thought her upturned little nose and wide mouth very attractive. Of course, in his current state of isolation, he would probably find any young woman appealing. Abstinence did that to a man. Right now it had him thinking he preferred little upturned noses to all other kinds.

"I personally did not know any of them." She pointed to the monstrous pyramid. "He must have been much admired, to have such a sepulcher built for him."

"He built it himself. Or at least began it, then left funds for its quick completion should he die early."

"You mean like the pharaohs of ancient Egypt. It is

said those pyramids were started as soon as a man became king, because each one dared not trust his successor to see it done for him."

An educated flower, it appeared. She had the kind of face that would appear fresh, friendly, and girlish even when she grew old. Bright doe eyes, full cheeks, dimples . . .

"Are you a visitor to the manor?" He knew she was not, but he wanted the conversation to continue.

She shook her head.

"Are you lost?"

"No. I was just curious. I suppose I am trespassing." She gave him a sly smile. "Like you?"

It was an excellent opportunity to explain who he was. Only if he did, she would most likely flee. His reputation had never been the kind to encourage nice young ladies to dally, and this past year even grown men treated him with caution. The Wicked Duke, he had come to be called, his valet had mournfully told him. So much for almost a year of living like a monkish country squire, concerned only with the welfare of his neighbors.

That had been his brother Ives's idea—that correct and moral living would lead people to think the best of him. Ives tended to be too optimistic about his fellow man.

"I am not trespassing. I am allowed to be here," he said. "It is required of my situation. I am not a poacher, if that is what you assumed."

"Oh." Her color rose. She glanced to the musket and hares. "Of course. Why have hunting lands if no one hunts?

No doubt a duke has many huntsmen. The wonder is that I did not see one today before this."

"I am such a sure shot that Aylesbury does not need an army to fill his kitchen and the winter pots of his tenants."

He ambled closer, watching her much as he watched his prey when he hunted, looking for signs she would bolt. He hoped not. This simple exchange had him enjoying himself more than he had in weeks. Months. The sap had begun to flow strongly now. Given half a chance and the slightest encouragement, he might pluck a pretty flower today. Sniff his fill of its nectar's scent. Nibble and lick the velvet surfaces of its petals—

He put such considerations out of his mind. He was not really a wicked duke. Well, not with the daughters of county neighbors. Not normally, at least.

Only he could not remember seeing her about in the county in the past. "Do you live on one of the neighboring properties?"

She thought before answering, which he found peculiar. "Yes and no," she said.

Even more peculiar.

"I am visiting a relative," she explained. "He has offered that I live in his home. I am dependent on him, but I am not sure I like the idea of being that dependent."

"He sounds to be a generous man. Perhaps you would do well to allow him to help you even more than he has."

"It does sound generous, doesn't it? Since he is not by nature that kind of man, I am suspicious." She blushed, and made a little waving motion with her hand. "I am sure all will be well." She turned her attention once more to the monstrous sepulcher. "Do not tell the family any-one said so, but it is not well carved, perhaps due to its haste in construction. The figure of this man here is un-natural in appearance, and almost deformed in the way he is twisted."

As was the character of the person whose body lay beneath the pile. "That is the thing about grave markers—it is considered rude to take them down later. It will remain as you see it for generations, I expect."

"Maybe the new duke will grow some ivy over it."

She paced between the other markers. He trailed along, far enough not to alarm her, but close enough to catch the scent of rose water. She even smelled like a flower. He won-dered if it were warmer inside the little chapel, and tried to remember if there were any cushions that might make a rough bed.

Not that he was so wicked as to seduce an impover-ished young woman related to one of his neighbors. And if he were that wicked, which half of him contemplated being and the whole of him badly wanted to be, he would never do it in a chapel on a cold stone floor. Even driven mad by isolation and boredom, he had some standards.

The tree canopy broke above the center of the grave-yard. She stepped into a pool of sunlight that formed beneath it. The golds in her hair shined brightly and her eyes took on the color of violets. He pictured her hair unbound, falling freely around her shoulders, mussed from a night in bed.

She peered down at his father's marker, as plain in design as his brother's was bold. "I used to live in this area," she said. "Years ago. I remember this duke. He was known as a good man."

"He was one." A good man, but not perfect. Still, not bad. Not twisted and not wicked. "When did you live here?" No images came to his head of a girl who looked like her, but she could not be more than twenty-two or so. If by years ago she meant even five years, he would have paid no mind to the girl she had been when she last inhabited his world.

"It has been a long time. Still, I know some people."

"Then you will not feel uncomfortable if you attend county assemblies. There should be one at the next full moon."

For some reason that brought her full attention on him. She examined him suspiciously. Her gaze spent a good amount of time on his garments.

Her nose rose. Her lids lowered. Her back stiffened. "I think you have been misleading me, sir. You are no huntsman."

"I never said I was a huntsman." The man offered a slow smile while he said it.

"You allowed me to believe it."

"I allowed you to conclude I was not a poacher, which I am not. We never talked about my specific situation here. I am curious, however. What gave me away?"

"Your coat and your boots. In the shade their quality

was not apparent. But here, in the sun, with you—" *With you so close.* She almost said it. He *was* close. Somehow, as they chatted, he had sidled nearer. So she could see the fine wool of his coats, and the superior craftsmanship of his boots. The hat, with its low, flat crown, still had little to recommend it, and his beard indicated he bowed to no fashion, but he was higher than a huntsman in the duke's entourage of servants.

"Then there was your mention of assemblies. I doubt a huntsman attends them, or thinks of them so readily. Your speech is educated too." She listed the evidence, some of which she only now gathered as she surveyed him. "I think I know who you are."

A twinkle of humor entered his eyes. They were dark and intense but not threatening or unkind—at least she did not think so, even if his proximity caused her some discomfort. She did not experience fear as such, but a jumpy nervousness, as if this ride might turn out unlike what she expected on setting off, and this man was the reason.

He was a stranger, after all. Nice coats notwithstanding, she had been too quick to enter into conversation with him.

"Who do you think I am?" he asked.

"The steward."

"The steward." He laughed quietly. "First a poacher, then a huntsman, now a steward. I am rising quickly in your esteem. If we dally another ten minutes, you will proclaim me the duke."

She burst out laughing, and he joined in.

"Do I look like a steward?"

"Not at all. Hence my mistake. I think your master is in London raising the hell he has long been reputed for enjoying, and without him here, you enjoy a more rustic practice in your grooming."

He felt his face. "You mean the beard?"

"I do."

"You do not care for it?"

"I do not, but my opinion does not signify. I assume you shave immediately when the duke comes down from town."

"If I shave it on my own, will you dance with me at the next assembly?"

His tone of voice possessed a flirtatious softness, but that was not what dazed her. Something to it that she could not name—a very masculine current—took her aback.

"Do not shave on my account, sir."

"Are you saying you will not dance with me under any circumstance, or you will even if I do not shave?"

"I—uh—if we are properly introduced, I may— That is—" She stammered like an idiot. It seemed he had come closer yet, except he had not moved.

She glanced around. Here she stood in a graveyard, talking to a stranger who in the last moment had revealed himself to be a formidable presence. It was as if he exercised a power that urged her toward more familiarity, and more physical closeness. He might have removed a cloak under which he hid his true self, and revealed the ability to mesmerize like a magician.

She was not immune to the spell he cast her way. She found herself hoping he *did* ask her to dance at the next assembly. At the same time, she could not ignore a sense of impending danger. This coincidental meeting had become too familiar, in spirit if not in words.

Gathering up her skirt, she turned to her horse. "I must go."

He bent and picked up the long train that made a riding habit inconvenient for anything except riding. "I will help you onto the horse."

"The wall will do. It is how I dismounted, right there where that tree stump rises halfway up the wall. I am very agile, and Calliope is very well trained."

"If the horse moves, you will hurt yourself. Also, you will appear very clumsy clamoring up first onto the stump, then the wall, then the horse."

"No one sees me to care if I appear clumsy."

"I will see it today. If you were not so pretty, I would stand back and enjoy the theater. However, I prefer to help you mount with some grace."

She could think of no way to dissuade him. She certainly should not allow him to do anything more than hand her up the tree stump onto the wall and hold her horse, however.

She explained all of that once they arrived at Calliope. He looked down at her as if she had just spoken in Chinese. Her heart beat hard.

He draped her train over her arm. "Are you ready?" His voice teased, as if they were about to do something audacious.

He stepped very close. She smelled leather and something spicy. His hands firmly closed on her waist. Her feet left the ground.

He did not hoist her up in one quick swing. Rather, he lifted her as if she weighed nothing, slowly. So slowly that for a long spell her face remained near his and he looked deeply into her eyes. So slowly that her body felt the warmth of his. Her breath left her.

Then she was sitting on Calliope, embarrassed and awed.

He looked up. "Did you think I was going to kiss you?"

"Of course not. What nonsense. You don't even know my name."

"If you think a man needs to know a woman's name before he kisses her, you are very innocent. Too innocent to talk to strangers in the woods." He handed her the reins and managed to cover her hands with his as he did so. Warm hands. Strong and surprisingly soft. "I will make sure we are properly introduced very soon, since it matters to you."

He walked away, picked up his musket and hares, and disappeared into the woods.

She wished she had left first, with a kick to Calliope and an arch retort. Instead she had gawked at him like a girl with whom no man had ever flirted before.

Which was almost true.

CHAPTER 3

"The trunks have arrived," Marianne's mother said, as soon as Marianne arrived on the third level of Trenfield Park.

She, her mother, and her cousin Nora had taken a coach here from Calne, but the trunks came by wagon. They contained all of their worldly belongings, other than what they packed to bring with them.

"Were you riding?" her mother asked, noticing her habit. "Sir Horace said he wanted you to accompany him. He made that clear at dinner last night."

"I can ride on my own too. I hope you do not think I need his permission or his company. That would be comical for a woman my age."

She experienced contrasting emotions while she watched her trunks being carried into her bedchamber.

The move back to Gloucestershire meant a return to her girlhood home. So why did she not experience more joy?

Perhaps because she was no longer a girl. Maybe because it did not appear her change in circumstances heralded any forward steps, but only those of retreat. It would disrupt her secret employment, for one thing. She was not sure she would be able to transfer that occupation to a new locale, and she had enjoyed making a few shillings that were just hers.

Her mother followed the servants in, then shooed them out after they set the trunks down.

"Finally, after five years of impoverishment, we are back where we belong." Mama's voice announced the victory, but so did her person. She wore one of her best dresses. A small lace cap perched atop dark curls dressed in high style, as befitted the chatelaine of a big country home.

"We were not impoverished. Nor is this our home again," Marianne reminded her. "We are here as Uncle Horace's guests and dependents."

"Better here than in that hovel of a cottage in Cherhill. And it is only his home because of an accident of fate."

Marianne did not think the death of her brother Thomas seven years ago had been an accident of fate, but rather a tragedy. Even this small reference opened a nostalgic place in her heart. She still missed him, and not because it meant Sir Horace had inherited upon Papa's death.

Mama aimed a critical eye at the chamber's furnishings. "I will tell Sir Horace that you must have new drapes. We both must. And dresses. You can hardly attend assemblies and dinner parties with what is in those trunks. It is all out of fashion now." She gave one trunk a little kick with her toe. "Bad enough you rode out in that habit. It barely fits you anymore. I hope no one saw you."

Only the steward of Merrywood Manor, a man with dark eyes and magnetic aura. "No one who matters." With her newly reclaimed position, Mama would probably think a steward beneath them, even if he were educated and responsible for an entire estate.

Marianne often disagreed with her mother. She definitely did about the last five years of their lives. She had liked the pretty cottage in Cherhill where they lived during that time. She loved the rolling hills, and would miss seeing the big, white chalk horse on the downs every morning from their kitchen window.

No one interfered with them there. Uncle Horace left them alone. Even after he sent Nora to live with them three years ago, he rarely inquired after them. When, during his surprise visit before Christmas, he explained that he expected their return in the new year, Marianne had greeted the command with dismay.

He only accepted hers and Mama's presence so they could continue seeing to Nora's care. They would now be beholden to him in new ways, however. He would probably issue demands the way men tended to do. He might grow curious about Marianne's activities or friends, and lay down rules she did not think she should have to obey. He might even create problems with Nora, if he did not defer to Marianne's experience in handling his daughter.

Nora. "I must go see how my cousin is faring before

I unpack. This has been a very large change for her, and she was quite agitated in the coach yesterday."

Mama did not appear to hear her. She looked out one of the windows. "He has let the garden go. I will have to rectify that, along with many other things. Well, what can you expect of a man in a house with no woman to keep things sorted properly? Your father would have done no better had he not married me. Yes, it is a very good thing that I am back."

"We can tour the garden, and you can explain your plans, after I visit Nora."

Mama heard this time. "Oh, Nora— Sir Horace is up there with her now."

"He promised not to do that without me. Just last night we agreed—"

"He came looking for you, and even waited, but finally went above. He had dressmakers with him, and they can hardly sit here all day until you return from a ride no one knew you were taking."

Marianne was out the door before her mother finished. She gathered the stupid train of her habit and went up the stairs as quickly as she could. As she neared her cousin's chambers, she heard an argument.

Uncle Horace's voice rose and fell. Nora's cries contained the frantic notes that Marianne knew too well. Her cousin's episodes of frenzied high emotion had become infrequent while she lived in Cherhill. Normally Nora retreated into a quiet, almost lifeless passivity, which Marianne found equally troubling, if less disruptive.

Now, the second time in two days, Nora sounded like a

madwoman. "I won't," she screamed. "Tell them to go away. I will not stand for it, or for them. I do not need new dresses, since I will not be going out." The sound of china crashing to pieces punctuated her rant.

"Damnation!" Horace roared. "Hear me, daughter, you will indeed have a new wardrobe, and you will be going out, and you will comport yourself as I say. I have plans for you, and will no longer indulge you." Horace's fury made every third word ring loud and high, as if he intoned from a stage.

Marianne pushed open the door to her cousin's chambers.

Her uncle swung around. "Thank God. Where in hell were you?"

Nora ran to her. Marianne embraced her and spoke soothing words while she petted her head. She noted the remnants of a blue and white hair gatherer on the floor. She looked over Nora's shoulder at the two cowering dressmakers. "Send them away, Uncle."

Horace raked his gray hair back with his bony fingers. He was a tall man, with vivid blue eyes and sunken cheeks in his gaunt, long face. Marianne always thought Horace looked similar to her own father during her father's last year, when he was dying.

"I'll not have you indulging her either. There has been too much of that. It is time for her to take her place in the world."

Nora cringed closer. Marianne stared at her uncle. "Send them away, and take yourself elsewhere too," she repeated firmly. "She will not calm until you do."

He cursed, but he shooed the women out, and made to follow. "Get her sane, then come and see me in the library," he barked.

Once they were alone, Nora's frenzy quickly died into little more than heavy breaths. Marianne continued holding her. She took in the chamber, and her anger spiked.

Uncle Horace had put his daughter in a small, obscure spot, one that visitors would never see if Nora continued to be a problem. It held a small bed and table, and had no dressing room. An open trunk stood near a wardrobe, the servant's unpacking left unfinished when Horace invaded.

Nora extricated herself. Calm now, eerily so, she sat by the one small window, on a wooden chair of little comfort. Pale of face and hair, large eyed and reed thin, she stared out at—what? Perhaps she did not look at anything.

Marianne believed that most of the time Nora's vision turned inward, at thoughts and ideas she never shared. Perhaps that was not true either, though. Maybe her cousin's mind remained blank most of the time, just the way her expression did.

She had not always been thus. Once vibrant and bright, she had emerged from a bad illness when she was fifteen in this altered state. The fever had done it to her, the physician explained. Or perhaps on that day that she took ill after being out in a storm, she had been hit by lightning. Or fallen from the horse. Whatever the cause, her brain had been affected. Nothing else could explain the change in her.

Marianne walked around the little chamber. Putting

Nora here was an insult. It was as if Uncle Horace sought to punish his daughter for that which she could not affect. Forcing them all to come back here had been selfish and cruel too. He had not cared at all when Marianne explained she did not think it wise for Nora to move from the cottage in Wiltshire.

She stood beside Nora and stroked her fair hair. "I will tell your father that this chamber will not do. I am sure an error was made."

"I like it here. It is a comforting size. I do not want my old chamber. I will not be happy there."

Thus could Nora speak most clearly and express logical thoughts. If, when she did so, her eyes did not remain opaque, one might never know she was damaged. One might also never guess that sometimes Nora could inexplicably become very emotional. Dangerously so.

Those fits had ceased while she lived in the cottage. However, as they rolled toward this house through the neighboring countryside yesterday, one had emerged. It had taken Marianne a half hour to calm her cousin, and she had ordered the coachman to delay their arrival until she could.

"I will move up here with you, then," she said. "It will be like it was in the cottage. The two of us sharing a chamber."

Nora shook her head, her blank gaze still fixed on the grounds below. "I do not want you here. I do not want anyone here. There is one window and one door, and it is small and simple. I like it. I feel safe here."

I can hide here. I can be forgotten here. I shall never leave and can go quietly mad without interference here.

"Mama and I are going to tour the garden so she can make a list of chores for the gardeners. Come with us," Marianne urged.

Nora shook her head.

"I will see you at dinner, then." She pressed a kiss to Nora's crown.

Again Nora shook her head.

Marianne began walking to the door.

"He thinks to marry me off. That is why he wants me to have a new wardrobe," Nora said.

Marianne halted and faced her. "I am sure you are wrong."

"He said things just now about making myself look pretty. I know what he is planning and thinking." She turned her head and gazed into Marianne's eyes. "I won't do it. I will kill myself first."

Marianne wished she could treat that threat lightly. Instead it caused a bolt of terror to pierce her heart. "Do not say such things. Think of how I would mourn."

Nora's gaze returned to the window. "I do. But for that, I would have done it already."

M arianne closed the door to the library after she entered. Her uncle paced near the fireplace, pretending to read the titles on the books' spines.

They were actually her father's books, carefully chosen

and bound over a lifetime. Horace had inherited them
along with everything else her father had owned. Because
the inheritance was entailed, the premature death of her
brother during the war had ensured it would all go to her
father's brother instead of her father's son.

Horace pivoted when he heard her step. Nora had
calmed better than he had. His color still high, he gestured
her to a settee. Before he sat on the chair nearby, he walked
over to a decanter and poured himself some spirits.

"Are you going to offer me some?" Marianne asked.

He looked over, startled.

"I have always wondered why, if men need spirits to
fortify themselves after a period of high emotion, or before
an unpleasant task, they do not assume women might as
well," she said.

"It isn't done, is why."

Horace arranged his long limbs in the chair. The way
he sat, sunk back, rump low and knees high, reminded
her of her brother, who had also been very tall and lanky.

"I need to tell you something." He gazed at the amber
spirits in his glass. "It is not the kind of thing one talks
to women about, but I see no choice. Without you aware
of all of it, I doubt you will know how to manage her
now."

"How ominous a preamble, Uncle."

"More embarrassing than ominous. Embarrassing,
and infuriating, and I'll be damned if I will live with it
any longer."

"By any description, it sounds like I will be a good deal
less happy once I hear it."

He took his time broaching this subject. He let her wait while he drank the contents of his glass.

"What you know about Nora's brush with death three years ago is true. It is also incomplete. The horse did return without her, and she did come down with a bad fever, and she may have even been struck with lightning. However . . ." He swallowed what was left in the glass. "Her condition is not the result of fever alone."

"What else could affect such a condition?"

He shifted in the chair, as if it no longer fit him. "While in fever, she spoke of what happened." He flushed, and looked away. "She was violated that day. Seduced, perhaps, but used." He glanced askance, a man desperate for escape. "The physician said there had been some blood on her skirt, but it was assumed that when she fell off the horse . . ." He sniffed. "My beautiful girl, my adorable child, ruined."

The revelation horrified Marianne. Nora had only been fifteen then, and barely that. "Is it thought she rode out to meet someone?"

"I think the rogue pursued her secretly, then lured her away from home for his nefarious purposes."

"That would mean it was someone local, Uncle." Marianne wished she had some of those spirits now. "Surely you are in error. Who would dare such a thing?"

"Someone so highly placed that my daughter would be little better than a kitchen maid to him. Someone known for years to be indiscriminate in his seductions, and wild in his excesses. A man with no morals, and little sympathy with decent people." His jaw clenched. "She mentioned who it was while in her fever."

"If so, why did you not swear information against him? She was *a child*."

"When you hear the name, you will know why I did not act thus, especially on the word of a girl not right in her head." He peered at her, his eyes narrow and gaze sharp. "She spoke of him several times as she raved in her delirium, and when she did, she would grow agitated in her bed. It was Lord Lancelot Hemingford. He has bettered his situation of late, of course. Due to the convenient death of his brother Percival, he is known now as the Duke of Aylesbury."

Marianne stood. She paced in an effort to control her emotions. She wanted to curse, or cry. "I refuse to believe even his station allows him to have his way with a girl, and leave her to the elements as he did. Good heavens, Uncle, you are a magistrate now. If you cannot see justice done, who can?"

"I intend to have justice, as you put it. The only kind that can be had under the circumstances, but a fitting kind." He gestured that she should retake her seat. After she had, he leaned forward and spoke confidentially. "I am going to make him marry her."

Nora had surmised her father's intention correctly, then. "She is not fit for marriage. Surely you can see that."

"Tosh. When the duke proposes, she will be her old self again. What woman would not come around at once at the expectation of being a duchess?"

"Truly, she will not. She guessed your plan. She told me upstairs after you left that she will kill herself first."

"People always say things like that when they want their way."

"Dare you risk she would do it? If ever a woman might, it is she."

"That is why you are here, Marianne. Why your mother is already making free with my home and giving the servants orders. Why you will dance at parties again, and meet some man who will support you throughout your life. Unless you want to live on the pittance my brother left you, you are to convince Nora to have that wardrobe made, and to step outside of herself enough so I can see her get her justice. Nora is still beautiful, if a little vague. Once he meets her, he will not be averse to my plan, I think. Assuming she is not raving, of course."

He sank back into the chair. His pose formed a dismissal. Marianne stood.

"What if it is not what she wants, Uncle? What if she accepts the wardrobe, and steps out, and meets this duke, but when the proposal comes, she does not want it?"

"What she wants does not signify. This is a matter of family honor."

Biting her tongue, and furious that her uncle expected her to be an accomplice in this scheme, she strode to the door. As she did, she heard Uncle Horace muttering to himself. "Wants it? Hell and damnation. Of course she will want to be her seducer's duchess, or she is truly mad and it will be Bedlam for her."

CHAPTER 4

Riding with Uncle Horace proved useful in some ways, Marianne decided.

Although a wealthy man now, he fawned like a green squire whenever they passed a person of a higher station. He introduced her to everyone, and many remembered the daughter of Malcolm Radley.

Horace insisted on riding right through Dutton, the village near Trenfield Park, so neighbors could either approach to complain about something or make the same joke about his position. *Have a good batch of rogues for the petty sessions, do you?* His role in organizing a local militia during the war had gotten him knighted, and that in turn had gotten him made a justice of the peace. He loved the status, and presiding over trials.

Sometimes he responded at some length about the sessions. Marianne had a particular interest in local legal proceedings, and she paid close attention to those conversations.

He stopped to talk with other people on social matters that interested her too. She did not approve of gossip, but she always listened to it. This day it helped bring her up to date on the region.

Eventually all the conversations rounded toward one topic she truly cared about, and her uncle's responses to the questions worried her.

"And how is your daughter, sir? Is she visiting with Miss Radley here? Has she come back?"

"Nora is doing very well, thank you. Very well indeed. She was a bit tired from the journey, but I expect she will be riding out with me soon. A few years of quiet has done her the world of good, and she is her old self again, I am happy to say."

When they finally left the village and rode farther west, Marianne kept quiet for fifteen minutes, but then could do so no longer.

"Why are you telling people that Nora is fine? You know she is not."

"If she chooses to be fine, she will be, is what I think."

"You are wrong there. It will be cruel of you if you persist in this plan of yours, or force her to a level of sociability beyond what she wants."

"Am I to take the advice of a girl barely of legal age, after all my years leading men and knowing what is in people?

Once she has a decent riding ensemble, I will expect her to join us. If you come as well, that should reassure her."

"I do not care for how you expect me to lure her into doing what you want, especially since I do not think it is the wise course for her."

"I only expect you to ease her back into normal behavior by providing the friend she has come to know in you. Would you have her do it without your presence? Say the word, and that can be arranged. You and your mother can go make your own way without any further worry of my daughter."

Marianne was about to argue, but her uncle's attention became arrested by something across the field on their left. He narrowed his eyes on the dark form, and a thin smile broke on his face.

"You complained at our slow pace most of the morning," he said. "Well, follow me." He kicked his mount into a gallop.

Marianne pushed Calliope to follow, and they tore across the barren field, charging toward the man on horseback. As much as she enjoyed the speed, Marianne did not look forward to what could be another half hour of Uncle Horace being obsequious with one of his betters.

Uncle Horace had become a parvenu. Knighthood had given him airs. He obviously wanted to shed his current circles for far better ones.

The man they approached saw them coming. Did she imagine his whole body sigh at the prospect of engaging with Horace? Certainly his seat on his horse shifted and his posture sagged. Then, immediately, he caught himself and sat erectly again. He even trotted in their direction to meet them.

Horace hailed him as they closed in. "Your Grace, what a fortuitous coincidence."

Your Grace? The Duke of Aylesbury? Uncle Horace aimed too high now. She blanched at the idea of meeting the duke, let alone sitting by while Uncle Horace imposed on him in order to further the terrible scheme about Nora's marriage.

"A coincidence that has become quite frequent of late, to my delight," the duke said, putting a subtle pause before *delight* that had Marianne mortified and staring at her horse's neck.

"Allow me to introduce my niece, Miss Radley," Horace said.

She had to look up then. The eyes that met hers startled her speechless. Dark and intense, she had seen them before. In the graveyard. The poacher-huntsman-steward was actually the Duke of Aylesbury.

More embarrassment flowed, but soon indignation followed. He might have told her. With what she now knew about him and Nora, she had no desire to be introduced. She could not imagine why Uncle Horace kept grinning.

"I see the beard is gone, Your Grace," Horace said.

"You are the first to see me denuded. I had my valet do the deed this morning."

"Your brother's influence?"

"Ives is unaware, and will be shocked when he visits. A more compelling reason forced me to give up the warmth and comfort. A lovely lady indicated that she would not allow me to kiss her otherwise." He looked right at Marianne. "I suspect she thought I would never do it. It is the sort of thing only the most conceited woman would really expect of a man. Don't you agree, Miss Radley?"

"Since Your Grace would not want to kiss the most conceited of women, the one you speak of will probably be astonished to see you thus."

Marianne felt her face getting hot. He spoke as if she had promised a kiss if he shaved. She had not, she was sure, not that she could remember much of what she said in the last few minutes of their first meeting.

She forced herself to look right at him with her best expression of indifference. It was then that she saw one reason he might favor beards. A scar, thin and ragged, meandered across his right cheek. An old scar, from the looks of its pale and puckered path. It did not totally mar his face, which, she had to admit, was otherwise handsome now that she could see all of it. Shaving revealed his firm jaw and his full lips. He was not typically handsome, but attractive in a rough, sensual way.

No doubt many women found his attention enticing. Girls might too. Girls like Nora had been three years ago.

"I trust you are not planning any nuptials with this lady who demanded you give up your beard." Horace sounded far too interested.

Marianne hoped the duke would declare himself in love with someone, so perhaps Nora would be spared her father's ridiculous scheme.

"You are nothing if not proper, Sir Horace. I speak of one kiss and you hear vows."

"I assumed if you mentioned this lady in front of my niece, the lady was someone you intended for more than one kiss."

A naughty twinkle entered the duke's eyes. "I do, Sir Horace. Eros be willing, that is."

Uncle Horace flustered and flushed. "Sir, I ask that you restrain your innuendos while my niece is present."

"She appears less shocked than you, sir. However, let us ride. I promise to behave when we stop." He turned his horse and used his crop to take it to a gallop.

Horace charged after. Marianne followed. She wished her uncle had chosen a different path today.

The rogue had all but named her as the woman for whom he shaved, and all but announced dishonorable intentions. Did he think her such easy pickings that she would not mind? Perhaps some women cooed and giggled when he began his seductions in such a public and bold way, but she was made of different stuff.

And for him to think that she would entertain even one kiss after what happened to Nora marked him as bad and without conscience. He must have known who Nora was, and now that he knew their relationship, his silly flirtation with her should have ended.

They pulled up at the base of a hill. "The prospect from up there is impressive," the duke said. "Other than family, few have seen it since it is deep into the estate, and no charted road comes to it." He began leading the way up.

"We are honored you invite us to share this private prospect," Uncle Horace oozed.

Marianne wanted to hit him. Just yesterday he had

almost been in tears when he described how this man had misused his own daughter, but now he fawned like the worst sycophant.

"Do I speak out of turn in asking how things fare between you and Lady Barnell, Sir Horace?" the duke said over his shoulder.

Uncle Horace chortled. "I like to think the lady is not without interest in my attendance, mild though it may still be."

"Be bold, Sir Horace. Nothing less will do with a widow."

"Thank you for your advice, Your Grace. I fear if I were as bold as some men, the lady would leave the county for good, however."

"You refer to me, I think. I disagree, but it is not my place to give you advice. I can only wish you well."

Marianne forced Calliope up alongside her uncle. "Are you speaking of Baron Barnell's widow?"

Horace glanced askance at her, annoyed. "We are."

"You have indeed set your sights high, Uncle."

"I remind you that I am not without position in the county, Marianne."

"I only wonder if you are too optimistic regarding the lady's views on the matter."

"Give me a few weeks, and her views will be much improved, I assure you."

The prospect from the top of the hill indeed proved impressive. At its crest one could look down on farms and fields for several miles. Marianne made all the right sounds of appreciation, but her mind remained on other things.

If Uncle Horace proved successful in wooing Lady Barnell, Mama would immediately be displaced.

If in turn he were successful in marrying off Nora, there would be no need at all for Mama and herself in that house.

It sounded as if Uncle Horace had neglected to inform them of part of his plan. He intended their residence in his home to be a fairly short one.

It would not do to tell any of this to Mama. Uncle Horace was bound to fail on both counts. As long as he chased after the widows of peers, and with the likelihood of his preposterous plans for Nora going nowhere, Mama's rule of Trenfield would probably last forever.

"Do you like it?"

The voice by her shoulder startled her. While Uncle Horace paced along the crest, admiring the landscape, the duke had moved his horse next to hers. He looked into her eyes, disconcerting her.

"The view is lovely."

"I meant do you like that I have shaved?"

"You certainly appear less rustic."

"I am to receive no more praise than that?"

"You do not need praise from me. I expect that you possess very fine looking glasses, and can assess your own visage, whether bearded or not."

She could not say what she really thought. He appeared far more handsome now, with his bone structure and firm jaw apparent, but also less friendly. More ducal and severe. Perhaps that only came from her knowing his identity. She sensed a touch of imperiousness in him, however. An expectation that as a duke, he should of course get what he wanted, including her compliments on his shaven face.

"I will expect that dance at the next assembly now."

"Do you always attend the local assemblies? That is good of you."

"Make no mistake about it, Miss Radley. I am not good. Ask anyone and that is what you will be told. Ask your uncle. As for assemblies, I never attend them. This one, however, promises to be more pleasant than the others."

"If you rarely attend, the circle around you will be thick when you do. Dancing may prove impossible."

"It will not be nearly as thick as you would think."

"Perhaps my cousin Nora will come with me. She is my uncle's daughter. You may know her. Nora Radley."

"I have not been introduced, and the name brings up no memory of her. I am sorry if she thinks it should. I did not spend much time here over the recent years. Until I inherited, my preferred abode was in London."

He did not even remember her name. Marianne bit her tongue so she did not upbraid him then and there. The scold screamed in her mind, however. *You scoundrel. You toyed with her and flirted and arranged an assignation when she was barely out of the schoolroom. She rode out to meet you and you seduced her, and left her to find her way back alone with a storm brewing.*

"Unfortunately, she may not come. Three years ago she was caught in a tempest and took to her bed with a severe fever that affected her mind. My uncle tells everyone she is much recovered, but she really is not. At least not entirely."

She looked for embarrassment again. She only saw signs of some sympathy. At least when Uncle Horace attempted to make this match, the duke would know of Nora's condition, however.

"That is sad to hear. Perhaps with rest and time she will indeed recover entirely," he said. "Now that you and I have been properly introduced, I will call on you and we can take her on a carriage ride. Perhaps she would like that."

You seduced her, you idiot. You ruined her. She will not want to be within a mile of you. "We are barely settled in, and have much to do still. I am afraid that carriage rides for pleasure will have to wait a good while for all of us."

"It is rare for people to refuse me their company, Miss Radley. More common are those like your uncle, who gallop across fields to interfere with my day and to curry favor. When I call you will indeed agree to a carriage ride with me. Your uncle will insist on it. If he lusts after Lady Barnell's connections, he will be apoplectic if you deny him the chance to have mine." He leaned forward and patted Calliope's neck. "As for how much pleasure there is on that carriage ride, that will be up to you."

Calliope moved closer, hoping for more petting from that handsome, masculine hand. Marianne struggled with the reins to keep the horse from snuggling too close to the duke's mount, and putting Marianne all but in the duke's lap.

Uncle Horace trotted his horse toward them.

"Splendid prospects, Your Grace. Splendid. It is a wonder your family has not built up here. If not a manor house, then villas to let."

"My brother considered the latter before he passed. Fortunately, no contracts had been signed. As for my building villas to let, my father would haunt me if I even thought twice about it." He led them down the hill, then pointed to the rough line through the field. "If you follow this, it will bring you back to where we met. I must take my leave of you now. I meet with my steward soon."

"Quite so, quite so," Uncle Horace said. "Splendid to see you today, Your Grace."

"We are honored by your condescension," Marianne added. Uncle Horace may have forgotten his place, but she knew hers, and it would behoove one of them to remind His Grace that just as one comported oneself a certain way with one's betters, one did so with one's inferiors too.

"The honor is mine, Miss Radley, since I made your introduction as a result. We will talk soon, Radley."

"Very soon, Your Grace."

The duke turned his horse and galloped away. Uncle Horace watched, a sly smile on his face. "Damnation, but that went well."

"If you force your company on him frequently, it is a wonder he did not cut us directly."

"He won't cut *me*. He will tolerate my company. He permitted the introduction to you and will do the same with Nora. I had his agreement on it months ago."

"Then he is kinder than he appears."

Horace grasped his riding crop, signaling that he intended to clear this field quickly. "Kindness has nothing to do with it. He knows I hold his life in my hands."

* * *

"May I take the curling iron to this topknot, Miss?" Katy, the servant assigned to her, posed the question hopefully. Having been promoted to lady's maid out of necessity, Katy wanted to show her abilities with needle and thread, dressing and undressing, and now the curling iron.

Marianne nodded, since there was no reason other than stubbornness to refuse. At the cottage they had all shared old Jane, but now Mama had taken her as her private servant, so she and Nora had to contend with two girls who had never been properly trained.

Marianne's real reason for wanting to be stubborn had nothing to do with that. She had not spent this long dressing in five years, and being required to do so now irritated her. She envisioned hours of each day now being devoted to her grooming. This morning the maid's arrival had interfered with her writing an important letter, which still awaited completion in her bedchamber.

"Did you enjoy your ride with your uncle yesterday?" Katy asked while she singed a lock of hair with the iron.

"We had a few good gallops, which was better than I expected. We visited the village and I met many people. I was introduced to the Duke of Aylesbury."

"The duke? Oh, my." Katy's round dark eyes grew larger in the looking glass's reflection. "An honor, I am sure, but one I could have done without, if it were me."

"Surely you are not afraid of him."

"He is said to be very wicked, miss. Not only the normal kinds of ways men can be wicked either." She lowered her voice. "It is said he done in his brother. The coroner has left the matter open all this time. Nine months it is. The magistrates are sure they will find enough to have the lords hold a trial. If he were not a duke, he would've swung by now."

"Killed his brother? The last duke? I find that hard to believe."

"He was in the house when it happened. Poison, it is said. The physician implied as much. That family insists it was a malady of the gut, but no one believes it." She lifted another strand of hair. "I'd stay far away from that one, miss. Not that it is my place to advise you, of course."

Was this what Uncle Horace had meant when he spoke of holding the duke's life in his hands? As a county justice of the peace, Horace was responsible for investigating crimes and presiding at the petty sessions.

But if he believed Aylesbury to be a murderer, why was he talking of a match with Nora?

Marianne watched the curls form on her crown. Her uncle's true plans and motivations fell into place along with each lock's unfurling.

While Uncle Horace might truly believe Aylesbury had seduced and ruined Nora, it was not family honor he pursued in his scheme. It was connections, and improving his status, just as it was with his pursuit of Lady Barnell.

Would he sacrifice his daughter in order to advance his own position in society? Being in a duke's circle probably brought all kinds of opportunities and benefits. Even marriage to Lady Barnell would become attainable if one of

Horace's female relatives married a duke. The financial expectations alone after such a match would be considerable.

She would confront Uncle Horace about all of it. She would tell him she had guessed his intentions, and that she would not allow him to use Nora thus. The duke would hardly treat Nora well if he were blackmailed into marriage. Uncle Horace's avarice should not go unchecked.

"Katy, are there any other stories about the duke? Is he known to take advantage of local women, for example? Even as a girl I remember he had a bad reputation."

"A rake, you mean? Oh, he is wicked that way too, miss. Everyone knows it and says so. But as to local girls, I can't say I have heard of it, although it would take a brave one to accuse such as him. Of course, he is so rarely here, except the last nine months, that is. Why, when he began living in that big house, there were some of his servants who did not know who he was, he visited so rarely in the past. That is why his being there on the night his brother was poisoned is so suspicious. Of all the nights to come down from town, why that one if he is innocent?"

"It would be a tragedy if a mere coincidence of domicile caused a man's name to be ruined, Katy."

"His name is the least of it, don't you think? Even dukes can hang for murder, although I was told they get a silk rope if they do."

"Does he live there in isolation? For a man with his tastes, that would make the manor house a luxurious prison, but a prison all the same."

"His brothers visit, and their wives. There's stories

aplenty about those two as well. One just married a woman whose father is a criminal, it's said. He was in Newgate for months, but released. A mistake, it was explained. More a matter of a duke's son wanting it to be a mistake is the common thinking."

Marianne tucked that morsel away for later chewing. "He cannot be enjoying his inheritance much if only family visits on occasion."

"I think being rich would entertain me enough on its own. However, his life here has been very quiet, even more than that of the last duke, his brother. There has not been a party there in years. Even the events held for the tenants and the county years ago are never done now. I remember going to one of those when I was a child."

Marianne remembered too. There had been summer festivals back then, with the whole county invited. She had been with her father at one when he spoke with the old duke—the current one's father. The two had talked about sheep and barley.

"So nothing of interest goes on at that big house. How unfortunate." Except a possible murder. That was very interesting.

Katy finished with the last curl, and poked at it all with her comb's tail. Marianne looked at the result. It appeared lopsided and frizzy. She would have old Jane explain a few things to Katy.

"Get me dressed now, quickly. I have a letter to finish, then I need to visit my cousin, and then I intend to go to the village."

After dressing, she left Katy and returned to her writing table. There she finished the letter she had started. It was to Nora's half brother, Vincent, the son of their mother by her first marriage. Vincent was an officer in the naval service. She wanted him to know about their change of domicile, and also to assure him of Nora's health, although she had no idea when he would receive the letter.

Writing to Vincent always put her in a bittersweet mood. As a girl she had formed emotions for him as he grew older and taller. It seemed that every month her feelings deepened. He was the only man she had ever loved.

She had foolishly formed expectations. Especially after her father died, she had built dreams around Nora's brother. Only then he had entered the naval service, and was no longer in her life, so she did not see right away that he did not think of her the same way.

At least she had never poured out her emotions in a letter to him, although she was tempted to during those first months after she moved to Wiltshire. She had kept her dreams to herself. Thank goodness for that, because when he never expressed similar feelings himself, she had slowly awakened to the truth and accepted reality.

She folded and sealed the page, and debated how to post it. This was another problem with moving back here. For the last five years, letters to and from Vincent and others could come and go without Uncle Horace knowing about it. He did not like Vincent, however, and now he might forbid the correspondence when he became aware of it.

Hoping her visit to the village would solve the dilemma,

she set out a clean sheet of paper. She stared at it. Did she dare try to continue this other correspondence she had begun in Wiltshire?

If so, she definitely could not post the letters from this house, or receive the responses. She would have to hope she could find a business in the village that served as a mail drop, and rely on the proprietor's discretion.

She dipped her pen and began writing. *To the* Times of London . . .

CHAPTER 5

The Times of London

. . . *thus I conclude the most interesting cases brought up at the Michaelmas quarter sessions in Wiltshire.*

Finally, your correspondent will find himself spending the winter in Gloucestershire. Even as he awaits his departure for that region, news of its social developments has reached him. Justice of the Peace and Knight of St. George, Sir Horace Radley, has received as visitors in his home there the widow of his brother, Malcolm Radley, and their daughter. His own daughter, who had been visiting her cousin and aunt at length, has joined them. Readers may remember that Mrs. Malcolm Radley entertained Sir

*Horace in Wiltshire in December, before he returned
to his home near Cheltenham to celebrate Christmas.*

Elijah Tewkberry

Lance drank coffee in the library of Merrywood Manor. After noting there was correspondence in the *Times* from his county, and even about Miss Radley, he set aside that impressive paper and picked up instead the little broadside published out of Cheltenham every Tuesday.

He never read this paper, but now he found it almost interesting. He paused over the death notice of an elderly neighbor he thought had passed away years ago, and over the news that another neighbor had bought a new carriage and pair. He found the advertisements a revelation, since he never shopped anywhere but London. Finally he turned to what he was really looking for. A notice on the back of the sheet announced an assembly two weeks hence, to coincide with the full moon. Lady Barnell would host it in her home.

Two weeks seemed a long time. Miss Radley might be gone by then if she declined her uncle's invitation to live in his home. She had not sounded happy with the notion.

He was debating whether to ride over to Radley's house today or tomorrow, when a servant announced the arrival of his own visitor. A minute later his brother Ives strode into the library, looked in his direction, and halted in his tracks. His green eyes bulged dramatically. He covered his heart with his hand and feigned a swoon.

"Spare me the courtroom histrionics," Lance said.

"I am truly overcome. It has been so long since I have seen you properly shaved that I barely recognized you. Did your valet tie you down while you slept, and do the deed out of pique with your eccentricity?"

"It was not eccentric, but practical. Why risk a nick if no one will see you?"

"And someone will see you now?" Ives's brow furrowed. "I hope you are not planning to come up to town."

"I may." Lance had no such intention, but his brother's attempts to govern his movements had grown tedious months ago.

Instead of launching into one of his harangues about why that was not desirable with suspicions about Percy's death still at large, Ives merely sat and stretched out his booted legs. Thus did sexual satisfaction mute even the loudest lion. Marriage to Miss Belvoir had wrought many changes in Ives, some of which Lance did not welcome. It was harder to goad him now, for one thing.

"I suppose you are very bored here," Ives said with uncharacteristic understanding for the endless ennui of being rusticated. "Come up if you want. I doubt you will get into any trouble, because there is no one in town now."

"If that is the case, I will stay here, where I at least see a few souls when I go riding."

Ives barely heard. The newspaper had garnered his attention. Angling his head, he read the announcement on the back. Suddenly alert, he shot Lance a glance of curiosity. "Are you so bored now that you are planning to attend this assembly? If so you must warn the lady. I doubt she is expecting a duke."

"Thank you for the lesson in county etiquette. Whatever would I do without you, Ives? No doubt just bumble along, embarrassing myself."

That set Ives back for a moment. No longer, however.

"Are you going?" He tapped the paper.

"I don't know why you care."

"I find it odd, that is all. You have not attended one of those since you were—" He paused and calculated. "Seventeen. After the last one, it was widely known that you were no longer welcome at them."

"Sixteen. As for the unfortunate events of that evening, and the general censure that followed, it was much ado about nothing, and in my defense, I was a boy."

Actually there was no defense, which did not bother Lance at the time, or now. And the much ado had been about something worthy of the reprobation that rained down upon him. It had cut his bad reputation into stone as far as this county was concerned.

"That you were a boy was part of the fun. She was not a girl, after all. And your being a boy is all that kept her husband from calling you out. If you attend this one, someone is sure to revive that story for the general entertainment of all, and the undoing of all that your recent virtue has built."

Ives had turned into a lawyer again. He was correct, however. There were other parts to the story that would live again, such as the fact that Percy, that weasel, had been the one to send the lady's husband into that garden. He had found his wife on all fours with her skirt pushed up to her shoulders, and a boy of sixteen taking his pleasure.

"If I choose to go, I will go. Let the county gossip anew. Virtue is a terrible bore anyway, and I grow tired of pretending to be other than I am."

That pulled Ives totally out of his marital calm. He sat upright. He stared at the paper. His gaze sharpened. One could all but hear his brain parsing and poking at all he had seen and heard the last few minutes.

"Who is she?"

Lance decided to finish his coffee.

"Whoever she is, you must not."

"Must not what?"

Ives glared at him. "You should come up to London when I go back."

"When will that be?"

"A day or two, no more."

"So you rode down with no other intention than to visit me for a day or so? How good you are." They both knew the word *visit* was too polite. Lance was in a type of prison, and Ives had appointed himself gaoler.

"I thought you would want company."

"I am long past that. The hares and grouse keep me company enough. The servants remind me I still walk the earth."

Ives frowned. "It has been almost a year since Percy died. I will call on the coroner and tell him it is time to put all of this nonsense to rest."

"I suspect it remains open because someone wants it open. You are not to worry about it, however. You have already done enough of that for both of us."

Ives, subdued, withdrew into his thoughts. Rather suddenly he jolted out of them. "Nicely done, distracting me like that, making me feel bad for you, and absolving me of any further duty."

"I am glad you liked it."

"It won't work. I again ask, who is she?"

Their half brother Gareth would have given up by now. Ives was nothing if not tenacious. That helped make him a renowned barrister. His willingness to badger a person proved useful in the courtroom.

"What makes you assume there is any she?"

"You shaved." He pointed to the paper. "You intend to go to that assembly. Your eyes have a gleam I haven't seen in almost a year. You are in pursuit, and you are not hunting hares, deer, or fowl, although I wager there is a pretty chicken in danger of getting plucked."

Lance stood. "I am going to ride. I need to visit one of the tenants. Come with me if you want." He strode to the door. Ives caught up.

"Stop frowning, Ives."

"I frown for good reason. If you will not say who she is, it is worse than I thought."

Much worse. That is what unrelenting virtue did to a man.

"It is said that the lady left within minutes of the gentleman," Mrs. Wigglesworth confided. "That is one too many coincidences if you ask me." Her emphasis on *coincidences* dripped with innuendo.

Mama glanced askance at Marianne, to see if her daughter had grasped the implications of the gossip. Marianne pretended to be perplexed. Mrs. Wigglesworth should not be speaking about such things in front of an unmarried girl, but Marianne accompanied Mama on her calls just so she might hear such interesting news.

Mrs. Wigglesworth's plump face drew long with shock at her own revelations. A short, round woman, she favored large caps that covered most of her gray hair. Her green dress, while attractive, left too much of her abundant décolletage exposed, and its color made her white skin appear sallow, in Marianne's opinion. If this was how the local dressmakers influenced fashion in the county, she would have to insist that Uncle Horace send Nora to London for her new wardrobe.

"Did the servants at the inn tell people about this?" Mama asked. "That was indiscreet of them."

"It is not every day that such notables stop at this village's inn, my dear. There is a far better one just outside Cheltenham. The servants can be excused for revealing too much in their excitement, even if they should not have done so."

Marianne was delighted to learn the servants were indiscreet. "I fail to see how these coincidences signify," she lied. "It is a lot of excitement about nothing, it appears."

Mrs. Wigglesworth gave Mama a meaningful look. Mama returned one. They both smiled indulgently at Marianne.

"Perhaps you would like to visit the garden," Mama suggested. "Mrs. Wigglesworth and I can then talk about other insignificant things without boring you."

Marianne tried to determine if Mrs. Wigglesworth

looked to have additional interesting news in her. She decided not. "I think I will stroll in the village instead, and look in the shops."

"I will come with the carriage and find you," Mama said.

Taking her leave, Marianne slipped out the door and hurried down the road to the village. Once there she darted into Howard's bookshop.

From the first time she had seen him, Marianne thought Mr. Howard did not look much like a bookseller. She always pictured such men as thin and spectacled, and serious like tutors. Mr. Howard instead stood tall and fat, had a florid face and manner, and possessed wild red hair whose curls stood on end. He might be a tavern owner or a sheep farmer, from the looks of him.

He greeted her warmly, and immediately opened a drawer behind his counter. He handed over two letters and gave her a big smile.

Marianne noted one of the letters was from Nora's brother Vincent. As for the other, she had no choice but to depend upon Mr. Howard's discretion, but surely there were limits to that.

"Do you not find it odd that I will be receiving these letters, under this name, from this gentleman, Mr. Howard?"

"I would be lying if I said I did not find it odd, but I find many of the letters I handle odd, Miss Radley. You would be amazed at how odd some of them are." He grinned. "You might say that handling odd letters is one of my stocks-in-trade."

A fairly lucrative one. She paid a shilling a month for

this mail drop. If even ten others did so, too, Mr. Howard made a goodly sum for the service. She suspected most of his income derived from his handling of odd letters. He would not want to jeopardize that with indiscretions.

"You are not to worry about it now," he said. "No one sees them but me, like I explained. No one will know."

"It is a rare person who can be privy to so many secrets and feel no need to divulge them, but I know you are such a person."

"I am at that, miss. Do you have anything to mail today?"

She opened her reticule and handed him a letter. An odd one. She fished out the coin needed to send it to London. Then she tucked her mail into the reticule, and left so Mama would find her strolling along the shops.

CHAPTER 6

The Times of London

. . . In financial developments, Mr. Vickers of Gloucester will be selling in his shop the miniature conservatories made at the behest of the Brazilian Botanical Company, which has discovered that their plan to have sailors take said conservatories to gather rare plants, and care for them during transport back to England, has met with no success. It appears the sailors, who were happy for the payment, balked at the notion of sharing their ration of fresh water with their botanical pets. Mr. Vickers will sell the little glass boxes for a shilling each.

Regarding county notables, the Duke of Aylesbury, who for months has sported enough facial hair *to pass as either an ancient philosopher or a ship-wrecked sailor, has shaved. The resulting appearance caused him to be misidentified by at least three county residents when he recently visited Cheltenham. Your correspondent wonders if His Grace conceded he would be unable to persuade enough men to follow his hirsute designs in order to start a new fashion, or if the beard had interfered with his normal activities, in particular the enthusiastic hunting of pretty fowl for which he is famous.*

Elijah Tewkberry, Gloucestershire

Lance pretended to examine the books in Sir Horace's library. Sir Horace attempted to fill the void of time by chattering about county matters.

Eventually neither one of them could ignore that more time had passed than expected.

"I have come at an inconvenient hour. I will return another day."

"No, no, your call was not at all inconvenient. I am sure that my niece will be here soon. Very soon. Imminently now, I think. I beg you to wait a few minutes more." He pointed his nose toward the servant standing near the door. "Refreshments for His Grace. See to it."

"I do not require any, as I said."

"Some brandy, then." Horace made a dancing amble toward a table with decanters.

Lance was about to demur when the door opened. A servant's head bent to the ear of his colleague keeping watch. That footman then advanced on Sir Horace, and bent to that ear in turn.

"They have returned," Horace announced with delight. His finger twirled at the servant. "Tell Mrs. Radley and Miss Radley to join us immediately."

Lance glanced out the window and judged the passage of the day. If he invited Miss Radley on that carriage ride as he had intended, they would have no more than a couple of hours before dusk fell.

Said lady soon burst into the library with a worried expression. She halted, looked around, and exhaled with relief. "When the servant said *immediately*, I thought perhaps . . . Nora . . ."

She collected herself just as another woman joined her. Older but no more than forty years or so, and still very handsome, this one had dark hair, but eyes of similar color.

Sir Horace introduced her as the widow of his late brother. Mrs. Radley executed a deep curtsy. Her daughter followed suit. Lance bowed. Sir Horace beamed.

"How good of you to call, Your Grace. We are honored," Mrs. Radley said.

"I was on the road and thought your daughter might agree to a short ride with me. With your permission, of course. You are welcome to come, too, or send her maid if you prefer." *Send the maid.* He could always lose a servant. One direct glare and the maid would disappear.

Not that he had any intentions that would require such a tactic. However, one never knew.

"My daughter can accompany her," Sir Horace said. "Surely that will keep everything proper enough."

Lance liked that *enough*. Sir Horace was not above bending a few rules if it suited him. "I would be happy to have her join us, if she is agreeable."

"Uncle—" Miss Radley darted a scolding glare at her uncle. Sir Horace pretended not to see.

"Go up and get her," he instructed her. "Tell her I think it would be very good for her health to go out in the fresh air. She has remained inside too long."

Vexed, but without recourse, Miss Radley departed. Her mother took a chair and made attempts at small talk. Lance heard little of what he and she said.

Too much time passed. Sir Horace excused himself, promising to return. Instead, ten minutes later Miss Radley reappeared with another young woman, this one little more than a girl. Very pale, with hair almost colorless it was so blond, she appeared childlike in her yellow dress and wore a large-eyed, fearful expression. It appeared she had been crying.

"Let us go," Miss Radley said. "Now, if you do not mind." With that she turned her cousin and steered the girl out of the library.

"But His Grace has not been introduced to her," her mother called after her.

"I will do it," came the curt reply that echoed in the entry hall.

Lance followed them out. By the time he caught up, Miss Radley and her cousin stood beside his carriage.

Miss Radley no longer hid her pique. She left her cousin and pulled Lance aside. "Nora did not want to come, as you might imagine. My uncle would not abide by her decision, and we had a scene while he browbeat her into it. I beg you to make this a quick ride, and if she does not choose to speak, please be kind enough to allow her that."

"Of course."

Reassured, Miss Radley brought him over to the girl and introduced them. Nora never looked at him through it all, nor as she entered the carriage. When he sat across from the two of them, he concluded that Nora would be an even better chaperone than a servant. Her gaze settled on the window and he doubted she heard anything he said.

He handed Miss Radley a carriage blanket. "Perhaps you would both be more comfortable with this."

She took it and draped it over her cousin's lap, and high on her chest. She took her cousin's hand in hers.

"You care for her," he said.

"In every way." A flinty spark entered her eyes. "She has not changed much in appearance in the last three years. Don't you agree?"

"As I said before, I would not know. I am sorry." He was glad that his admission that he had no memory of this neighbor did not evoke a hurt reaction in the girl. She merely continued her perusal of the passing countryside.

Miss Radley's chin and jaw tensed. She looked like a person swallowing words that choked her. "Perhaps when you met her, you were in your cups."

"That could be." It was time to talk of other things. "Were you out making calls?"

"Yes. My mother has many old friends to see. She lived here for a long time before we moved away."

"When Sir Horace inherited?"

She nodded. "My brother, Thomas—"

"I did know your brother. I was sorry to hear of his passing."

"Entailments being what they are, once he was gone it all went to my uncle. He decided we would be happier elsewhere. He gave us a family property in Wiltshire to use, so he did not wash his hands totally of our support."

"Now he has called you back." He glanced at Nora, who remained removed from their conversation and from the world itself.

"We were better off in that cottage." She squeezed Nora's hand. "She was, at least. I think I was too. Yet here we are, and I will make the best of it." She looked out the window. "Where are we going?"

"I thought we would go to the lake. It is not far."

"That would be pleasant. I have not been there in years. It was kind of you to invite us."

"I hope that you will in turn be kind, and call on me. Along with your mother, of course."

"I am sure you are far too busy to receive us."

"I promise I will. If you come in the next day or so, you can meet my brother Ives. He has come down from London for a short visit."

That interested her. "Did his family come too?"

"He left his new wife in London. She has embarked on an intensive course of study with the intention of going to Padua to enter the university there. It is ambitious, and she has thrown herself into this endeavor with my brother's full approval."

"How very, very interesting. She sounds to be a remarkable woman. If he approves, he must be an equally remarkable man. What is she studying?"

He spent the next fifteen minutes telling Miss Radley all about Ives and his new bride. By the time he finished, they were at the lake.

His property line ran down the middle of it. For decades both owners had allowed anyone to row or swim here, and in summer one could always find people about. On this wintery day it was deserted.

"Let us take a turn along the water's edge," he said.

Miss Radley glanced at her cousin. "I should stay here."

"The carriage is warm, and she has the blanket. The coachman will remain with the equipage. She will be safe."

Miss Radley turned to her cousin. "Nora, I am going to take a short walk. Do you want to come along?"

Nora shook her head. "I will be fine here, just as the gentleman said."

Overcoming her hesitance, Miss Radley allowed him to hand her down. They walked through the grass to the lake's edge.

"It looked bigger when I was a girl."

"Isn't that always the way it is. When I was fifteen I realized it was small enough I could easily swim across, although it looked like an ocean when I was a child."

They strolled along the bank. "When you said you would call on me and demand a carriage ride, I did not think you meant it," she said. "As you can see, Nora is not grateful for the opportunity."

"I am sorry she was obligated to join us. I would have been glad for your company alone."

Such subtle flirtation did not come naturally to him. Since she did not so much as blush, he must have been very subtle indeed.

She frowned. "Are you very sure you do not recognize her?"

"Most sure. You seem to believe I should, however."

"Yes, I do."

"Miss Radley, if your cousin says we met, no doubt we did. I will be honest and say that even if she says I flirted with her, perhaps that is true. I confess that I do not remember all the girls I meet or flatter."

"No doubt you will forget me soon too."

"I did not say that, nor should you think it. A passing smile or flattery is not quite the same as calling on a woman."

She glanced back. Their stroll had taken them along a curve that removed them from view of the carriage.

"We should return."

"Let us row out a bit, unless you are too chilled." He coaxed her toward one of the rowboats resting along the bank.

If ever a woman were of two minds, this one was. She followed, however, and climbed into the boat. He pushed it off, and jumped in, then sat and took the oars. With a few strokes they were away from the bank.

Free of the overhanging tree branches, the late afternoon sun bathed them in its warmth. She untied her bonnet's ribbons, and removed and set it on the bench beside her. "It is very lovely here. So peaceful and quiet. I wish Nora had come with us."

He set the oars up, and let the boat drift. "I am glad she did not."

She looked lovely, awash in the gold of the sun's rays, surrounded by the deep blue of the lake. Her copper hair appeared on fire in places, as the sun set strands ablaze. Her wide mouth did not smile, however, and her deep blue eyes watched him cautiously.

"Why did you call on me? What is it you expect?" she asked.

If he were good, which he never had been, he would say something reassuring. He might even pretend to be wounded by her apparent suspicions. Since he was bad, wicked even, he did not bother.

"Surely you know. You may be innocent, but you are not ignorant."

W ell, that was blunt.

She had asked, however. She should not be vexed that he answered honestly. Yet she was. This man was so conceited that he assumed she would not mind such a bald allusion. Perhaps he saved more subtle words for better women than she.

"I am very ignorant as to your intentions in this boat right now."

He regarded her at length. She wished that did not affect her. He was not a man whose attention a woman could ignore, however, or remain immune to. At least not *this* woman. She suspected her susceptibility had much to do with never having had such attention before, from any man. Respectability plus no fortune equaled no male interest. It was an equation she had learned quickly, and made her peace with.

"My intention is to claim the kiss that you owe me."

"I owe you no kiss."

"You promised one if I shaved."

"I did not. I have reviewed that meeting at length, and I only said that perhaps, if we were introduced, I might dance with you if you shave. I said nothing about a kiss, nor did you even ask for one."

"I remember it differently."

"Your memory is faulty on many counts, Your Grace, so I am not surprised it is on this one."

"Please do not address me like that. Call me Aylesbury." He smiled. "I will call you Marianne."

"No, sir, you will not. I will not accept such familiarity."

"And I will not accept the formality of addressing you as Miss Radley, especially since another Miss Radley sits in the carriage." He leaned forward. "I will call you pretty flower, until you think more familiarity is acceptable."

It might be wiser to allow him to use her given name, rather than suffer this endearment. She tried to form a terse rejection of both, to no avail. The words kept scrambling. Lack of experience made her utterly incapable of handling this advance with anything resembling sophistication.

His position, with his arms on his knees, brought him very close to her. To her astonishment, he reached out and took her hand. The warmth of his touch flowed right through her glove, and up her arm. Then it kept going, as if he heated her blood.

He began removing her glove. She watched, mesmerized by the intimacy of the small act. His fingers slid along her skin as they coaxed the glove down, bit by bit. His devilish slow disrobing of her hand caused his fingertips to keep skimming her inner arm. Her breath caught, and a shiver slid from her neck to her stomach.

"What . . . what are you doing?"

He drew off the glove completely, and held her hand in his, skin on skin. "You will not allow me to kiss you on the lips, I am sure. But this is not dangerous or scandalous. If we had been introduced differently, I would have done it right in front of your uncle."

With that, he bowed his head over her hand, and kissed it.

Only it was not the kind of kiss a man might make to a lady's hand upon an introduction. Not a mere brushing or peck. He *kissed* her hand. Slowly. Seductively.

He hovered so his breath warmed her skin. Chills danced up her arm.

He pressed warm lips, then moved them so his mouth caressed her. She watched, mesmerized by the sight of his ardor, and by the effect it had on her. A new alertness affected all her senses. It felt like time had slowed to allow him to kiss at his leisure.

He turned her hand palm up, and kissed yet more. Prickly signs of arousal stirred in her stomach, astonishing her. Parts of her body that she rarely noticed came alive with sensations.

He gently nipped each fingertip. Each delicate pressure sent delicious shocks up her arm. Finally, he bit the pad at the base of her thumb. A scandalous pleasure tensed deep inside her.

The warmth of his lips edged over onto her wrist's pulse, and the sensation exploded.

She started, and pulled her hand away.

He looked at her. Not surprised. Not annoyed. He just waited while he watched her.

Her mind strove to form words to scold him, but her embarrassment would not allow them to form. Self-reproach for permitting such liberties came together neatly, however.

After one last, deep look into her eyes, he took the oars and began rowing again. It had been a knowing look, too honest in reflecting what he saw—a woman who had not resisted soon enough, considering what he had done.

When they arrived at the lake's bank, she clambered out of the boat and strode toward the carriage. She replaced her glove on her hand with difficulty, since she also carried her bonnet.

His boots fell into place beside her. "You can reprimand me if you want."

"And continue to be the lord's fool? I will only scold this far. You are not to do that again. Nor do you need to call again, since you have had the kiss you say I owed you, even though I owed you nothing of the kind."

"I think you may be right about that. I believe, now that I remember, that it was indeed a dance at the next assembly, as you claim."

"You are impossible, and very bad. I know all about you. I knew even when I was a girl, and I can see you are even *badder* now."

"I do not think *badder* is a word."

"Should I say *wicked*, as everyone else does?"

"It has a certain flair to it, while *bad* is a word so often used as to be boring. It is applied to all sorts of ordinary things. The food has gone bad. He had a bad fall. *Wicked*, however, is always about a person at least, and much more precise."

Between her embarrassment, and his teasing, she was flustered and at wits' end by the time they arrived at the carriage.

She hurried, to claim the sanctuary of having Nora nearby. When she saw the carriage window, however, all thoughts of the duke vanished. She broke into a run.

She pulled open the door. Her heart turned to lead and sank hard. "She is not here. *Nora is gone.*"

Aylesbury strode over, looked in, then called to the coachman. "Where did the lady go?"

The coachman rounded the carriage and looked inside. "I was here the whole time, Your Grace. Except the few minutes just now when I, um . . ." He looked at Marianne and flushed. "When I made a visit to the brush over there." He pointed to the other side of the road.

She strode to the bank of the lake so she could see down the road better. She prayed she would spy Nora's thin form and yellow dress strolling away. Instead the road showed empty.

Aylesbury joined her, scanning as hard as she.

She turned her gaze on the lake. Horror shouted in her head. Yellow could be seen in the water a few hundred feet away. She clawed at the duke's arm and pointed. "*Look*. In the lake."

"Stay here," he commanded her sharply. He called to the coachman to follow and started running.

She ran, too, cursing herself for not being more careful, fighting tears that blinded her.

Aylesbury walked right into the lake and swam toward the yellow fabric billowing atop the water. He dove. For a few horrible moments nothing happened. The worst sensation spread through Marianne, one of pending grief too profound to bear.

Then Aylesbury's head broke the water. So did Nora's. He started back, pulling Nora's limp body with him. Marianne gasped hard for breath, not in relief but in dread.

She reached them just as he and the coachman dragged Nora onto the bank. Her muslin dress, transparent now, showed her body in all its pale thinness.

Nora looked dead. There was no way to pretend she did not. She neither moved nor breathed. An eerie serenity had claimed her face.

Marianne fell to her knees and took Nora in her arms. "She warned me. I will never forgive myself for not keeping better watch, especially today when she was forced to—" She glared over at Aylesbury. "How careless I have been. I should have refused my uncle. Fought him today. I should have walked away into abject poverty rather than allow him to risk her like this."

Aylesbury reached for Nora. "She was not in long."

He turned Nora over on the ground, and pressed firmly on her back.

"Again, milord," the coachman said, watching with fearful eyes.

Aylesbury pushed again. And again. This time water streamed out Nora's mouth. He pushed once more.

Nora coughed. Then her shoulders rose and she coughed again and again.

Relief made Marianne weak. She embraced Nora's shoulders while the air entered her and consciousness returned. Nora remained face to the ground while she came back to life.

"What were you thinking, darling?" Marianne whispered in her ear while she cried out her anger with herself. "Forgive me for not knowing what his company would do, even for a short while. Forgive me for not standing up to your father. I will take care of you, and if it means we both leave that house, so be it."

Aylesbury had stood so Marianne could tend to her cousin. Now he bent down, turned Nora, and lifted her in his arms. He began striding back to the carriage, with the coachman and Marianne in his wake.

They bundled her into the blanket, and Aylesbury gave orders to make haste back to the house. Marianne held Nora the whole way.

A hearty footman carried Nora into the house.

"Take her to my chamber," Marianne said. "Find my uncle and send him at once," she commanded another servant.

Up in her chamber, Marianne had Katy remove Nora's

soaked clothes and dress her in one of Marianne's night-dresses. They tucked her into the bed, and built up the fire. Nora looked very small there. Childish and helpless.

Nora opened her eyes. She saw Marianne, and reached for her hand. "Do not scold."

"I will not scold *you*." With Nora safe and dry, however, her anger kept building. Anger at herself, for not being more careful, and at her uncle, for being so cruel, and at Aylesbury, for being so bad his whole life he did not even remember all the wicked things he had done.

Uncle Horace burst into the chamber and strode to the bed. Seeing his daughter awake resulted in a long sigh of relief that gave Marianne heart. At least he had cared enough to worry.

He collected himself. "See she is kept warm," he ordered Katy. "Get some sherry in her. That should help."

Marianne touched his arm. "Uncle, I would speak with you." She walked to the door.

In the passageway, with the door to her chamber firmly closed, she faced her uncle.

"Aylesbury said something about the lake," he muttered. "Could you not prevent it?"

"She did not fall in the lake. She *walked into the lake.*" Marianne spoke lowly, but the words came out clipped and furious. "She threatened as much. You demanded she accompany the duke on this ride, and this is the result."

"He is soaked. He went in after her. He saved her, the coachman said."

"*He is the reason she even did it.* Are we now to be grateful he ruined his nice coats to drag her out?" She turned on her heel. "He is still here? Good. I am going to tell him he is responsible, and that his actions today do not change that. I am going to let him know the damage he did three years ago, and—"

Her uncle's firm grasp stopped her in mid-stride. "You dare not. You cannot accuse him based on the fevered ravings of a woman."

"I can and I will."

"No. If you do it, I will say you are as mad as she."

"Are you so concerned about your forced friendship with this man that you will risk sacrificing your own daughter to your ambitions? Do not think I do not understand what motivates you. It is not Nora, or her welfare."

"How dare you speak thus to me. I will—"

"Throw me out on the road? Do it. I am not without resources or skills."

Her voice rang louder than she intended. She heard herself, and forced a calm on her demeanor that she did not feel in her heart. "You will abandon your plan regarding her marriage to him, or to anyone, until and unless she chooses to wed. Do you hear me, Uncle? If you persist in this, I will find a way to remove her from this house, even if I have to go into service to provide for her. She tried to make good on her threat today, and if ever there was proof that she will not accept marriage, that is it."

Uncle Horace's expression changed from fury to chagrin by the time she finished.

"I will not expect her to marry," he finally said. "In turn you are to promise that you will not throw accusations at Aylesbury. They cannot be proven, and such men have power you do not comprehend."

His quick capitulation surprised her. Perhaps how close they came to tragedy today added weight to her demand.

"I will go down and thank the duke for his help today," Uncle Horace said. "I will communicate your gratitude as well, in ways I doubt you could voice sincerely right now."

Marianne returned to Nora while her uncle descended the stairs. He had been right. After the events of the day, gratitude was the last thing she was inclined to give His Grace.

CHAPTER 7

The Times of London

. . . To conclude our letter, we can report that Lord Ywain Hemingford of Lincoln's Inn Fields, London, has arrived in Gloucestershire to visit his brother, the Duke of Aylesbury. It is unknown whether the visit is a matter of business or is strictly familial, but locals have noted that Lord Ywain was not accompanied by his new wife, whose father, Hadrian Belvoir, had Newgate Prison as his domicile in the autumn, an incarceration that has now been described as an error. It is assumed that his wife remained in London to continue her studies with her tutors.

Elijah Tewkberry, Gloucestershire

"There is no reason for both of you to be bored too." Lance ended his explanation of why his brothers should leave while they handed their horses to the groom.

That Ives dallied at Merrywood was bad enough. That Gareth had arrived yesterday did not bode well. It meant Ives had written and bidden him to come, in the hopes that Gareth could lure out of Lance that which Ives could not learn by badgering.

Ives wanted to know who "she" was. His lawyer's mind had concocted untold disasters waiting if Lance pursued a woman here in the county. Lance's refusal to go up to London with him two days ago only solidified Ives's view that something was afoot that required investigation.

"Just tell me where you went the other day, and I will leave," Ives said. "You took the carriage."

He referred to Lance's absence on the afternoon he called on Miss Radley.

"I told you I had the carriage take me to the lake so I could do some rowing. A man cannot live for weeks on end without exercise." They strolled toward the house. "If you persist in prying, I may invite you to box for a few rounds, in order to release my irritation with your questions while I exercise more."

"Have you developed a fondness for the lake of late?" Gareth asked. He always smiled when he pried, and he now beamed his most amiable expression in Lance's direction. Gareth's notable charm had ingratiated him with many ladies of the ton prior to his marriage, and it served him well with men too. It had probably, Lance admitted, created the bond he and Ives felt for Gareth even if he was a half brother, and a bastard.

"Not particularly. Why do you ask?"

"We visited today. We went out of our way to do so."

"We were riding. One rides here and there. We had no destination, so we could not go out of our way."

Lance would not mind telling them about that ride with Miss Radley. If Ives had not turned into, well, Ives, he might have. Today's visit to the lake *had* been deliberate, so he could take a good look at the bank of that lake near where Nora Radley had almost drowned.

He had seen no evidence that she might have fallen in. No marks in the mud. No disturbance of the weeds or brush. The bank was not especially treacherous there. In fact it sloped to the water, making it easy to just walk in.

Is that what she had done? Marianne's dismay suggested as much. It disturbed him that he might have come so close to seeing one so young take her own life.

He had mulled over the evidence frequently since he left Sir Horace that day. The outing's bad ending had done much to remove from his mind the slow seduction of Miss Radley's hand, and her apparent arousal from it.

They entered the house by the library's garden doors. No sooner had they done so than a servant stepped into the library and handed Lance a card.

Gareth craned his neck to read it. "Sir Horace. That is interesting. Perhaps he has come to inform you that the coroner will finally be settling matters regarding Percy's death."

Somehow Lance doubted it. An oblique reference to doing that, made by Sir Horace in the autumn, had yielded nothing yet. Little had changed since then. More likely Sir Horace was using the excuse of Lance saving his daughter to insinuate himself further into a friendship.

"I should see him alone."

"Certainly," Ives said. He and Gareth retraced their steps and retreated to the garden.

Sir Horace, upon being presented, took a deliberate pose so Lance might examine him and note his dress and stance. One foot forward, back straight, nose high, he gazed with aggressive self-confidence. His gray hair had been slicked back, making his gaunt face all the more angular in appearance. His eyes appeared as narrow slits of bright smugness.

Sir Horace looked to be a man who intended to have his worth known today.

Lance could not imagine why.

"Will you have some brandy, Sir Horace?" Lance went to the decanters, since he knew one of them at least would imbibe.

"Thank you, Your Grace."

Glasses in hand, and asses settled on chairs facing each other, they sipped. Then Sir Horace set his glass down and put his hands on his knees. "I have come on a very important matter, sir. Not a mere social call."

Hopefully, as Gareth had suggested, Horace was here as a justice of the peace, to inform Lance that the nine-month winter of his life was over.

"I will be clear and quick with it," Sir Horace said, eyeing Lance with a steely glint. "I have come to advise you to marry my niece, Marianne Radley."

Lance rarely found himself astonished. Now his surprise was such that he wondered if Sir Horace had gone mad.

That amazement soon gave way to a profound irritation. He had suffered much the last nine months, in part due to this man's intransigence. He had of late tolerated Sir Horace's company during rides he intended to take alone. Now this. Sir Horace had gone too far.

"How good of you to worry for my domestic contentment, sir."

Horace rested back in his chair. "You do not like my presumption, I can see. I remind you that I am not only a mere neighbor, and one below you in rank at that. I am a justice of the peace."

"How does that signify to the matter at hand?"

"I've the means to make you swing, Your Grace. I've proof enough you poisoned your brother. Like most men, I want to better myself, so I offer a bargain. Marry my niece, and I will not only keep this proof to myself, I will tell the coroner to close out the matter."

Lance knew a moment of relief that Ives had gone into the garden. While normally of even temper, Ives was quick to fight when provoked, and if he sat where Lance now did, Sir Horace would soon find himself thrashed bloody.

Not that Lance took the threat, and the arrogance with which Sir Horace said it, without rising rancor.

"Do you expect me to trust that you have this proof?"

"If you've a bit of sense, you will. I've a person who will swear he saw you by your brother's food that night. Food prepared on a tray to go up to his private chambers. Saw you fussing with it. He came to me first, and I convinced him to tell no one else. Yet. If he lays down this information, however, that is all that will be needed, and you know it. You and your brother did not like each other. Lots of animosity for years. Then, with his passing, you got all of this." His hand waved around the library, implying all that lay beyond.

As Lance listened, a raw emptiness spread out from his gut. He had come to know the sensation well these last months. It usually emerged at night, during his darkest hours, and he had resisted naming it for a long time. Ignoble fear. Pending doom. It evoked the insidious temptation to panic that all trapped men felt.

"Who is this person who claims to have seen this?"

Sir Horace laughed. "Let us just say it is someone I can put my hands on quickly enough, who will speak if I ask it of him."

"Damnation, whoever it is, he lies. I did not even dine here myself, so I have no idea of where and when my brother did."

"So you have said, many times." Sir Horace picked up his glass and sipped some brandy. He appeared pleased with himself, and unwavering. Protestations of innocence would do Lance no good.

"Why your niece?"

"You find her at least moderately appealing, if you called. And my daughter . . ." He looked down at his glass. "My daughter is not suitable due to her illness."

Lance stood. Hands in pockets lest he succumb to his urge to punch Sir Horace, he paced away.

He did not need to ask why Sir Horace wanted this marriage. Any relationship to a duke brought advantages. It nearly always could be exploited for financial gain. Sir Horace's ability to get close to a man of influence would bring him influence in turn. Others would curry his favor, and offer him partnerships.

Most likely in the years ahead, if this marriage happened, Sir Horace would be sitting here many times, demanding some favor or another that would ultimately enrich him and his new friends.

"I will add some honey to the pot," Sir Horace said. "I have considerable influence with the coroner. Not only will you not swing if you agree to my plan, but I will also see that you are exonerated. At least officially. He will change his determination from unknown causes, to natural causes."

Lance would have liked to dismiss this new offer, but it pulled at his soul. The suspicions about him had made time stand still. With such a sword hanging over a man's head, he could never be truly free.

As for the "at least officially"—there would always be some talk of it, but without the official exoneration of this crime, the common references to it would never cease, no matter how virtuous a life he may lead.

"You are assuming the lady will have me."

"What woman would not?"

A willful woman. A smart woman. "I'll not have you coerce her, as you are coercing me, if I agree to this. One partner in such a match is bad enough."

"I am counting on your seeing that no coercion is necessary. Women aplenty have made fools of themselves over you. What is one more?" Sir Horace gazed over with a wizened spark in his eyes. "Woo her if you choose. Play the lovesick swain. Seduce if necessary. I leave the details to your expertise."

"And if she proves intractable? There is no way you can force her to accept a proposal when it comes. All my expertise may be for naught."

Sir Horace chuckled. "Possibly, possibly. We will consider that problem should it arise. I am sure it will not." His mirth died. "Do we have a right understanding, Your Grace?"

It was a hell of a bargain, and one not to accept if there were any other choice. "I need to think about it."

Sir Horace got to his feet. "Think all you want, but not too long. The coroner has been restless for several months now, and it can go badly if he is left to his own conclusions."

"I'll be damned."

Ives muttered the curse for the third time. Or was it the fourth?

He and Gareth sat with Lance in Lance's dressing room. A bottle of port, its contents almost depleted, stood on the dressing table. Glasses dotted the chamber.

Lance had sent for them when it became clear he would not sleep this night. Now they all sat half foxed, ruminating over the news he had shared about Radley's visit.

"No, *I'll* be damned, from the looks of it, no matter what I do," Lance said. "Have you no advice? No insights? No calls for action? No *solution*?"

That made his brothers alert.

"What do you think of her?" Gareth asked.

"What he thinks of her does not matter," Ives said. "Lance, you cannot agree to marriage on these terms. He is bluffing. Lying."

"Or someone is lying to him," Gareth said.

"Let us assume it is the latter. Not because I trust Radley, but because he appeared far too sure of himself. If there is indeed a person willing to hang me with a lie, who might it be?" Lance grabbed the bottle, poured some, and passed it around. "A servant in this house, I expect, since only the servants and I were here. There is no one else to claim to have seen anything."

"That hardly helps," Gareth said. "There must be forty of them. How would you ferret out the scoundrel?"

"Actually, there are seventy or so," Lance said.

"Eighty-seven, counting the ones on the grounds," Ives corrected.

How like Ives to know.

"Yet not all eighty-seven would have excuses to be where a dinner might be prepared or transported," Gareth offered.

Lance waved that idea off. "Any of them could find an

excuse to explain how they came to see me at my nefarious deed. We are stuck with all of them as possibilities."

More silent rumination.

"I am going to put Radley off," Lance said. "I will attend on the lady, and allow Radley to think I am going to propose. While I dance attendance, I will find out who this witness is."

He set aside his glass and closed his eyes. Attending on Miss Radley—Marianne—would not be difficult. He had intended to anyway, to occupy his time. He did not like the idea of being required to court her, however. No man would. Just as no man, least of all a duke, would allow the likes of Sir Horace to dictate his choice of wife.

"Here is a problem," Ives said. "If you pursue the lady in order to garner some time to find this liar, it will create expectations. From Sir Horace. From her mother and the county neighbors. From her. If it goes on very long, it will be assumed by all that a proposal is imminent."

"I will ensure the lady will not have me. I will arrange it so she throws me over before it reaches any proposal."

"Oh, of course. You will merely do what dukes always do to discourage women from wanting to be wealthy duchesses of incomparable station. We should have thought of that, Gareth." Ives cocked his head. "How do dukes manage that again? It has slipped my mind."

"She already does not care for me much," Lance said. "And after what happened to her cousin at the lake—" He glared at the port, annoyed it had made him loose-lipped.

Ives's sudden frown looked like canyons emerged on his brow. "I knew you took us there for a reason. What happened to her cousin at the lake? And why were you at the lake with her cousin?"

Resenting every word, Lance explained Nora's accident, and his suspicions about what had really happened. "Miss Radley said a few things that led me to think it was no accident too," he concluded.

"Why did she do it?" Gareth asked. "Why would Miss Radley think this was her cousin's effort to harm herself?"

Lance searched his memory about the confusion after they pulled Nora out. "It was not clear, but she blamed herself. And me. My arrival, and my offer of that carriage ride, seemed part of it."

"That explains why it is Marianne Radley whom Sir Horace now throws at you, and not his daughter. I was wondering about that," Gareth said. "Her state of mind does not allow marriage, from the sounds of things. In particular, it does not allow marriage to you."

"I did not even know her before that carriage ride."

"But she knew you, or of you. She knows you are a duke, if nothing else."

They all knew what the something else might be. Being thought a murderer was not the kind of thing to reassure a very young, very frightened girl who was not right in her head.

"It explains Radley's threat and blackmail. His daughter made her views most clear, and he can't risk she will do it again. So he turned to the cousin," Gareth said. "Now he will not have to talk you into marrying a madwoman either. You might have balked at that, especially with your duties to the title and the family."

"Is this other one the 'she'?" Ives asked, proving he had not missed one word of what Gareth said.

"She?" Gareth looked curiously at Ives, then Lance.

"Lance showed evidence of a blooming fascination when I arrived. I guessed it was why he took off without a word that afternoon, and I was right. So, again, is Marianne Radley the 'she'?"

Damnation. "I will admit that I chanced to meet her, and thought her company might alleviate the unending tedium of my days. She is, and was, by no means a fascination."

"So you will woo the lady, and ensure she does not like you at all before you are done," Ives said. "And while you woo and pursue, you will find out about this lying witness. It is not much of a plan, but I am at a loss for a better one."

"I will be doing one other thing," Lance said, the decision coming to him with a certainty he had not felt about anything in the last nine months. "I will be making sure I am never again the victim of schemes like Radley's, and that any fool who chooses cannot threaten me with exposure of a crime *I did not commit.*"

A bolt of anger crashed through him while he spoke. He hurled his glass into the fire with his last word. The flames jumped as they consumed the remnants of the spirits.

"I am going to rid myself of the damnable suspicions that follow me like a pending tempest, and that will never go away no matter what is done. I am going to ignore your advice, Ives, and stop living like the saint I have never been, and instead become an avenging angel."

He glared at his brothers, waiting for them to try to

soothe the unholy fury that gripped him. All he saw were
two men watching him with concern and, God help him,
sympathy.

"How are you going to do that?" Ives asked.

He grabbed the bottle, got up, and aimed for his bed. "I
am going to find out who did kill Percy, damn it."

CHAPTER 8

The Times of London

. . . *With that reassurance to readers regarding the health of Lady Jersey, who continues her long residence in Cheltenham, and our description of improvements intended at one of that spa's pumps, we now must conclude our notes regarding that town.*

In other county news, a widow of very high station has found herself attended upon by a man of merely respectable fortune and birth. Society watches to see if the lady will be persuaded the gentleman is worth the relinquishment of both her independence and the control of her considerable income. Local wags think that unlikely unless the gentleman strikes a bargain

with the devil to give him new youth and at least a
fair amount of wit.

Elijah Tewkberry, Gloucestershire

Marianne stepped out of the silk dress. The color of ice
frosting a lake, its hint of blue enhanced her eyes.

"We will have it ready for a final fitting on Monday,"
Mrs. Makepeace said. Her daughter Mrs. Trumball
began helping Marianne into the outdated green muslin
she had worn to the dressmakers.

Uncle Horace had generously offered to have this dress
made for the assembly next week. Mama was getting one
too. He had not even objected when Nora refused to
accept one herself. Perhaps he really had given up on the
idea of forcing Nora into social situations.

These visits to the dressmakers in Dutton had become part of life the last week, as Marianne's days had
followed life's inevitable preference for routine and pre-
dictability.

She usually spent the mornings with Nora, and by
week's end had even coaxed her cousin out into the garden
to watch the men rehabilitating the plantings to Mama's
instructions.

Every few days she joined Mama on her calls. Normally they visited the village too. Twice now they had
taken the longer carriage ride to Cheltenham, however,
for better shopping or for other errands.

Mama had deigned to make use of the Dutton dressmakers due to the press of time, but she let the women

know that if the resulting dresses disappointed in any way, all further wardrobe additions would be procured in London.

With such a prize dangling, the dressmakers found their best materials, such as the lovely ice blue silk that Mrs. Makepeace now folded with care. Marianne stepped from behind the curtain into the shop's little sitting room while she buttoned her gray wool pelisse.

"It was very bad of you to demand they remake four of our other dresses, too, and for no extra money," she said to her mother while she pulled on her gloves. Behind the curtain, the women hurried to straighten up the workroom for the grand lady who would be fitted next.

"They are charging too much for these new dresses, so I am only evening the accounts. You must be alert to that, Marianne. Shopkeepers will want you to pay more if they think Sir Horace's fortune is behind you."

Marianne tied on her bonnet. "While you are being fitted, I think I will take a turn outside."

"Do not be long. I do not want to have to wait for you."

Promising to return soon, Marianne slipped out of the shop.

She marched down to Howard's bookshop, and took care of her business there. Before leaving she broke the seal on a letter from London. The editor of the *Times* had written to Elijah Tewkberry, and informed him that the sum of five shillings had been deposited in the London bank account designated for any payments.

Unfortunately, he had also written that some of the letters were not suitable for the *Times*. Her letter regarding the woman and the eloquent gentleman who took chambers at Dutton's inn had been rejected. He advised that Mr. Tewkberry should expand his circle of papers should he want to sell such gossip. He even provided the address of a gossip sheet, and said he had been told they paid handsomely for information. He hoped, however, that any news of true importance would first be offered to the Times.

She would never meet this editor, but she would someday express her gratitude. Eighteen months ago, after attending the quarter sessions in Calne, she had written up a report of a murder trial, complete with dialogue from the proceedings. On a whim she had sent it to the newspaper. Assuming such a missive from a woman would not find favor, she had plucked the name Elijah Tewkberry out of her head.

To her amazement, a bank draft had arrived four days later. As it was made out in Mr. Tewkberry's name, she had been unable to do anything with it. Since Vincent was in London at the time, she wrote and asked him to open a bank account there in both her name and that of Elijah Tewkberry. He had done so, never once asking why, or even who this man was. If she had harbored any remaining hopes regarding Vincent's interest in her private life, his utter indifference to the reasons for her unusual request made the truth very clear.

After that she had the newspaper deposit payments in that London account, then had a bank in Calne transfer the money to it. Thus she maintained the illusion that her correspondence came from a man.

This money earned from her correspondence had become more important all of a sudden. She did not trust Uncle Horace to permanently set aside his intentions to use Nora in some marriage scheme. Should he take such steps in the future, she wanted to have money to make good on her threat to remove Nora from the house.

Which meant that Elijah Tewkberry needed to correspond more frequently. She hoped she could find enough respectable news to avoid approaching the gossip sheets, but if it came to that, she would swallow her pride and do it.

Joining Mama on calls would provide some. Uncle Horace, it appeared, would be another source. Just last night he had described a humorous event that took place at the petty sessions he presided over. She intended to start attending those herself. Unfortunately, the really interesting transgressions were only brought forward at the quarter sessions, and the last one at Michaelmas had ended before she left Wiltshire.

She debated whether she had time to walk all the way out to the Blackthorn coaching inn, to chat with the servants and see if they had any information that might point her toward something useful. She had formed an acquaintance with two talkative maids there when she stopped by while out riding. That was something else that had changed since Nora's "accident" at the lake. Uncle Horace no longer demanded her company on rides. Rather, he seemed to encourage her to ride on her own now.

Deciding she did not have time to walk all the way to the inn and back, she strolled along the main lane in the village, stopping on occasion to look in shop windows. She was peering into a tailor's shop when a voice behind her interfered with her thoughts.

"Rare to see you here in the village, sir," a man said loudly. "As it happens, I've been wanting a word with you."

"I have time for two words, Mr. Langreth. I regret that you waited to share them. I always am happy to speak with a neighbor."

Hearing Aylesbury's voice, Marianne became most attentive, but bent to pretend close study of a waistcoat on display in the window.

"Talk between neighbors is one thing. A right understanding is another, Your Grace."

"You appear vexed, Mr. Langreth."

"I am, sir. I am. I have been after that sly thief Jeremiah Stone for almost a year, and when I finally catch him red-handed, he gets off at the petty sessions, due to you, when he should have been bound over for a judge's trial."

"You must refer to those hares found with him when you detained him. As the magistrates said, there was not sufficient information to assess his guilt. Or at least that is what my steward reported."

"He is a poacher! Everyone knows it. He makes free use of my land and everyone else's. I swore down information as such."

"Why was he not convicted, then?" Another man spoke now. Marianne strained to see him in the glass panes' reflection, but all she could make out were three dark heads clustered together on three tall male forms.

Another figure, this one shorter by a head and white-haired, pointed at Aylesbury. "They said *he* had to swear, not me, that is why. And he would not. Nor would his steward in his stead. You may be so rich you can afford to allow poachers a free hand, Your Grace, but the rest of the landowners here are not so favored by Providence."

"Mr. Langreth, I am sorry to have denied you your pound of Mr. Stone's flesh. We all know his circumstances, however. He is little more than a boy, and he cares for his ill father and his six siblings. Furthermore, there is no proof he poached on my lands that day."

"He had the damned hares in his damned sack, along with a damned trap. He was crossing the road between our properties, leaving yours and going to mine. If that is not proof he was poaching, what is?"

"Finding him *on* someone's land with that trap, or those hares," the other voice said. "Of course my brother would not swear information against this Mr. Stone. He could not prove Mr. Stone had in fact gotten those hares in his forest."

"Hell of a thing. I've been asking you to put your people after him, and when I catch him myself it doesn't count in the law!"

"Mr. Langreth. I sympathize that you think your property rights have been violated by poachers. There are some I would gladly see punished," Aylesbury said. "However, what little Mr. Stone may take from my land feeds an infirm father and a passel of children, all of whom might starve if he is taken from them."

Silence greeted that. Then boots stomped away. "Hell of a thing!" Mr. Langreth yelled to the village at large.

"I am surprised this Jeremiah Stone was not convicted," another new voice said.

"Sir Horace Radley woke up that morning in a generous mood," Aylesbury said.

Marianne sneaked a look over her shoulder. Aylesbury stood with two other men, not more than fifteen feet behind her. They all appeared related, although not a one of them truly looked like another. Dark-haired, all of them, and tall. Of the three, Aylesbury was perhaps the least typically handsome, yet she thought his particular version of handsome the most compelling.

As if feeling her quick glance, he turned. In the window's reflection she saw him facing her back, looking at her.

"Miss Radley, is that you?"

She feigned surprise at seeing him. He walked over and looked in the shop window. "Are you considering the purchase of a man's waistcoat? There are a few women who favor such things, but I do not think you would find one flattering."

He had noticed she had been at the window for some time. "I was thinking my uncle could use a new one." It sounded stupid, but it was all she had.

"You should advise him against getting it here. This fellow does not cut well." He looked toward the lane. "Our meeting is a happy coincidence. I would like to introduce you to my brothers. They are visiting for a week or so."

She could not refuse, so she found herself receiving

close inspection by Lord Ywain Hemingford, and Mr. Gareth Fitzallen. The latter was a beautiful man with a winning smile. The former might be beautiful, too, but with a subtle hardness that his own smile did not soften.

"Is your mother with you?" Aylesbury asked.

"She is completing some business with the dressmaker. I should return to her."

"We will walk with you." Aylesbury made to do just that, so she walked too. His brothers followed.

"Your cousin is well?" he asked.

"She is much recovered, thank you. I believe her ordeal from that day is firmly in the past."

"That is good to know. I have been concerned for her."

She began to think well of him for that, until she remembered that in the past he had been so unconcerned that poor Nora was found in the mud, after rain poured on her for hours.

"At least she suffered no fever this time." She could not resist saying it.

As soon as they approached the dressmakers, her mother came out the door. Mama must have seen her escort through the window, because now she pretended to look far and wide for Marianne, making a display of her search. She feigned surprise to see her daughter nearby with three gentlemen.

"Your Grace!" Mama dipped a curtsy. "Marianne, you have collected an impressive group of friends in such a short walk."

Aylesbury did the introductions. "You have not called on me, Mrs. Radley. I expected you by now."

"It has been my intention to do so very soon, Your Grace. Hasn't it, Marianne? We are well settled now, so we would be honored to call."

"I look forward to it. Do not dally, or my brothers may be gone. That would disappoint them, since they have so little society here other than my company."

Marianne doubted either brother wanted to sit in a drawing room while Aylesbury flattered her mother. However, both brothers smiled, nodded, and joined in cajoling Mama to make her call very soon.

"We will take our leave now," Aylesbury said. "I regret we have business to attend." He bowed to Mama and her, and all three brothers walked back toward the tailor shop.

"Well. *My.*" Mama let her shock finally show. "When he invited me to call the day we met, I did not believe he meant it. Such things are said all the time out of politeness. I certainly did not think he meant it so much that he now scolds me for neglecting him."

"Do you know the third one? Mr. Fitzallen?"

"The old duke took a mistress early on, and kept her until he died, and that man is the result." Mama turned back to the dressmaker. "If we are going to make a call on a duke, I must tell Mrs. Makepeace to enhance those ensembles they are doing over, and to complete it immediately. Come along, and pick out some trim for your mantelet. We will call the day after tomorrow, I think, not tomorrow. We do not want to look too eager."

Considering the gleam in Mama's eyes, Marianne suspected they would look too eager even if they waited a week.

* * *

"You both must stay now. Ives, invite your wife to join you. She can study here as well as in London." Lance made the demand as they strode down the lane. "Gareth, since Eva is with child, she does not have to come."

"How good of you," Gareth said.

"I am not going to request it of Padua on your whim, so she will not be coming either," Ives said.

"It is not a whim. It will be much easier for me to devise ways to see Miss Radley if there is a woman or two about. Otherwise I am left with dull calls in Sir Horace's drawing room. I can hardly make good progress that way."

"Good progress on what?" Ives asked.

"On being so bad she won't have me. Gareth, when they call, you are to attend on the mother. Attractive older women find you irresistible. Distract her, et cetera."

"There will be no 'et cetera.' I am a married man. I am not going to flirt with Mrs. Radley to accommodate your progress."

"Perhaps after today you will not have to concern yourself with the lady, or with Sir Horace," Ives said.

Lance thought that unlikely, but was willing to try anything.

Today's visit to the village had been Gareth's idea. At breakfast he suggested that, as Percy's next of kin, they all call on the coroner and express familial concern. They would press on him that the question regarding the circumstances of Percy's death left the entire family in a type of limbo.

They walked past the village's two taverns, either of which Lance thought would be a fine place for such a meeting. They turned a corner and instead entered a coffeehouse. Thaddeus Peterson, the coroner, favored this establishment over the others, being an abstemious sort of fellow. The son of a local landowner, he bided his time until he inherited his father's estate.

He sat on a divan, reading the *Times* and drinking his coffee. A thin, fair man with curly blond hair, his soft face appeared as bland as Lance knew his character to be. Many years ago, he and Peterson had boyhood friendship. Then Peterson grew up into someone who did not remember how to have fun.

"Peterson. What a fine accident, finding you here," Lance said as they descended on him.

Peterson gazed up in surprise at the phalanx of Hemingfords hovering over his divan. "I am always here in the afternoon, except on Fridays when I make calls. I ride out at two o'clock each day, and take coffee here, then ride back at four."

"Do you, now? I had forgotten what a pleasant place this is." Lance pulled over a chair. Ives sat on the divan's arm. Gareth propped his ass on the edge of a table. They all smiled at Thaddeus.

Peterson took one more look at his paper before setting it aside. "You interrupted my pondering the news reaching London." He tapped the paper. "Do you know this Elijah Tewkberry who is serving as the paper's correspondent in this county?"

"I have never heard of him," Lance said.

"One of his letters mentioned me," Ives said. "I do not recall meeting him, however."

"I have no idea who he is," Peterson said. "He wrote he was visiting here this winter. I have not heard of a family with such a visitor."

"Not everyone parades their visitors down Cheltenham's lanes," Gareth said. "I think you have no idea who I am, either, and I have visited the county many times over the years."

Peterson eyed him thoughtfully. "I confess I would not recognize you, or even guess who you are, except that you are here with these two. You must be the old duke's by-blow."

"Lance did not want to disturb you when we saw you in here, but I insisted," Gareth said, ignoring the slur with what Lance thought was admirable patience. "The unresolved matter of my eldest brother's death weighs on me. On all of us. As the coroner, surely you can come down one way or another. Your determination of causes unknown has stood for nine months."

Peterson glanced at Lance. "I am surprised you press me on it. After all, it may come down the one way you would not like."

"There is no evidence of any crime," Ives said.

"The physician—"

"The physician only said the stomach pains might indicate poison. *Might*," Ives said. "If after nine months there is no proof he was poisoned, it is time to lay the matter to rest, don't you think?"

Peterson folded his arms over his chest. He glared at

each of them in turn. "I do my duty as I see it. When a possible murder is on the table, and of a duke at that, I do not clear the plates in the name of expediency."

Ives looked ready to argue. A subtle gesture from Gareth stopped him. Gareth pushed away from the table and sat on the divan next to Peterson.

"No one would want you to do anything contrary to your sense of duty. We merely expressed our frustration with having his ghost still without rest."

Peterson relaxed. "I thank you for that. I confess to experiencing some of that frustration myself."

"Were you friends?"

Peterson hesitated. "He was amiable enough with me, and greeted me, and we spoke at assemblies and dinner parties. He called once or twice, on a matter having to do with my official duties." He glanced sharply at Lance. "He did not insult me at least, or cut me, or turn his wit against me."

"It sounds like a friendship to me," Gareth said. "We knew there were those in the county who mourned him as we did, even if we did not know all of their names."

Peterson nodded.

Gareth stood. "Let us leave Mr. Peterson to the revelations of Mr. Tewkberry. It is almost four and he will want to finish his coffee in peace."

Ives did not like it, but he followed Gareth and Lance out of the coffeehouse. Back on the main lane, Gareth stopped and turned to Lance.

"He hates you. Why?"

"Perhaps he was insulted when I dropped him as a friend. You know how it is. You have a boyhood acquaintance with whom you might on occasion play knights in the woods, but then you get older and realize that boy has become a very dull man, so you stop seeking him out." He gestured toward the coffeehouse. "Would you be friends with him now?"

"He spoke as if you did not merely stop seeking him out. He implied you insulted him."

"I suppose, when I was in my cups, I may have teased him once or twice, when we were both still very young. It was so long ago I have forgotten it."

"*He* has not forgotten it." Gareth walked on. "Did you also insult the justices? Is all of this personal, and a way to flog you for your past deeds?"

They repaired to one of the taverns. Over some ale, Gareth raised the question again.

"I will confess that if it had been Ives in the house that night, there might have never been one day of suspicions, let alone nine months," Lance said. "I have assumed from the beginning that it was partly personal, and revenge for my past behavior, but not by Peterson."

"He is speaking of the other justice of the peace," Ives said to Gareth. "Not Radley. Mr. Gregory."

Gareth swallowed a groan. "So not just the coroner, but one of the magistrates as well. Did you insult him too?"

"You might say so." Ives bit back a grin.

"What did you do?"

Lance never apologized for his behavior, but at this moment he felt some chagrin. "Seduced his wife," he muttered.

"Excuse me? You were talking into your cup and I did not hear well. Did you say you seduced the man's wife?"

"He did indeed, and not discreetly." Ives, who was always discreet, said the last with a tone of censure.

"He married a young woman, too young for him, and brought her up to London to show her off. In my defense, I did not pursue her, but one thing led to another—"

"So you did not just seduce his wife, you seduced *his bride*."

Gareth appeared shocked. Lance thought that took a lot of gall considering the topic was the seduction of another man's wife. His bastard brother had been notorious for that.

"With Gregory honing his ax, and Radley blackmailing you, and Peterson sulking about a slight from long ago, you will find no mercy there. I had hoped—well, it is safe to say that nothing less than making good on your plan to find the real murderer will exonerate you," Gareth said.

"That is why I intend to do just that."

"Here is the problem," Ives said. "What if we have always been correct, and he was not murdered? Then what?"

They all looked at each other. Leave it to a lawyer to point out the chasm on the path to salvation.

CHAPTER 9

"Smooth your mantelet. Straighten your hat." Mama's instructions came in a quick whisper after she and Marianne stepped out of the carriage.

Not just any carriage. Not the gig kept in the carriage house, or even the tilbury, either of which Marianne could have driven. On hearing the request for one of the carriages, and learning their intention to call on Aylesbury, Uncle Horace had insisted they use the barouche, and had sent a footman to accompany them and the driver. Both servants wore ancient livery that Marianne had not seen since she was a child.

She did smooth her sapphire mantelet. Mrs. Makepeace had added fur to its edge. A new bright sapphire plum adorned her bonnet. Beneath the mantelet, a pelisse dress of fine fawn wool sported a new border of brown embroidered with an intricate black design. The goal of that border was to increase the length of the dress due to Marianne growing an inch during their time in exile. The bodice had been let out an inch, too, to accommodate growth in another area.

Mama's green carriage ensemble now had plaid edging and new gold buttons. On leaving the house, Marianne doubted even Aylesbury would be able to tell both of them wore remade clothes. Mrs. Makepeace had done them proud.

Now, as her gaze spanned Merrywood Manor, her self-confidence wavered. Her family home was very large, but this manor house went on and on in every direction. There was probably twice as much again behind what she saw. This house would make anyone feel small, unless one was born to the manor to start.

Her mother muttered nonstop all the way to the door. "This will establish us again like nothing else will. And he insisted we call so he could receive us! I daresay you will find yourself with some eligible men dancing attendance on you when it becomes known a duke receives you and your family."

"I would not mind a beau."

"More than one, I hope. And not just any beaus. I have been making a list of the eligible bachelors in the county as I make my calls and hear of them. Much has changed on that count in five years, including your advancing years. Still, I am hopeful."

They presented their cards to the butler. He put them

in a little reception chamber while he went away. He returned soon, and led them to the drawing room.

"Don't gawk like a rustic," Mama warned as they stepped into the chamber.

It was all Marianne could do to obey when she saw the riches within. Hundreds of people would fit in the huge drawing room, and the many sofas and chairs would seat most of them. The ceiling soared above, replete with extensive moldings, and large windows lined one wall. Those windows were not composed of small panes of glass in the normal fashion, but with large ones lacking any leading. It was said the palaces of kings had windows like that.

Two of the largest carpets she had ever seen graced the floor. Her feet sank deeply into the one on which she stood. All of the fabrics in the chamber proclaimed the wealth of the owner. The drapes alone probably cost more than Uncle Horace's income in a year.

"Stand proud. We are more than presentable." Her mother did not sound nearly as confident as her words.

"I think even if we dressed in sable and the finest lace, we might not be presentable enough," Marianne whispered back.

They inched farther into the chamber, taking it all in. Then another set of doors opened, and the duke entered with his brothers.

Greetings. Bows and curtsies all around. A few mild flatteries from Mr. Fitzallen, along with a most charming smile. Tea arrived and they all sat and sipped.

"Will you gentlemen be attending the assembly?" Mama asked after some small talk.

"Regrettably I will not be staying that long," Mr. Fitzallen said.

"It is only a few days away," the duke said, as if his brother's departure was news to him.

"A few days too many." He turned his attention on Marianne and her mother. "I will return to my wife tomorrow. My brother does not understand how a woman in the family way might grow anxious if left too long."

"Goodness, yes," Mama said. "How pleased you must be."

"Ives's wife is not so burdened. Since her nose remains in books, she will not miss him, so he will still be here," Aylesbury said. "We will go together, Ives. It has been some time for both of us."

Ives apparently was the family name for Lord Ywain.

"In my brother's case, the reason he has not attended county events in all these years was for the best of reasons, as I am sure you know, Mrs. Radley," Ives said. "However, if I am still at Merrywood, I will accompany him to this assembly, should he dare it himself."

Mama reacted with puzzlement at his allusion regarding the hiatus. Then she must have understood, because her face went slack, her eyes widened, and a blush spread. Marianne itched to demand further explanation. She would have to badger Mama later.

"Would you like to see the garden?" the duke asked. "Gareth, let us escort the ladies there by way of the gallery. Gareth is a renowned art expert, Miss Radley. He can talk for an hour about any painting we own, but I promise not to allow him to bore you too much."

"My mother is fond of gardens. She is currently remaking the one at my uncle's house."

"You must tell me all about it, Mrs. Radley," Mr. Fitzallen said, offering his hand to help Mama rise.

Mama appeared too bedazzled to move. What woman would not, with the attention of such a beautiful man showering down on her? Mr. Fitzallen had not flirted, or done the slightest thing to cause Mama's reaction. He merely was a man as handsome as the devil, with a smile that had Mama breathless.

She collected herself, and accepted his escort out of the drawing room. Lord Ywain drifted along in their wake. Aylesbury stepped into place alongside Marianne.

"I am pleased you called," he said.

"I cannot imagine why. The three of you must have better things to do than entertain us."

"Not many. You would be surprised at how uneventful it is here. It quickly grows very boring."

She would not be surprised. Leisure was the product of privilege, but an unending supply of it could be burdensome. That was one reason she took such joy in caring for Nora. It gave her life a purpose that would be difficult to find otherwise.

"Is that why you lived in London for so long?" They strolled the long gallery of paintings. Up ahead, Mr. Fitzallen stopped occasionally to point something out to her mother. Mama's gaze tended to gravitate to the face of the man, not the canvas under discussion.

"In part. Perhaps it was one third of the reason."

"And the other two thirds?"

Mama and Mr. Fitzallen had paused again. The duke did, too, and looked at her. "Once my brother Percy inherited, this house ceased being a home to me. Or to Ives either. We did not rub well together, Percy and I, and once he became the duke, the lack of mutual sympathy increased."

"Once he became lord, did he lord it over the rest of you? I think it is probably a rare man who does not succumb to the temptations of power, even with family members."

"How perceptive you are. You know the human heart very well for one so young."

They moved on, slowly. More slowly than Mr. Fitzallen up ahead. The distance to Mama stretched longer with each step. Marianne looked at the paintings as she passed, but she did not have time to really examine any of them.

"You could make this house less boring," she said. "You could entertain London friends. You could invite some neighbors for dinner on occasion. You might even open the estate grounds to the county for a day, the way your father used to do. Perhaps with a little time it would become a home again, and one that you enjoyed." She tried to quicken their path, to no avail. Aylesbury's steps remained ever so slow.

At the end of the gallery, Mr. Fitzallen opened a door, chatting with Mama all the while.

"I may try that. We will plot a fair for the county in the spring. You can help me."

We? "I— Surely there is someone here—"

Without so much as looking back, Mama followed her escort out of the gallery.

Aylesbury stopped again.

"The lady of the house usually directs the servants in such things, and I do not have one. What do I know about the sort of food to be served, or the decorations? Your advice will be essential. We do not want everyone later saying it was a poor affair."

Marianne kept one eye on the gallery, where Ives still lingered, studying a painting. "I am sure you know ladies more suited to the task than I. I have never managed a household, or been responsible for entertaining." She gestured broadly down the gallery. "My mother, however—"

"I am sure you would be successful in every way. I can tell when a person has good taste." Aylesbury took her hand in his. "I would be both pleased and honored if you gave your help in this."

She stared down at her hand, then up at him, then at the distant, distracted figure of Ives. How careless of Mama to leave her like this.

With one finger on her chin, the duke coaxed her gaze back at him. He looked deeply in her eyes. A little panic swelled in her chest. She could not look away.

"Do I have your agreement, pretty flower?" he asked.

Agreement for what? Oh, yes, helping with that county event. "I suppose so."

"I am so glad."

A smile. A subtle one. Devilish, confident, and dangerous. She seemed surrounded by haze now. The gallery barely penetrated her consciousness.

Did she step forward, or float? She moved, that was certain, as the duke gently pulled her toward him while he eased back, toward the wall. Now she could not see the gallery even if she wanted to, because a very large statue blocked her view of it.

Warmth on her face, as his hands cupped her head. Her mind absorbed what he was doing too late. By the time she realized his intention, his lips had already pressed hers.

Who knew being naughty could be so sweet? Who would guess the Wicked Duke would kiss so gently? He lured her into compliance, as if he touched the parts inside her that wanted to be kissed because he knew they were there. He made love to her mouth much as he had to her hand in the boat.

It was the first real kiss she had ever had, and his lips on hers felt absolutely perfect. Wonderful. Its effects on her were a revelation too. Such a small thing, a kiss. Yet it fascinated and vanquished her. A titillating pleasure lapped through her that defeated her conscience when it belatedly emerged.

I shouldn't, but . . .

He kissed her more fully.

I must stop this at once. Only I do not want to . . .

He drew her into an embrace.

This is scandalous, and yet . . .

His kisses became more ardent, less gentle. His hands caressed her back and hips, evoking wicked thrills unlike she had ever experienced, or even guessed could be felt.

I must not, I should not, I . . .

His tongue urged her lips apart. His tongue began a slow dance inside her mouth, shocking and mesmerizing her at the same time

"Lance, I am going out to the garden. Why don't you

allow Miss Radley time to see it too? I am sure by now the art has begun to bore her." Ives's voice crashed through her euphoric daze. It did not sound far away at all.

Aylesbury stopped kissing her, but he did not release her for a few moments. Then he gave her a look such as she had never seen in a man's eyes before, and set her away from himself.

"If you insist, Ives. However, we have both discovered new things about this old Greek god here. His entire stance appears different from this angle. Don't you agree, Miss Radley?" He stepped away and into the gallery's long hall.

She took a deep breath to collect herself, and stepped out as well. "Very different. Far less languid, and much more angular." She forced herself not to touch her hat, to see if those kisses had set it askew.

Ives stood fifteen feet away. He smiled at his brother, then her. He turned on his heel and walked away.

She felt herself again. Enough to continue walking down the gallery. Astonishment at her own behavior blotted out most of her thoughts. Except one.

She had been bad, and the duke had been *badder*, but . . . being kissed by him had been glorious.

"What pleasant ladies." Gareth offered his view of the visit while Lance sat with him and Ives out on the terrace, watching the sun set below the treetops of the forest.

"Mrs. Radley appeared captivated by you," Ives said. "So much that she did not notice the absence of her daughter."

"She realized it right before Miss Radley emerged from the house. Did the paintings make Miss Radley dally in the gallery, Lance? If she likes art, perhaps she and Eva would get along well," Gareth said.

"She was not admiring art. She was with Lance." Ives puffed deeply on his cigar. "Damned good thing I interfered. Two more minutes and . . ." He finished with a long glare at Lance.

He was not going to explain himself to Ives, especially Ives at his most sanctimonious. Besides, right now, he could not even explain himself to himself.

He had intended a stolen kiss, no more. A minor bit of naughtiness. He had assumed that would shock her. Scare her. It would set the foundation for his ensuring she thought him too bad to consider.

Instead she had allowed it. Her breathless acceptance had been fuel to his own heat. Where they were and who they were ceased to matter.

Damned good thing indeed that Ives had interfered.

"As I explained, we were availing ourselves of different views of the statue. From the side, the rear, and so forth."

"From the sounds I heard, you were not studying that Greek god's ass. I never knew the acoustics in the gallery were so good."

Gareth grinned. "Are you saying there was some etcetera taking place, Ives?"

"Only of the mildest sort," Lance said.

"Well, having done my duty today, and allowed you the privacy to shock Miss Radley—"

"She did not look shocked to me," Ives muttered.

"—having procured you that privacy, I will make my departure in the morning," Gareth said.

"I need you to stay until after the assembly. Who is to distract her mother that night if you are not oozing your charm?"

"Ives will do it. I must leave."

"Ives will *not* do it," Ives said. "You will have to employ your talent for disarming ladies and manage it on your own, Lance. I will accompany you to the assembly, so that I can stop you from thrashing someone when you are insulted, as you are sure to be. I will not distract Mrs. Radley by any means, however, least of all charm."

"You have both become much less useful since your marriages. Also very staid. I hope, if I ever wed, that I do not lose my sense of adventure and fun as you both have."

"If you are not careful, you will wed very soon." Ives stubbed out his cigar, emphasizing each word with a little smash. "Scaring off Miss Radley to the point where she turns down a proposal from a duke may be harder than you think."

"Or require some very shocking behavior and revelations," Gareth said.

"I can manage both, if necessary."

"Of course you can," Gareth said. "It is Ives who doubts your plan, not I."

Upon returning home from the call on the duke, Marianne went looking for Nora. Guilt as much as love sent her to her cousin's chamber.

To allow Aylesbury to kiss her was scandalous. Her lack of resistance had been disgraceful, and she did not pretend that her inexperience excused her. That she now did not regret it nearly as much as she should reflected far worse on her character than the act itself, however.

She should be mortified, not only due to compromising her own virtue, but also because that kiss had been most disloyal to Nora.

To her surprise, Nora was not in her chamber. A crisp breeze entered through the open window. *An open window!* Panic burst through her heart. She rushed to the window and forced herself to look down on the ground below, terrified she would see her cousin's broken body there.

Relief poured out when the view showed nothing of the sort. Nora stood on the terrace, however, with her gaze fixed on the gardens. Abruptly she started walking, right into the plantings.

Marianne hurried down to the terrace. She could not see Nora from there, however. The garden was far too formal to obscure a person easily. Where could her cousin have gone?

In a far corner of the garden, the door of a greenhouse opened, and Nora walked out carrying a potted plant. A man stood at the threshold to the greenhouse, watching Nora walk away. He saw Marianne notice him, and came toward the terrace, following Nora.

"Look what Mr. Llewellyn gave me, Marianne." Nora admired her little plant. Her lips turned up at the edges while she showed it off.

Marianne stared. It was the first time in three years, she was sure, that she had seen her cousin smile.

"I am going to find a place in my chamber for it." Nora carried the pot into the house.

The man sauntered forward. He was a big fellow with dark hair, and quite young. His kind eyes and ease of movement appeared at odds with his size. "She has been sitting here by day a lot, Miss Radley. It seemed rude to ignore her. I hope I was not out of place in speaking to her at times."

"No, not out of place. She spoke back?"

He smiled softly. "A little. Not much. She finds the gardening interesting, I guess. I said yesterday that if she wanted a bit of that for herself in her chamber, there were pots to be had. Today she just showed up when I went in the glasshouse, and asked for one."

"I thank you for your kindness to her. She is not— that is to say, she is—" How to describe Nora?

"I understand. I had an aunt like that. Lost in herself, she was." He walked to the terrace steps. "Best I get back to those pots now. Good day to you."

Marianne turned to go back in the house, only to see Mama at the French doors, mouthing something through the glass. Marianne shook her head and pointed to her ears to indicate she could not hear. With an expression of exasperation, Mama came out to join her.

"We must talk."

"Indeed we must. The most amazing thing just happened. I saw Nora smile."

"Oh, tosh, Nora, Nora, always Nora. We have bigger

things to discuss. Come with me." Mama led the way to a bench against the wall that afforded some privacy.

"We must plan how we disclose our visit today. Do we let it be known before the assembly, or wait until that night? The duke is sure to acknowledge us there. Goodness, he may even ask you to dance."

"I think I may not go."

"Why ever not? Do not say it is because you want to keep your cousin company here. I will suffer a fit if you do."

She wished Mama knew everything about the duke. She wished she had not promised Uncle Horace to keep that history a secret.

"He kissed me today, Mama."

Her mother frowned and drew back. "Who did? That gardener I saw talking to you? I will have him sent—"

"The duke did. Aylesbury."

Her mother's mouth fell open and stayed that way for a ten count.

"Where? When?"

"In the gallery, after you and Mr. Fitzallen left." Marianne covered her face with her hands. "I am sure his other brother knows too. He was still there, in the gallery. I think he guessed what happened."

Mama's face flushed deeply. She grasped Marianne's hand in hers. With her other hand she pressed her bodice, over her heart. She appeared ready to swoon.

"This is outrageous."

"Yes. I blame myself for not seeing—"

"Scandalous and bold."

"Very bold. I am so embarrassed—"

"Such behavior is not to be condoned."

"I am very sorry, Mama—"

Mama squeezed her hand. She cocked her head. Suddenly she appeared most calm and very thoughtful. "Then again, he is a duke."

"What has that to do with anything? From what I have heard, he is prone to such outrageous, bold behavior."

"Being a duke does not excuse him, of course. However, it does make some difference."

"I do not see how."

Her mother turned to her and took both her hands in her own now. "Let us say at the assembly he dances with you. That will only make eligible men all the more interested. If the right one ends up proposing, that little kiss in the gallery will be seen by you in a different light."

It was not a little kiss, but she did not think it wise to explain that. Nor should she mention that this had not been the first kiss of any kind.

She definitely would not admit she had enjoyed both examples of bad behavior on Aylesbury's part.

Mama stood. "We will let his interest in you be seen at the assembly. We will not discuss our call at Merrywood before that, so it is all the talk that night. And you will most certainly come, Marianne." She walked toward the house.

"He will think I am encouraging him. That I welcome his advances."

"Oh, daughter, do not be a fool. Must I be blunt? If he chooses to toy with you for a brief spell, it is worth your while to suffer a few kisses. He is *a duke*."

*   *   *

Marianne found Nora in her chamber, dripping a bit of water into her pot.

"Mr. Llewellyn said it should have indirect light. Do you think he meant to put it in a place like this spot here?"

"I expect so. It is bright there, but the sun will not beat down on it through the window."

Nora tied a bow around the pot. She sat in her wooden chair and watched it. "Perhaps if it does not die, I will get another one too."

The conversation with Mama had disheartened Marianne. Much like her uncle, her mother sounded willing to accept behavior from the duke that she would never accept from another, all with the hope it would enhance her position in the community.

Perhaps Mama thought that not only her daughter might attract an eligible man if a duke danced with her. Maybe Mama thought she might too.

It was an unworthy thought, but perhaps not an incorrect one. The biggest problem with Mama's plan, aside from the risks to her daughter's reputation, was it would mean being disloyal in the worst way to Nora.

Marianne decided to broach the topic with the person they should be considering first and foremost.

"Mama and I paid a call today," she said.

Nora looked over, almost interested.

"We called on the Duke of Aylesbury. He received us. You remember, he called here last week."

"I remember."

Marianne waited for more of a reaction. None emerged. "He may call again, Nora."

"Do you like him?"

"I don't know. Do you?"

Nora shrugged. "He is a man like all men. They are by nature bestial, except for Vincent. I don't care about any of them one way or another."

How odd. "Your father thinks you may have cause to dislike the duke quite a lot. He thinks . . ." Marianne sought the mildest way of saying it. "He thinks you had a tendre for him years ago and that after . . . flirting with you, he ended his attention." She held her breath, bracing herself.

Nora petted a few leaves of her plant. "Papa is very stupid at times. We should not blame him for that. It is just the way he is."

Had Uncle Horace been wrong? He had sounded so certain, but Nora appeared indifferent.

Marianne went over and bent to embrace Nora's shoulders. She angled her head to look in her cousin's eyes. "So if I dance with the duke at the assembly, you will not mind?"

"It is not for me to mind, is it?"

Feeling better, but also confused, Marianne walked to the door.

"Marianne," Nora said.

"Yes?"

Nora turned her pot to get a different view of the plant. "Dance if you want, but be careful, dear cousin. He is a very wicked man."

CHAPTER 10

To the editor of the Times of London, *from Gloucestershire:*

The recent petty sessions are still being discussed in the county. Of foremost continued interest is the case of Mr. Jeremiah Stone, who was acquitted of poaching. Information was laid down by Mr. Langreth, who apprehended Mr. Stone on the road that separates his property from that of the Duke of Aylesbury. Mr. Langreth was astonished when the duke refused to lay down information too. Since Mr. Stone apparently was leaving the duke's lands when he was caught, and had not yet helped himself to game from Mr. Langreth's lands, the magistrates

*were left with no complaint from the owner of the
game in Mr. Stone's possession.*

*Mr. Langreth was heard to upbraid the duke in
the village of two weeks later. In response, the duke
declared that he would never lay down information
against Mr. Stone. Local opinion among landowners is that the duke has given poachers permission
to steal at will. However, a careful consideration of
the argument does not support that accusation, in
the opinion of your correspondent.*

Elijah Tewkberry, Gloucestershire

The dress slid over her petticoat like a fall of water. The
luxurious sensation of the fabric transported Marianne
to another world.

"Oh, miss. You are too lovely," Katy said. "Please sit,
so I can fix this around your neck. Your mother said you
are to wear it, and I was to accept no objections."

Katy secured the necklace. Made of fine silver fili-
gree, it managed to set off the dress and add a bit of
dazzle while remaining discreet.

The looking glass reflected a person Marianne had
never seen before. Her dark red hair displayed more curls
than normal, thanks to the curling iron. Her pale skin
showed some flush, thanks to a bit of paint. Her neck
appeared longer than usual, no doubt due to the low
décolletage of the dress.

She did not look like a girl, she admitted. Her maturity

showed when dressed and groomed like this, in ways her more casual attire did not reveal so readily. In her own mind her appearance had frozen when they moved to Cherhill, when she was seventeen. Now, tonight, she saw how much she had changed.

A girl no longer. Most women her age were married and mothers by now. She would look to be what she was tonight—a mature, unmarried woman, with one arm and leg already on the shelf.

In that light, perhaps Aylesbury's behavior had not been nearly as bad as she claimed. With her, at least. The episode with Nora had been another matter.

Lifting her reticule and her wrap, she went to her mother's chamber. Old Jane finished tweaking a few tendrils, then brought over Mama's silk shawl.

"You are lovely tonight, Mama." She noted how Mama's reflection did not appear all that different from her own. At thirty-nine, her mother qualified as not old yet, or even far into her middle years. Perhaps she actually would receive proposals if men thought a duke favored the family.

"Thank you. You are very lovely yourself." She stood. "Let us go. Your uncle sent up word the carriage was ready some time ago."

"Did you inform Lady Barnell that you are coming?" Ives asked the question as they rolled toward the lady's house in the moonlit night.

"I wrote her a little letter a few days ago, saying we would both attend."

"I hope Sutton is not there tonight."

"Who is Sutton?"

"The man whose wife you fucked in the garden when you were sixteen."

"Oh. Yes. That Sutton."

Poor Ives, to feel obligated to cover his errant brother's back. And sides. He claimed to be coming to hold off a fight if anyone issued insults. Lance knew the one likely to throw the first punch would be Ives himself.

That volatility was his brother's main failing. Maybe the only one that mattered. Otherwise the gods had smiled on Ives. Of the three of them, he was tallest, and probably the strongest, although their father had bequeathed them all enough in those areas.

The brother not so blessed had been Percy, the firstborn. It had become obvious by the time they all reached the age when boys either grow or don't that of them all, Percy would grow the least. He had taken after their mother in that way, and in others that did not favor him. Ives and Gareth were handsome as sin, and Lance liked to think he at least muddled along there, but Percy—well, Percy's face had been ordinary and boring. Even outright ugliness might have been preferred to such utter lack of distinction.

He had known. Percy had resented every gift any of them showed. One would think being the heir, with expectations he would be rich as Croesus, would be compensation, but Percival could not abide that he had not gotten more than the rest of them in everything.

"What is wrong?" Ives asked.

"Nothing. Why do you ask?"

"You are stroking your face. Your scar. It is something you only do when you are deep in thought about—"

He stopped the instinctive action, resenting that Ives had noticed a pattern to it. "Tonight, if anyone at any time asks where I am, you are to say the gaming room."

"And if you are not found there?"

"It will be assumed I departed for the ballroom."

"You must be careful. Should the lady lack the presence of mind to defend herself, as happened in the gallery, you must draw some lines of your own. It has entered my mind that she may be an accomplice to Sir Horace, and more than happy to ensnare you. It would not be the first time it was attempted with a peer."

"I do not think she is aware of his visit to me. I cannot prove it, but I do not think she is an accomplice."

The carriage stopped. A trickle of people still dribbled into the house. Ives hopped out and Lance followed.

"If you are correct, I again say you must be careful. It will be a hell of a situation if you are found in a compromising situation with her. You count on the lady rejecting you, but she won't be able to then."

"Do not worry. I have learned a few things since I was sixteen."

"I so enjoy watching the young people dance. Don't you, Marianne?" Mrs. Wigglesworth posed the question while she fanned herself. They sat in chairs against one wall of Lady Barnell's ballroom.

Mrs. Wigglesworth wore a dress the color of wine tonight. It sported an unfortunate curve of dark lace halfway down the skirt that accentuated her rotund figure. Two long feathers on her headdress in turn curved down on either side of her head. The result was that Mrs. Wigglesworth, who tended to be a composition of circles on the best of days, tonight appeared quite round indeed.

Other women sat with them along that wall. A whole line of chairs and benches stretched out in either direction from their prime spots in the center. Other matrons sat here, as did one or two wallflowers. This was also the place for those on the shelf, young women like Marianne herself.

She had only agreed to take a place in the line because Mrs. Wigglesworth liked to gossip. For the last half hour, tidbits and morsels of social news had flowed into Marianne's ear as the county walked past them. Now the well had gone dry. Marianne was trying to find a way to take her leave.

Mrs. Wigglesworth angled for a most private word behind her fan. "Do not despair, my dear. I have told Mr. Thaddeus Peterson to do his duty tonight, and request a dance of you and the others past eligibility. As a bachelor, he has an obligation."

Peterson. How did she know that name? "How kind of you. I hope you did not have to threaten him in some way before he agreed to this odious task."

"He did not express enthusiasm, I will admit, but as a gentleman it did not come to threats. Who knows, he may even form a tendre for you if you acquit yourself well. You could do worse. He is his father's heir, although the estate is not large. And of course he is the coroner, which reflects the respect he holds in the county."

Of course, the coroner. Elijah Tewkberry had made it a point to learn his name. "Can you point him out?"

Mrs. Wigglesworth peered over the crowd, then aimed a bejeweled finger to their left. "Over there, with your uncle. The shorter man, with cropped blond curls. He may not be impressive, but he will come into two thousand a year."

Mr. Peterson and Uncle Horace looked to be in deep conversation on a serious matter. Marianne decided to wait until Peterson made his request for a dance, should it ever come.

Her mother approached. Mama was not one to sit on chairs against a wall. Not tonight of all nights. However, Marianne could tell that the absence of a certain duke vexed Mama.

"Lady Barnell is most distraught," she reported.

"I expect she is," Mrs. Wigglesworth said. "She let everyone know Aylesbury was attending. Half the county did not believe her, but all of the county showed up to see if he did. The crush is impressive, although uncomfortable. She will be humiliated if he does not come now." Mrs. Wigglesworth did not seem sympathetic to Lady Barnell's plight.

"Dukes move to their own clocks," Mama responded. "I am sure he will arrive soon."

"He has not deigned to socialize with any of his neighbors for fifteen years. I can see no reason why he would now, with everyone still wondering about his brother's untimely demise."

"Really, that is such old gossip," Mama said. "If you cannot come up with something better, you will lose your reputation as the most notorious scandalmonger in Gloucestershire."

Mrs. Wigglesworth's eyes narrowed. "Are you defending him? Now, that is interesting. I hope that his greeting you in the village, along with his brothers, did not turn your head. Word of that flared and died quickly, it was so dull. Everyone knows that, unlike their eldest brother, those three have no friends in this county, let alone you."

Mama's smile thinned. Her eyes brightened dangerously. "I will have you know that—"

"Mama, I think I would like to speak with Lady Barnell, if you would join me. I want to thank and compliment her for tonight."

Dragging her glare away from Mrs. Wigglesworth, Mama joined her. The two of them walked the edge of the crowd, looking for Lady Barnell.

"Thank goodness we did not tell anyone about that call at Merrywood," Mama said. "If he does not show tonight, we may never do so."

"What did Mrs. Wigglesworth mean about only the eldest brother having friends here?"

"She is just talking, which is all she knows how to do. However, she probably refers to how the last duke, Percival, did condescend to receive his neighbors, and call on some of them, and at least acknowledge them. He truly lived here, unlike the others, who rarely even visited."

"He was well liked, then."

"People speak well of him now. Of course, since I

was not here for most of his time as duke, I would not know much more than that."

"There is Lady Barnell. I think she will not mind our interfering with her conversation."

Uncle Horace had positioned himself so the lady in question had to suffer his attention. More matronly than Mama, but dressed in an exquisite dress no doubt commissioned in London, Lady Barnell looked up at Uncle Horace with an expression of bland politeness.

Uncle Horace must have thought whatever he said to be witty, because he laughed at his own words. The lady barely smiled.

"Sir Horace, I am sure you will not mind if we join you," Mama declared. She artfully positioned herself between Horace and Lady Barnell, and pulled Marianne next to her. They became a wall over which her uncle peered.

"My daughter wanted a word with you, but feared addressing you alone would be an imposition," Mama said.

Marianne launched into flattering her hostess about the decorations, the music, the food. Lady Barnell had indeed outdone herself. Some might say she had overdone herself. The assembly was more like a ball than a county gathering.

"Zeus."

Uncle Horace's exclamation interrupted Marianne just as she was finishing. She looked over her shoulder at her uncle, then in the direction of his gaze.

Behind Lady Barnell, the double doors that gave out to the stair landing had opened. Two men stood right outside them.

A servant walked forward. "The Most High, Noble, and Potent Prince, His Grace Lancelot, Duke of Aylesbury, and Lord Ywain Hemingford," he announced. He had not proclaimed anyone else's arrival.

Lady Barnell closed her eyes and collected herself. With an expression of pure bliss, she turned to her exalted guest. Mama beamed a satisfied smile at Marianne.

The chamber hushed and all eyes turned to the duke. Marianne slipped from her mother's side and sought obscurity in the crowd.

No one missed how Aylesbury and his brother greeted Mrs. Radley after speaking with Lady Barnell. Mama accepted the attention like a queen would from a courtier.

The moment of theater over, the guests returned to their conversations. The musicians played again. The *tableau vivant* inside the ballroom fell apart.

Just as Marianne moved toward the terrace doors to disappear, Mrs. Wigglesworth appeared with Mr. Peterson in tow. She made introductions. Mr. Peterson asked Marianne for a dance.

Everything about the man made her want to yawn. His expression seemed incapable of animation. The way his eyelids lived at half-mast gave the impression it was all he could do to stay awake.

Unable to politely decline, but wishing she had made it to the upper terrace doors, she accompanied Mr. Peterson into the line forming for the dance.

"Mrs. Wigglesworth says your family is well known in the area," Marianne said.

"We have been here for generations. I knew your

father, although it was my own father with whom he was friends."

The dance began.

"Are you not also the coroner?" she asked when they came together again.

"I am indeed. I have been for three years now."

More dance steps.

"That must be a sad position."

"At times. It can be very interesting, too, and require careful thought."

It took some time before she could speak to him again.

"I have heard people mention how the last duke's death still occupies you. How distressing it must be, to be unable to determine the rightness of a decision after all this time."

He said nothing in reply. When the dance ended, he escorted her back to where he found her. "Do you have a particular interest in a coroner's duties, Miss Radley? Few people do."

"I think it must be fascinating. I hope you do not think me morbid for saying so."

"I am not morbid myself, so I would never think that about you. Death comes to us all. Like birth and marriage, it involves documents. I merely ensure those legal papers are accurate."

"Much like a vicar."

He almost smiled. "Yes, that is a good way to put it."

"Perhaps on occasion, at assemblies and such, you will regale me with your more interesting cases. Such as that of the last duke."

Half alert now, he stepped closer and spoke in a smug

voice. "I would be happy to. As it happens, on that particular matter, I will confide there may be a resolution very soon." He put a finger to his pale lips.

She made the same gesture and nodded. "I assure you, I am very discreet, sir."

"Miss Radley, I had no idea you were so sympathetic. I would have begged an introduction days ago. Would you accept my escort to the dining room for some refreshments?"

Elijah Tewkberry should be elated to agree to that escort and the resulting half hour of conversation. Miss Radley, however, did not want to go at all.

"I hear there is a wonderful cake," Mr. Peterson cajoled.

"She does not want cake, Peterson," a voice interrupted. "She promised me a dance, and I am claiming it now."

Aylesbury loomed at Mr. Peterson's shoulder. Without another word, the duke held out his hand to escort Marianne back to the dancing.

"It is a good thing I spied you over in that corner," he said as they waited for others to take their places. "Peterson is bad for one's health, he so lacks vitality."

"No one could accuse you of that, Your Grace."

"Aylesbury. I told you. Did you not believe me?"

"I noticed your rescue deprived me of the opportunity to decline this honor, Aylesbury."

"If you had truly wanted to decline, you would have found a way, even if it meant eating cake with a man much less interesting than I am."

Marianne tried to pretend she did not notice the attention they garnered as they joined the line. In order to avoid the eyes aimed her way, she had to look at the duke, however. He, on the other hand, smiled left and right to whomever he saw watching.

He asked after Nora as they danced. He complimented her dress. He admired her mother's impressive presence. Soon enough the dance ended, and he escorted her back.

Peterson was gone. Nor did the duke stop in that spot. Rather, with her hand still resting on his, he kept walking, right through the doors to the upper veranda.

Their dance ceased to interest people as soon as it began. Marianne trusted not too many eyes saw them leave. Nor was the veranda deserted. Two women chatted at one end, and three men enjoyed cigars not far from the doors.

"You might have asked me if I wanted some air," she said.

"And risk having you decide you did not? That is not the way I do things."

They stood near a lamp. It sent amber light up onto his face. A handsome face, remarkably so, but the scar appeared harsher and deeper in that abrupt chiaroscuro.

He noticed her looking at it. He touched it lightly with his fingertips. "Do you find it repulsive?"

"Not at all."

"Some people do."

"It cannot be ignored, but when someone notices it, that does not mean they are repulsed."

"For many years, when I was younger, that was all I saw in their eyes."

"And now?"

"I learned not to give a damn what people think."

"Then why did you ask me what I thought?"

He smiled. "You are not supposed to be more clever than a duke when you talk to him. It isn't done."

"Since you don't give a damn what anyone thinks about you, you will not be offended when I say that I do not care if you are a duke."

"Far too clever now."

"Then I will leave you, and return to my seat by the wall reserved for women on the shelf."

She turned to leave. He stepped away from the lamp and stopped her with a hold on her arm. "Do not go. If you stay, I will tell you how it happened. Almost no one knows."

She looked at his hand on her, and then at where those women had been talking. They were gone now, as were the men. They were alone on the terrace.

"Did you tell everyone to go inside?"

"Did you hear me do that?" He looked around. "Perhaps they were cold. Or maybe they preferred to give me wide berth. Or wanted me to have privacy with you. It does not seem fair, does it? For the whole county to be deprived of the terrace because a duke has use of it. Let us remedy that." He crooked his finger, beckoning her to follow him.

Her sense of caution at high mast, she followed him to a set of stone stairs that led down to the lower terrace. "I am not such a fool as to go down there with you. I do care what is thought of *me*, and you play fast with my reputation now."

"It is in clear view of anyone up there, but out of hearing. I daresay others will venture down if we do."

She looked up, then down. The upper terrace was a shallow balcony overlooking the larger lower one. Although only the full moon illuminated that terrace, anyone up here could see it.

Swallowing her misgivings, she ventured down. He brought her to the terrace wall near the garden, the part most visible from above.

"So now you will tell me the secret of that scar? Is it from a duel?"

He did not appear inclined to speak. She glared at him boldly, daring him to renege on his promise.

He lounged against the wall, with his arm and elbow resting on its top. "Since your return, what have you heard about my brother?"

"That he was not as bad as you, and perhaps even good."

He laughed at that. "I would not go so far as to damn him with goodness. He could be very careless at times." He touched his cheek. "He did this, for example."

"Were you practicing with swords?"

"Percy ceased being serious competition at swordplay by the time I was twelve. No, this was a game gone awry. Two boys up to no good. I matured before him, and began to sport hairs on my chin and face. Just a few, but enough to annoy him."

"I expect he did not like that at all, to have a younger brother becoming a man first."

"One day, when we were together, having fun for the first time in memory—he and I had long before begun avoiding each other—we found ourselves in a servant's chamber where we should not be. Percy liked to snoop on people. So there we were, and we opened the box with that man's shaving materials. The razor fascinated my brother. He suggested he play valet, and shave off those hairs."

She suddenly knew where the story would end. She held up her hand. "Please. Do not describe it. Such an accident must have been horrible."

"It was very dramatic. Blood everywhere. I staggered out of there screaming, blind from it. It took a surgeon to stitch it up, and I almost died from an infection before it was over."

"How terrible for you. For both of you. He must have experienced terrible guilt."

He gazed over at her. "Such guilt you have never seen. He cried until my mother insisted we never speak of it to him again. Poor Percy. All that grief. All those apologies. Begging my father's forgiveness. Such a sorry lad."

"It is understandable that you did not feel bad for him."

"I knew him very well, better than my father or mother ever would. I did not see guilt or sorrow in his eyes when he looked at me and no one watched. As I relived that afternoon over the years, I realized he had done it on purpose. He would look at my face when we were alone, look at that scar, and smile."

"Surely you misunderstood."

He stood straight. "I misunderstood nothing, pretty flower. I may be bad, but he was evil."

He was not joking. Her demand for the story of the scar had changed him. Altered his presence. Darkened him.

"That is a strong word."

"One that I avoided using for a very long time too. As a

boy, I merely thought him mean. He was the heir, and he loved using that in any way he could. To get his own way. To separate us from our mother by requiring all her attention. As I got older, I realized he hated me, and Ives, too, although Ives was young enough to miss the worst of it."

"Why should he hate you? As you said, he was the heir."

"He was smaller than us. He took after Mother in that, and in his frailty, and even in his features, which did not flatter him. He did not look much like our father, as we do. By the time I was ten I could beat him at any physical sport or game. When I put my mind to it, I could beat him in schoolwork too. So he set about getting back at us. There were many accidents such as the one with the razor, you see. And Percy was always involved."

She wished she had not encouraged this topic. The mood between them had turned serious. Also intimate. His darkness and her sympathy met in the space between them, each trying to absorb the other.

He looked to the upper terrace. "Now you have to share one of your secrets."

"I have no secrets." She had one, but if she revealed her correspondence, she would commit social suicide. No one could ever know about Elijah Tewkberry.

"Everyone has things they do not want to admit. Failings, or sins, or regrets." He looked over at her and smiled. "Private yearnings, or forbidden plans."

She shook her head, but each of his words called forth her inner thoughts and emotions. He was correct. Everyone had secrets in their hearts.

"Then I will have to guess." He cocked his head and

examined her. "I think in your heart there are many reasons you preferred that cottage to coming back here. I do not deny you your kindness in being concerned for your cousin's welfare. However, I think you came to enjoy your lack of expectations."

"What nonsense. Who prefers no expectations?"

"I speak of the ones others lay on your shoulders. People like your mother. Like them." He gestured toward the ballroom's door. "Marriage, for example. My guess is in Wiltshire there were no assemblies and balls where you sat on the wall reserved for ladies on the shelf. Nor did such as Mr. Peterson dare familiarity, all the while thinking you would never do since you lack a fortune."

She felt her face getting hot. And her head. "Thank you for articulating my situation with such precision. I might have missed its full implications without your help."

He touched her left cheek with his right hand. No one on the upper terrace would see.

"I have hurt you. I can be careless that way."

"No. Fair is fair." She turned her head enough for his fingertips to fall away. "After how I pressed you, I cannot complain if you try to bare my soul."

"I also think that there is a memory that sustains your heart," he said quietly. "A tendre from when you were a girl, for a man you could not have. Whatever the pain, you are content you were not deprived of that emotion. Better to have loved and lost than . . ."

She refused to react. She would be damned before she let him know he had been right twice.

"I also think—"

"You are not done? You will owe me more secrets if you tip the accounts."

"I also think that you enjoy where fate has placed your life. You must have learned the benefits of independence while away. You may not like sitting on the shelf for all of society to note and pity, but if it means keeping that freedom, you will do it."

She had a scold all ready, so as to end this when he finished this additional intrusion on her private life. She could not speak it. She could only look at him, both astonished and touched that with so little knowledge of her, he had surmised so much.

He stepped closer and took her hand in his. The ones not visible from the balcony. "I also think—no, I know—that you secretly like that I am bad, pretty flower. You enjoy my stolen kisses more than you are supposed to. The pleasure enthralls you."

He stood so closely she had to angle her head back to see his face. His expression sent excitement dancing through her. His intentions showed in his eyes. She looked up to the balcony. Not a person could be seen. She could not be sure they had complete privacy, however. She dare not allow another of those stolen kisses.

He moved, keeping her hand firmly in his. He pulled and coaxed at the same time, taking her toward the end of the wall where the building blocked the moonlight and created a black patch of shadow.

She went with him willingly. She could never claim she did not. She tripped after him. Surprise, not resistance, made her unsteady.

He tugged her and she fell against the hardness of his body, into his encompassing embrace. She could see nothing but felt everything—the strength in his arms and chest, the fine wool of his coats, finally his warm palm on her cheek, holding her face. She allowed it because he had been right. The pleasure enthralled her.

Dangerous. So perilous. She did not care. She closed her eyes and accepted how this newly discovered excitement compelled her. The sensations created a vitality in her body and an obscuring euphoria in her mind. Kisses to her mouth, neck, and body demanded she surrender all her senses to his command.

She wanted to. She ignored misgivings that quietly scolded. The changes in her body were too wonderful to reject. If this stopped, she would weep.

More movement. More stairs. He guided her, the kisses never stopping, holding her so she would not fall.

The scent of earth and damp. Stones beneath her shoes, then grass. Patches of moonlight, then more shadows, deep and hidden. Her wrap caught on a bush, stopping them both.

He released the fabric from the branch, then swept her up in his arms and carried her the last few yards. She watched the barren trees overhead give way to stones. Curving stones. She raised her head and looked around. They were in a tiny round garden folly with a domed vault. A circle of evenly spaced columns framed rectangles of moonlit woods.

A little sense returned. The misgivings spoke louder. *Dangerous. Reckless. Ruinous.*

"You are determined to prove how bad you can be, aren't you?" Her voice sounded distant and dreamy, just as the thought had been.

He paused and looked down at her. "Yes."

He sat on a bench and pulled her onto his lap. He kissed her again. Her conscience proved unable to compete with the sweet pleasure that coursed through her, rising higher like an incoming tide.

And when she was submerged, floating in need and bliss, he revealed just how bad he intended to be.

Lance assumed Miss Radley would frighten easily. A few aggressive kisses and embraces in dangerous proximity to the assembly should be enough. Instead she did not react with fear. Rather she permitted his boldness, and made good on his observation that pleasure enthralled her.

Had it been nothing but a gambit, that would not have mattered. Instead he lost sight of the why and where of it, and even the reason for the who. He blamed her innocence on that, and her ignorance. Both charmed him. Ensuring she was very enthralled indeed became his goal.

He pulled her wrap away while he kissed her. She did not notice its absence. He lowered his mouth to the exposed soft skin of her décolletage. Her head lolled back. He paused and looked at her face in the moonlight. Eyes closed, lips parted, she had become a picture of sensual ecstasy.

He kissed her flesh again, then lower. While he nuzzled the velvet of her body, he cupped her breast with his hand.

She did not startle or scream. The only sound from those lips was an *ah*, part of a sharp intake of breath. A little surprised and a lot joyful, that *ah* hardly discouraged him.

He should stop now. She was an innocent. And yet . . . clearly it would take much more to shock Miss Radley.

He caressed her breast. Her body flexed. Her deep arousal shuddered through that movement. He kissed the crook of her neck while his hand moved. He inhaled the scent of her. Images formed in his head. Erotic images, of Marianne naked and waiting, inviting him to be as bad as he could imagine.

His own fire crackled until he burned. He sought her nipple through her garments. He inwardly cursed at the tactile evidence she wore stays. He found the hard nub from the way gentle whimpers rode her quickening breaths when his caress passed over it.

His last lucid thought before the fire scorched his mind was that the plan was to buy time with her uncle by luring her along. Too much shocking behavior, and she might refuse his attention too early.

That thought disappeared in the blaze, before he had half the fastenings of her dress undone.

When she realized how his hand worked, she broke their kiss and looked, glassy-eyed, over her shoulder, perplexed. "What—?"

"I do not want to ruin your dress's lovely silk." He kissed her neck's pulse.

"I do not think . . . "

"Good. Do not think." He teased her breast ruthlessly. She lost interest in his other hand.

The dress loosened. He slipped his hand under the sagging neck of the bodice.

Damnable stays. At least these laced in the front. Impatient and more aroused than he had been in years, he urged some slack into the top of the laces with his finger. He managed just enough to allow him to caress the true softness of her breast.

"Oh." She looked down, wide-eyed, at his hand thrust beneath the top of the stays. He rubbed the hard tip. She closed her eyes. *"Ohh."*

He would ensure there were many more melodic *ohh*s. He would undress her properly and lie her down in a bed and take great care and time to teach her how her body could take her to another world, one where she would taste eternity. He would—

Only he would not. There was no bed here, only damp ground and hard stone. He could not take his time, because they were at an assembly. He could not undress her more either.

Those realities did not cool him. If anything his desire turned hard. Savage. He wanted her, damn it. She wanted him too.

Convinced of that, sure of it within the truths known by a brain deranged by lust, he sought a caress from his new lover, in return for those he gave. He took the hand already resting between them and on her thigh, and moved it a few inches, onto his lap.

Had he thrown her into a bath of ice water, she could not have reacted more strongly. One second she was limp on his lap, being pleasured to the point of moaning. The next she was on her feet, a human exclamation mark, staring at him.

Mouth agape and breathing deeply, for a five count she just stood there, her eyes reflecting confusion, as if she still sorted out what had just happened.

He reached for her. "Forgive me. You enchanted me to where I forgot myself." He tried to coax her back. If this ended now, like this, with him in this state—his whole being howled at the notion.

No longer confused, she jerked her hand out of his. Her eyes narrowed viciously. She took one step forward, swung, and planted her fist right on his face.

Hell. Damn.

It was all he could do not to really howl, in pain. *Why, the little—*

He stood abruptly and walked away so she would not see either his astonishment or his anger. He looked out into the garden while he found control of his fury. Neither of them made a sound for a while.

"I am . . . I probably should not have done that," she finally said. "I was just so surprised that I—"

He turned to see her flustered shrug. "You are stronger than you appear, pretty flower. Who would ever guess you could deliver a punch like that."

"It was not very ladylike, was it?"

"I have never had a lady do it before, so I guess not."

"Thank you for not punching me back. It would have only been fair if you had." She began rectifying her dishabille. She pulled her bodice higher and looked to check how it would appear over the stays.

"Gentlemen do not punch ladies. Only scoundrels do."

She stopped fussing with her garments, but made a gesture to them. "You will admit I had cause."

"I will admit I expected too much. As for that—" He gestured to the dress. "I heard no complaints."

"You did not ask permission either."

"You were too busy groaning with pleasure to talk."

Her eyes narrowed again. He didn't care. His face hurt, damn it, and she had been most willing. The only good part of this denouement of their tryst had been that a punch in the face obscured other pains he might otherwise be suffering.

At least she did not deny anything. If she had claimed she had fought valiantly for her virtue, he would lose all respect for her. As it was, right now he regretted only that he had been too impatient. A little more finesse on his part, and who knew where it might have led.

An unworthy thought, that. But an honest one.

She reached behind her to try to fix the dress. "Will you leave me now, to find my way back alone?" A bitter note tinged her tone.

"Of course not." What a hell of a thing to say. He wanted her to think him bad. Wicked. Not a boorish scoundrel. "We will plot it most carefully, so no one knows you were here."

He went over, turned her around, and fastened the dress. He led her over to the columns, so he could see her in the moonlight. Her headdress appeared none the worse for the last half hour. The bodice did not reveal his interference with the tightness of her stays' laces.

He lifted her wrap and draped it over her arms. "Trust me, nothing in your appearance would lead anyone to think you were with me."

"Unless they know you are very experienced in such things. I expect there are women who were far more enthralled than I was, who walk away just as neat."

"You are right. That is one of my God-given talents. I can ravish a woman with nary a lock on her head out of place afterward."

From the look she gave him, she assumed he was serious. "How do I get back in there with my reputation intact?"

"I will bring you to the open garden, and you will go in alone. I will find my way back later. If your mother asks where you have been, tell her that you sought some privacy out in the cool air, to think about the overtures Mr. Peterson made to you."

They began the trek on the path through the little woods.

"Mr. Peterson did not make overtures, whatever those are."

"Whatever those are, indeed. You would not know them if you heard them. I all but printed up a broadside announcing mine, and yet I kept astonishing you."

"I do not believe him to be bad like you."

"All men can be bad, pretty flower. And will be if offered the chance. But you are right, not bad like me. I am far better at it than the likes of boring Thaddeus Peterson."

They walked some more.

"You are being a little rude," she said. "You sound piqued."

"Forgive me. Someone punched me and I was

constrained from defending myself. Also, interrupted pleasure does that to a man. Leaves him piqued. Did you not know that?"

No reply. Hell, she did *not* know it.

The woods' edge came into view. The open garden, with its boxwood and paths, stretched to the terrace.

"You go first. I will make sure you get in safely, watching from here," he said.

She faced him, and touched the cheek she had punched. Then, ever so gently, her fingertips fluttered over the other one, and the scar.

She removed her hand. "What would have happened, if I had not . . . stopped it?"

I would have bent you over that stone railing and lifted your skirt and taken you.

"I expect we would have come to our senses soon." He gestured to the garden. "Now, go. We have not been gone nearly as long as you probably think, but long enough to be missed."

CHAPTER 11

Marianne paused while she washed the next day. The water in the basin showed the remnants of the tint of paint she had used on her cheeks and lips. She had sought her bed quickly upon returning from the assembly, and dismissed Katy as soon as her dress was removed. Already absorbed by thoughts that would make sleep long in coming, her washing had been absent-minded and incomplete.

She gazed into the looking glass. Her hair, still half up now, had not been properly brushed. She slowly untied her undressing gown until she could see her breasts. The same breasts so recently fondled by the duke. Thinking about that now caused her nipples to tighten, as if her dressing room did not have a comfortable fire warming its small space.

They—no, *she*—had been careless and reckless. The duke had risked nothing. What was one more mark on his reputation, if the world discovered him with Miss Radley in dishabille, alone where they should not be?

Their conversation on the terrace repeated in her mind. His honesty about his brother had stirred her sympathy. There had been no love between the two of them, from the sounds of it. His tone, a touch bitter and a lot sardonic, during his description of his brother, had her now wondering if perhaps he *had* used that poison.

She tried to push that thought out of her mind. She was only trying to paint him as worse even than he was, in order to claim some right to indignation. The intimacy his revelations created might have weakened her, but he had hardly imposed on her. Ignorant and curious and too aware of her advancing years, she had allowed it, up until she hit him. She had enjoyed every delicious moment.

Thank goodness there would be no more temptation. She was sure having her fist slammed into his face killed any interest he had in toying with her. She should be happy about that. Relieved. Instead she felt a little sad.

She finished washing. She was about to accept Katy's help to dress, when a female voice called her name.

Katy froze. She looked over. "Excuse me, miss. I'll see who that is. Not your mother, I am sure."

"It sounded like—"

"Yes, miss. I am sure it is one of the servants, though."

Except none of the servants would call her Marianne.

A moment later Katy returned, barely hiding her surprise. Nora followed in her wake.

"I had to find you," Nora said. "Look. A letter came from Vincent."

Her eyes held sparks Marianne had not seen in three years. Not even when Vincent last visited them in Cherhill nine months ago had Nora reacted like this. She looked *happy*.

Marianne gestured for Katy to leave. She took Nora over to a little settee and pulled her down beside her. "What does he say?"

"His ship is in Southampton. He is going to go to London, then come here." Nora's expression fell. "Papa will not receive him. He will journey all this way, and I will not be able to see him after all."

Uncle Horace's aversion to Vincent had an understandable birth. When he married Vincent's mother, the woman displayed little art in her efforts to have her son by her first marriage given a place in Horace's legacy. After Horace inherited from Marianne's father, the cajoling turned shrill. Her uncle's solution was to pull strings to get Vincent into the naval service, so he would be out of the house and her uncle's life.

For a few moments, the realization she might see Vincent revived her girlish emotions. Then she realized the true reason for the excitement she felt. He was an old friend. She could use a friend right now. Perhaps seeing him would remind her that no matter what her fortune, she had not been born to be a duke's toy.

"There may be a solution," Marianne said. "Whether I can arrange what I have in mind will be up to you."

"Tell me what it is. I so want to see him."

Marianne embraced Nora's shoulders. "If he cannot come here, perhaps we can go to him. In London. I am sure I can bring the two of you together if we go there."

Nora did not smile the way Marianne had hoped. Instead her expression went slack and her eyes filmed, as if a series of thin colorless silk veils descended, one by one.

"Papa would never receive him there either."

"Let me worry about that. Will you do it? Come to London with me? Mama would come, too, I am sure."

"And Papa?"

"I will tell him we are going to buy you that new wardrobe he insists upon. He will not want to stay for long if he comes. Few of his friends will be there in winter." She kept her scrutiny on Nora, to see if this plan would evoke interest, indifference, or something worse.

Nora only gazed at the letter in her hand for a long while.

"I will have to go out," she said. "To the dressmakers and such."

Hope bubbled in Marianne. Nora had not rejected the idea. "Yes. And to the park, perhaps, to meet with Vincent. Other than that, you will not have to do anything you do not want to do."

"If you promise I will not have to talk to anyone except Vincent, or make calls or meet strangers . . . If you will stay with me, I will go."

Marianne squeezed her shoulders and kissed her

cheek. "Give me the letter. I will write to Vincent and tell him what we are plotting, after I speak with your father."

"It has turned into an impressive bruise." Ives offered the opinion while he and Lance rode the estate's farms after an hour of hunting fowl.

Lance touched his left cheek. The sight in his looking glass this morning had not been pretty. A scar on one side of his face, and a discoloration the size of a little fist on the other.

"You need to watch where you are going," Ives continued. "You will be the joke of the county if it gets around that you walked into a door's edge while distracted by a pretty woman."

"No one saw it."

"No. No one did. Odd that, since it was when you were in the card room. Or else the smoking room. I used so many excuses for your absence that I can't know just where you were at the time."

Thus it had gone all morning. Ives probing for information, and Lance pretending he did not hear.

"You are being deucedly silent today," Ives said.

"A man likes his own thoughts at times more than a companion's relentless inquisitiveness, no matter how artfully that curiosity is cloaked."

"So you find me too curious now."

"I do."

Ives laughed. "It is as I thought. Your strategy last night did not work at all. You pursued, but she dodged and avoided and was not at all shocked because you never got her alone."

"Damn, you are too smart for me, Ives. I had hoped to hide my utter failure, but that shrewd mind of yours bests me once again." He kicked his horse to a canter and aimed across a field toward an isolated cottage. As he neared, he slowed to a walk. Ives fell in beside him.

A boy of about twelve years emerged from the cottage. He was lanky like boys are when they are growing fast. His shirt barely covered his chest and its sleeves ended four inches from his wrists. He waved toward them, peering through straw hair too long and in need of washing.

A woman appeared at the cottage door, holding a child in her arms.

Lance rode up, unhooked two of the birds he and Ives had shot, and handed them to the boy. The boy thanked him, but Lance had already turned his horse before the words ended.

"Isn't that James Badger's farm?" Ives asked.

Lance nodded. "He died last summer." James Badger had been a tenant since they were boys.

Ives looked over his shoulder. "Didn't he marry—"

"Yes."

Ives looked again. "That boy. Is he yours?"

"No."

"It is good of you to let them stay, anyway. Percy would have had the steward put them out by now."

The steward, a man who knew his business in land management, wanted very much to put Badger's family out. He had explained how all of that worked, as if

Lance were too stupid to know that an estate's income derived from rents and would be poorer if it had tenants who could not pay for the land they worked.

"The parish helps," he said, lest Ives think him too stupid too. "I am counting on some strapping man wanting to marry Badger's pretty second wife before spring comes."

"If one does not?"

"I will tell the groom to train the boy. He may have thanked me, but his eyes were not on me or the birds, but on my horse."

He aimed toward the road, then down it to a clutch of cottages, all in a circle. A few others dotted the landscape nearby. All of these tenants worked farms, but generations ago a duke had placed all their cottages here, close together, as if he played at making the start of a little village that never developed.

He left birds at all the doors, dropping them from his saddle as he and Ives rode by. They began circling back to the road.

Ives stopped. He gazed across a field to one cottage apart from the rest by a good five hundred yards. It showed the need of repairs to its roof. "You should either put someone there, or take it down."

"I should, I suppose. I probably will." He would burn it one day. He was not sure why he had not yet.

"Are you preserving it in case you are accused, to serve as testament to his true character? You said once you think it contains evidence of his sins. If so, I must tell you that it will not matter. The courts do not accept as an excuse for murder that the person murdered was worthy of death."

"You are such a lawyer. Since I am not, it never entered my mind it might be seen as an excuse for murder."

"Then why?"

"Damn it, you are a nuisance today." He sighed, but did ask himself the same question. *Why?* "I suppose to remind me, in case brotherly sentiment ever gets the upper hand." Then he kicked his horse to a gallop, so he would not have to pretend patience with his brother.

They handed their horses to the grooms back at the house.

"I am returning to town tomorrow," Ives said while they walked into the house. "You will have to find ways to shock Miss Radley without my help."

Lance aimed for the library, and the brandy.

"Unless, of course, you have already done so." Ives's words followed from a few steps behind.

"First you say I totally failed, and now you say I have seen fast success."

"It occurred to me that your bruise may be the result of fisticuffs. Perhaps one-sided. It looks like someone punched you; only, if so, it was not a big someone. I initially discarded the notion, but your mood today makes me reconsider it."

Lance poured some brandy. Ives angled his head this way and that, examining the bruise. "She did not pull her punch, from the looks of it. Hell, I wish I had been there. I can only imagine your surprise."

"If you share your ridiculous theory with anyone, I

will make sure your face looks far worse than mine does now."

Laughing, Ives backed up, then turned to leave. "I won't tell a soul. Except Padua. And maybe Gareth. That means Eva will learn of it, so the sisters Neville may eventually hear the tale. And Eva's sister and cousin, and—" The door closed behind him, while the list continued.

CHAPTER 12

Nora rested her head in her hands and sighed. "When you said we would tell Papa we were coming to London to buy new wardrobes, I did not think we really would do it."

"You expected me to lie?" Marianne flipped another fashion plate showing a simply designed dress. Handsome, she thought. Practical too. She set it on the little stack where she reserved the ones she liked.

"Not lie as such, just . . ." Nora made a gesture to the plates. She had set aside only two, and even those at Marianne's urging. "It will be a waste, at least for me. I will never wear any of it."

Yet another reference to how she intended never to change her seclusion from society. Marianne had hoped that Nora's willingness to come to London meant Uncle

Horace had been wise in moving her back to Trenfield Park. While Nora appeared more normal these last days, her view of life had not changed at all.

She wondered if she could convince Vincent to aid in nudging Nora along. He had written that he expected to arrive in town today. There would have to be a good deal of subterfuge once he did. Uncle Horace had come up to town with them, to take a hand in letting the house they were using for a fortnight, and probably to keep an eye on the bills.

She who intended to make those bills worthy of Uncle Horace's concern warmed Marianne's shoulders. Mama reached around and flipped through the little stack of plates. "This one is too young for you. This other is too plain. You are not purchasing the wardrobe for a governess, daughter. I can see I will have to take a hand in your wardrobe as well as my own."

"It is not as if I have done this before."

Mama kissed her head. "That is why you must make the most of it now. For five years we lived in deprivation, but our fortunes are on the rise. You need to look your best."

Having a social life improve did not mean one's fortune got any better, as Marianne saw it. It was foolish for Mama to hope that, if they turned themselves out fashionably, some man with a fortune of his own would lose his head and offer for the hand of a woman of little income.

From the looks of Mama's own stack of plates, she had great expectations of her own that such an offer might still come.

Mama pulled forward plates of a carriage ensemble and a ball gown. "You must have both. And the trim on the pelisse must be sable."

"Uncle Horace will have apoplexy if I present a bill for a garment trimmed in sable."

"Nonsense. He was delighted that you proposed this visit to town. He told me specifically to make sure you did not deny yourself too much, as is your habit."

"I am sure he did not think we would be buying ourselves luxuries like sable. Now, please go and help Nora. I am inexperienced in these things, but she is utterly lost."

Across the table, Nora stared at the same plate that had rested in front of her for ten minutes.

Mama walked around the table and sat beside Nora. In a soft, cajoling voice, she encouraged Nora to consider a different plate.

Marianne returned to her own decisions. The carriage ensemble her mother had pointed out really was very nice. Perhaps, if she did not choose the sable trim . . .

It was rare for a duke to call on anyone, let alone a woman, and not be received. But that was what happened when Lance, deciding his bruise was barely visible anymore, rode over to Radley's house. He wanted his call to make it clear to one young woman that while their last match had ended in a draw, he was not done with her.

Upon being told Miss Radley was not at home, he stared down the footman. How dare this young pup, and that woman, use that old excuse on him? He wasn't some local farmer seeking to bore the ladies for a half hour. He was a duke, damn it. Everyone was home for a duke.

The young man rushed to offer that Miss Radley truly was not at home. The whole family had gone to London.

She had bolted. Run away. Hidden, for all intents and purposes. He should have picked up the pursuit at once and called the morning after the assembly, even if it meant facing her with her brand on his face.

Two days later, he entered his London home without ceremony or prior warning. That sent the household into a panic of frantic activity.

He noticed, barely, but ignored it all, especially the wounded tone of the butler's astonishment about this unannounced arrival.

Throwing his hat and redingote to a footman, he strode to the library, poured some whiskey, and sat at a table. Fifteen minutes later he handed three letters to the butler, to be delivered immediately. Then he called for a carriage, and rolled off to take some exercise fencing.

An hour into his practice with the foil, responses to his letters began arriving at Angelo's, per his instructions to the recipients. The first, from the family solicitor, promised to obtain the required information forthwith, and certainly by day's end. The second came by way of two visitors. Gareth and Ives arrived just as he was putting his waistcoat on.

Ives lifted the foil resting on a nearby table. "Practicing with Henry?"

"That is what one does here."

"That you summoned us *here* does not bode well. Nor does your demeanor. You appear out of sorts, Lance."

"Hell, yes, I am out of sorts. I rode hard all the way, stopping only when my horse required it."

"Then you missed my letter, sent yesterday. In it I urged you not to come."

"I would have ignored it if I had read it. This is a situation a man cannot leave unfinished. I'll be damned before I turn the other cheek either."

He thought that a witty, ironic comment. Neither of his brothers seemed amused. Instead they kept shifting their weight from one leg to the other, trying to appear normal when instead they reeked of concern.

"Zeus, we have not declared war on France again," he said. "It is a minor problem that will be remedied quickly. I merely need a little help to arrange it."

Ives's face assumed its most lawyerly, annoying expression. "Ask Gareth. I will not do it. I have been your second in this particular situation too many times already."

How like Ives to think one night of fibbing about a brother's actual whereabouts amounted to supporting him in a duel by serving as his second and arranging the meeting. "I trust you are not declining out of some fastidious sense of fair play."

"In part, yes. The cost is too great. I have pondered this at length, Lance, and I will not help you."

"Have you so quickly forgotten that you used my home to seduce Miss Belvoir mere months ago? Did I not play your second all that time, when the lady did not stand a chance? Did I lecture you on fairness?"

Ives flushed, but remained resolute. Gareth's expression did not bode well for help from that quarter either.

"You both wound me deeply. I require a simple thing. A dinner party will hardly put you out, since your servants will take care of everything. And while you may not find my pursuit of Miss Radley as gentlemanly as you paragons of propriety would like, the alternative is—"

"Dinner party?" Gareth interrupted.

"She has come to town, and I need one of you to invite her and her mother to—"

"Oh, hell. He does not *know*, Gareth," Ives said. "He did not see it. He has not heard—"

Lance held up a hand, stopping him. "See what?

Gareth turned to Ives. "Did you bring it?"

Ives reached in his pocket. "You must not have been reading the *Times* the last few days, Lance."

"I glanced at the political news."

"Well, this was in it two days ago." Ives handed over a section cut from the paper. "Promise you will remain calm, and not charge off and do something rash."

To the editor of the Times *of London, from Gloucestershire:*

The county gentry and squires enjoyed a delightful assembly hosted by the most gracious Lady Barnell. She made use of her own house rather than the

Cheltenham assembly rooms, opening her impressive
ballroom to her neighbors. Among the surprise guests
were Mr. C. B. Codrington and his wife, who took
lodgings in Cheltenham for the week as well. Of par-
ticular note, the Duke of Aylesbury made an appear-
ance, his first at any local assembly in many years
according to the guests. Lady Barnell welcomed him
most warmly, and he seemed much at ease despite
the long delay in having a resolution regarding the
events surrounding the last duke's death. The local
coroner confided to several guests that he anticipated
soon changing his determination from unknown
causes to something else, however, so perhaps His
Grace felt free to dance in a manner denied him
almost ten months now.

In other county news, Mr. Harold Fikes of Glouces-
ter has sold the land he owns in town to an industrialist
who intends a factory for the making of—

Lance dropped his gaze to the correspondent's name,
then threw down the paper. "Who in hell is this Tewkberry?"

Ives shrugged. "He was neither introduced to me at
Lady Barnell's nor pointed out to me. One would expect
a man who is sending news from the county to the *Times*
to be better known."

"He probably was not even at the assembly. He most
likely gathers his news through gossip," Gareth said.
"He may not know how this has stirred the pot again."

Lance gazed at him. "Stirred the pot?"

"Let us go get some ale," Gareth suggested. "We will explain it then."

Lance walked toward the door, pretending he did not see Gareth grimace in Ives's direction.

Settled at a table in the tavern, he downed the ale before reading that infernal newspaper correspondence again. His brothers chatted about some horse in some race, as if the three of them had met to pass a few hours on small talk.

"How has the pot been stirred?" he asked, interrupting Gareth's description of the horse's lineage.

"Ah. Yes. That," Gareth said. "Town has been very quiet. Not much to talk about in winter." He gestured to the paper. "Now there is."

"It has all been given a new life," Ives said. "Wherever we go, there is speculation anew. Our friends try to rise above it, but of course . . ."

"They are very willing to share with us what terrible things others have said," Gareth finished dryly.

"In other words, it is like last April again. Within the week the post will have carried every scurrilous suspicion far and wide," Lance said.

He wished he did not care. For all his bravado the last nine months, he had felt scandal's lash more than he thought he could. Possibly because it was not a middling sort of gossip, but discussions over whether he had murdered a man.

Not just any man, but his own brother. That was an especially unforgivable sin. Far worse than rutting like a stag in his youth, or disregarding propriety now. He had not loved Percy. He had not even liked him, and none of them mourned his death. But killing his own brother— knowing the whole world thought he might have that in him darkened his world more than he expected.

That cloud blocked more than the sun. It shadowed every emotion. It dulled his life force. He wanted—no, he needed—to escape the insidious slow death of the spirit he suffered. It was why he had asked the steward about the servants, and quizzed the housekeeper on who did what with the meals, from the start of preparation to the delivery to his apartment. Neither one had acted surprised by the questions. Perhaps they wondered why no one had asked about all of that before.

Now it would all start again. At the moment he did not even care if he ever learned who had done it instead, or who might be feeding Radley lies. The fresh wind given to the scandal's sails sapped his ability to even wonder anymore.

"I will just brave it out, as I have been doing. Although it is clear this will never pass, Ives. You were too optimistic about your fellow man in thinking it would."

"Since you are correct, it pains me to tell you that it is indeed just as bad as in the spring. Two men have crossed the line from speculation to slander. Publicly. Since you came up to town, you will hear about it very soon."

Lance absorbed that while he called for more ale. No wonder the two of them had rushed to Angelo's, together. They assumed he had come up to town because he had learned of these smears on his name. Ives had thought he wanted one of them to serve as a real second, after he issued challenges.

He should do it, of course. He could not let this stand. And yet—that dark weariness had settled on his soul again. He knew its weight too well. He had carried it inside for a long time now. Only recently had it lifted, and allowed him some joy. Since the day he spied a pretty flower in the graveyard, now that he thought about it.

"Do not tell me their names. I assume they were both drunk. Unless one of them is so stupid as to speak thus in my presence, we will pretend I do not know about the insults to my honor."

Ives looked surprised. Gareth did not. As a bastard, Gareth knew all about walking away from insults. If he had not learned how to do it, he would have been dueling once a month for the last fifteen years.

A man approached their table then. He bowed, and presented Lance with a letter, then turned on his heel and left.

Lance broke the seal and read the two sentences. The solicitor had been very prompt in finding where in London Horace Radley and his family were temporarily domiciled.

He pictured Marianne, lost to pleasure in that garden. He felt again her fist hitting his face. The urge to laugh cleaved through his weariness like a ray of sun through winter's gray light.

He stuffed the letter in his pocket. "Now, which of you is going to host that dinner party?"

CHAPTER 13

"It is all too rich," Marianne whispered to her mother. They sorted through fabrics for their wardrobe at a shop patronized by the best of society. The bolts created a sensory experience of color, texture, and luxurious touch.

Other women did the same as they did. One lady, who appeared to have a modiste as her companion, removed any fabric that appealed to her and had it placed in a very large stack on the counter.

"Stop it," Mama said. "Not one more word. It is unnatural for you to keep complaining about the cost, when you will not pay the bills."

"I am imagining the scene when those bills arrive for my uncle."

"Oh, tosh. His wife knew how to spend better than

most. I daresay Sir Horace expects much of the same from us. If he does not—" Mama shrugged, to express her indifference. Then she eyed that stack on the counter. "How rude. That woman is reserving the best for herself. She will not use it all, but she wants to make sure no one else can consider any of them until she decides first."

Marianne continued examining the fabric, trying to avoid doing the same as that rude woman. Most of what she saw would go in her own private stack if she could muster the courage to have one.

She had only given the clerks two bolts to put aside so far. She tried to narrow her choices so she would not be here all afternoon.

"Marianne." Her mother said her name in a whisper marked with urgency. "Look who just walked in this shop. *Look.*"

Marianne did not look. Her mother was always pointing out notables so they both could gawk. That her mother recognized so many of them spoke to the time before Papa died, when he and she would enjoy the Season in London.

She continued her perusal of the shop's wares, but gradually became aware of a hush descending on the patrons. Her clerk left her and disappeared. Soon not a sound could be heard. Except boots walking across the wooden floor, then stopping.

Her mother's hand closed on her arm like an eagle's talon. "You must turn around," she hissed.

Marianne turned to her mother, who looked into the shop with a broad smile. Exasperated, she turned to see what had put her mother in that mask.

Aylesbury stood not ten feet away, watching her.

Bows, curtsies, greetings, welcomes. Marianne performed the rituals, all the while her gaze locked on the duke's cheek. The remnants of a bruise showed in a little pattern of yellows and purples.

He noticed her noticing that. His smile, it seemed to her, took on a dangerous character.

The other patrons pretended to go about their business, but eyes remained on him.

"What have you there?" he asked, joining her at the counter. He fingered the green wool she had chosen, and the pink raw silk. Her mother hovered at her shoulder.

"Pretty. However, I think you need—" He looked up at the shelves, narrowing his eyes. He pointed. "That, there. The violet color."

Two clerks appeared out of nowhere. One of them reached to pull down the fabric. "It is transparent, made of the finest woven silk," the other said. "It will need an underlayer, of course. Either the same color—" He snapped his finger and pointed to his colleague to fetch another bolt. "Or, if the lady is adventurous, a different one. See how it plays with the light when over this blue. Each movement will transform the colors." Another snap, and another bolt came down.

"I think it would look best with no underlayer," the duke said. "Just layers of this. Maybe bound with a gold cord."

"You mean *à la sauvage*?" her mother asked. "Oh, my, that is not done anymore, Your Grace. It has been years since women dressed thus, and even then it was scandalous to many."

"True. Memories of my youth got the better of me. An underlayer it must be. The same color, though. Don't you agree, Mrs. Radley?"

"Absolutely, Your Grace."

Marianne went back to her own choices. No one had asked her which underlayer *she* wanted. Her mother stepped away to conduct her own shopping, but Marianne guessed all of Mama's attention would be on any conversation with Aylesbury.

The duke sidled close to Marianne's side.

"What are you doing here?" she whispered, not turning her head. "Men do not come to shops like this. Dukes certainly do not."

"We should. It is a feast for the eyes. As for why I am here—I went to your London address, and was told you had come here."

Bold of the servants to have shared that. The duke had probably intimidated them. She could not imagine any of the temporary servants, or even Katy and old Jane, refusing him the information if he required it.

"You are going to be very bored. My mother and I have several more ensembles for which we need to choose fabric."

"I will help. Are those the fashion plates there?" He reached for the sheets she had brought that rested on the counter. The clerk obliged him by handing them over.

Everyone in the shop watched, but pretended not to.

Marianne tried to appear blasé, but having Aylesbury review her new wardrobe mortified her. He studied each plate carefully. She could not imagine why.

"These are not a bad start," he said. "Although this dinner dress looks too old for you. All those ruffles at the neck are not becoming. Tell the modiste to eliminate them, if you have not already."

Thus did he meddle for the next half hour. The clerk agreed with every bit of advice His Grace offered. More decisive than she, he made quick work of her wardrobe, forcing her to pick this or that, both of which he approved, when she could not choose one on her own.

"It appears we are done." He set the plates down firmly, and with a vague gesture sent the clerk away. "Now you are free to join me this afternoon. I am going to the park. It has a spare but undeniable beauty in winter."

Mama appeared at her elbow. "How generous of you, Your Grace. You also have my gratitude for encouraging Marianne to not belabor the fabric choices. Now the modistes can get to work. I feared, with her changeable mind on the subject, that we would not have our new dresses for six months."

He laughed lightly. Mama laughed harder.

"It is a very generous offer, Your Grace," Marianne said. "However, I promised to spend the afternoon with my cousin. I dare not disappoint her." She winced as a pain shot through her foot. Mama had stepped on it, ever so invisibly.

"I will have to find consolation in giving you both a ride back to your house. My coach is outside."

"My uncle's carriage—" A sharp pain speared her side. She glared at her mother, who was all innocence and looked only at the duke.

"We would be ever so thankful, Your Grace," Mama said. "Allow me to have one word with the proprietor about sending the fabric to our dressmaker."

Mama made it a private word. Then she joined Marianne, and they paraded out of the shop with the duke in their wake.

"You did not have to jab me so hard," Marianne murmured.

"You were about to turn down a ride in a duke's coach. Sir Horace's carriage will go back without us," Mama whispered. "On the way, you are to recall that it was tomorrow afternoon that you promised to spend with Nora."

"I will not, because it is today."

Mama looked over her shoulder at Aylesbury, and smiled. She then bent her head close to Marianne's. "Listen to me, daughter. He followed you here. To London. I am sure of it. Do not be too proud or he may lose all interest in you."

"I do not want his interest. As it is, if anyone in that shop recognized him, I may be the subject of gossip."

"Gossip of the best kind. I explained all of that."

"Mama, he stood there and helped choose my wardrobe. If you saw that going on, what would you think? What do you suppose Mrs. Wigglesworth would think, and confide to all she met?"

Mama's expression fell. "I would not think—"

"Oh, yes you would."

Aylesbury's coach was big, polished, and bore his escutcheon on its door. Marianne wished he had not brought this one. Everyone would know who had dallied over fabric with Miss Radley.

He personally handed them in. Mama almost giggled when she settled on the fine velvet seat next to Marianne. Any concerns for her daughter's reputation had disappeared.

To their surprise, and Marianne's relief, the duke did not join them. "I will send you on your way," he said through the window. "Since I am deprived of company, I will shop myself instead of visiting the park."

Marianne began to thank him, but already he had walked away.

"You handled that without any art at all, daughter. We could have been seen riding in the park with a duke. Instead we will be carried home like so much baggage." Mama sniffed. "I am very disappointed. Very."

Nora twisted her hands together on her lap as the carriage approached Hyde Park. "I am so excited. I hope he is on time, because I cannot wait."

The carriage had arrived at their house soon after the duke's coach delivered its baggage. Marianne loitered on the first level so she could intercept it. The coachman merely nodded when she explained that she wanted to go out again soon.

He would probably take her anywhere she wanted, at

any time, she realized. He most likely would not feel any obligations to report any doings he thought Sir Horace should know about.

Having a rather dull life, all she wanted to do was go to a park. Now they were entering it through a big gate.

"You can see there is almost no one here," she said to Nora, pointing out the window. "It is too early for the fashionable set to ride here, and too cold for many people to even take a turn."

"Not many people, but there are some. Must I really get out and walk?"

"If you want to see Vincent, you must."

The carriage stopped a short ways inside the gate. The coachman opened the door and set down the stairs. Nora looked at that open door a long time. Marianne began to worry that her cousin would not leave, that even her beloved brother could not lure her to walk among society.

Then Nora screwed up her face and lunged for the door, almost falling before the coachman could catch her and help her down.

Marianne followed and together they strolled down the path toward the place where Vincent had written he would wait.

Aylesbury had been right. The park in winter did possess a special beauty. Silver clouds muted the colors and created a palette of grays, browns, and darkest greens. Did he really enjoy that beauty, or had it only been an excuse to request her company, the way Mama thought?

Mama's other conclusions ran through her head. Had

he followed her? Did he truly have an interest, even a temporary one? Would his attendance raise her worth as much as Mama thought?

She found that hard to believe. Men were not stupid. When all was said and done, she would still be a woman on the shelf who had so little income as to be pitiable.

Suddenly Nora bolted and began running. Marianne looked ahead and saw why. Tall, fair, and dashing in his naval uniform, Vincent hailed them from up ahead. Nora ran to him, threw her arms wide, and flung herself at him with joy.

Joy filled Marianne, too, and not only because her cousin was so happy.

"How long will you be in London?" Marianne asked the question while Nora snuggled within Vincent's embrace. He looked over her head at Marianne. "Only two days. Plans changed with my ship. I was lucky to get away at all."

Nora did not seem to hear. Vincent extricated himself from her arms and set her back a bit. "You are even more beautiful, Nora. I would not have said that was possible."

She *was* beautiful right now. Alert, happy, and full of life. Marianne prayed that three days hence even a fraction of that vitality remained.

"Papa does not know we came," Nora said. "We snuck away, and will again too. Marianne arranged it all. She was very sly."

"I was sly? You are the one who found a way to have the servants intercept his letters once we came to town."

Nora smiled. "I suppose I was sly, wasn't I?" She hooked her arm through her brother's and they all walked together. "I had to agree to get a new wardrobe so we could come to London. At least Marianne gets one, too, so I suppose I can suffer it."

Vincent laughed. "Suffer a new wardrobe? What a gem your father has in you, that you do not cost him thousands a year on clothing." He looked over at Marianne. "You also grow more lovely, Marianne."

He said it sincerely, perhaps. However, there was something lacking in the way he looked at her. Oh, she saw gratitude, for her care of Nora. And appreciation of her character. She had always seen all those good things in Vincent's eyes.

What she had never seen was love, or even fascination. She had never seen a spark of intimacy that went beyond their closeness due to his sister. Even now, as he flattered her, nothing about him hinted at a man's interest in a woman.

She remembered how she used to mind that deeply, how she had cried over him, too, because he never displayed any special affection for her.

She no longer cried or dreamt. That had stopped three years ago, when Nora changed. He arranged to visit them all in Wiltshire as soon as he could, and he wept after spending an hour alone with his sister and her blank, lifeless stare.

Marianne had comforted him, and seen his grief and his anger. What she had not seen, even as she embraced him while he wept, was a man thinking of her as more than the only chance Nora had of the help his career meant he could not give himself.

He looked over at her now, with warm affection, but nothing more. It was still enough to raise her heart, however. To bring her some joy. Still enough for her to rather wish things had been different. *It is better to have loved and lost . . .*

"I have been gardening," Nora told him.

"Have you now? Mucking in the dirt and such?"

"Don't be silly. That would never do. I garden in my chamber. I have some pots there with plants in them. I take care of them."

"It sounds to be a good pastime. Perhaps you will have one of those glasshouses just for your own plants someday, or convince your father to add a conservatory to the house."

Nora considered that. "I wonder if Papa would agree. Probably not. He is cross with me because I would not get married."

Vincent almost stopped walking. His expression darkened. He looked quizzically at Marianne.

"He has given up the idea," she reassured him.

"Was he mad?"

"I would say he was too optimistic. Nora convinced him to abandon the notion, I think. At least for now." She did not want to promise that Uncle Horace had given the idea up for good. For all she knew, once Nora's attempted suicide became history, her father would warm to making a good marriage for her once again.

"Papa is in love," Nora said. "I think he hoped I would marry well enough to raise him enough for the lady he wants."

That astonished Marianne. For someone barely noticing the world, Nora had surmised a great deal.

"Is that true?" Vincent asked Marianne.

"Fairly close, I think. I do not always understand my uncle's reasons for what he does."

"You are not alone. I never understood the man."

"Perhaps, if you called, I could convince him to receive you. It would be better if your relationship with your sister were not a matter of subterfuge."

Vincent looked at Nora, then at her. "The last time I called, he would not allow me to see her, despite her illness. Had he not sent her to live with you in Cherhill—" His jaw tightened. "He only did that for his own purposes, but good came of it. She has you, Marianne. You cannot know what comfort it gives me to know she does still."

She strolled on while Vincent described where his ship had been. He regaled his sister with descriptions of foreign lands and people. Marianne listened, but her thoughts dwelled on Vincent's last words to her.

He assumed she would always be there for Nora. He thought she would never marry, would never be faced with a choice between her cousin's care and life with a man. He had no reason to believe it would go that way, but he did.

To Vincent, she was not almost on the shelf. She had

been nailed there by her age and her lack of fortune several years ago.

V incent arranged a ride on the river the next day. As a naval officer, finding a vehicle that floated was easy. He procured a fancy pleasure boat that looked like a barge decked out for a party. On it they floated up the river as far as Vauxhall Gardens.

"I want to go with you when you go back to your ship," Nora said, right in the middle of Vincent's explanation of the fireworks held in the pleasure garden on some summer nights. "I can dress like a boy, and be your servant."

Vincent laughed. "That would be a fine thing. What if you were found out?"

"I suppose I would be sent home."

"Indeed you would be. Alone. I could not accompany you on the voyage back."

Nora pursed her lips. "We could make very sure I am not found out, couldn't we?"

He realized she was serious. "Darling, it is not done. You can imagine why. Sometimes, on very large ships, the captain's wife joins him if the voyage will be a long one. No one else has such privilege."

"Does your captain bring his wife? Maybe I could be her servant. She surely does not use a boy for it."

Vincent looked at Marianne helplessly.

"Nora, you are only sad because your brother must leave us today. You do not really want to do this, do you?

Who would take care of the plants in your chamber then? I will not have the time for it."

Nora's eyes misted. "If you become a captain someday, could you bring your sister instead of a wife?"

Vincent hesitated in answering. Marianne assumed that meant that perhaps maybe he could. Only he did not want to, did he?

"I expect someday I may have a wife, Nora. I could not leave her behind and take a sister instead. She would not like that."

"When? When will you have a wife? I keep waiting but you never do it," Nora said. "You promised once that when you married, you would take me out of Papa's house to live with you. Remember?"

Nora's good memory discomforted Vincent. "I will marry when I meet the right woman, I suppose. That often takes a long time."

"A very long time, it appears." Nora chewed on her lip, thinking. "I think you should marry Marianne. She would be perfect, and she is very pretty. Then we could all live together."

He did not laugh. Marianne gave him that. Instead, bemused, he looked at her with an expression that assumed she saw the humor in such a notion as much as he did. He expected her to jump into the conversation and tell Nora her suggestion was too strange to be tolerated.

Marianne said nothing. She just waited for Vincent to get himself out of this.

His expression fell. He looked away, embarrassed. "I

do not think Marianne thinks of me as a potential husband, Nora. We have been like brother and sister for too
long. Besides, she can do much better."

Nora reacted little. After a few minutes, she spoke as if
no time had passed. "That is true, I think. She can do better. After all, she has danced with a duke. With a wicked
Hemingford duke. With the new Duke of Aylesbury."

It was Vincent's turn to just wait, with astonishment
in his gaze. Marianne rather liked his dumbfounded
expression.

"Do not put too much weight on that dance, Nora," she
said. "He was only being polite, since we had met. Although
Mama insists that thus does a woman's value improve, I
doubt that is true." She looked at the bank of the river.
"What is that over there, Vincent, with the big garden?"

He returned to explaining the sites, but for the rest of
the day, Marianne would find him looking at her in a
different way than he had in the past.

A t dinner that night, Uncle Horace announced he
would be returning home in the morning, but that
the ladies should remain in London for the full fortnight
so they could have some fittings.

"How good of you, Papa, and how generous." Nora's
response took Uncle Horace by surprise. She never
spoke at meals, let alone to him.

Marianne could see that the time with Vincent had
yielded wonderful fruit. Nora remained animated and

talkative. She did not stare out her window. She seemed very normal this evening.

"Thank you, daughter. I am glad to indulge you. Perhaps one day when you are ready, you will in turn indulge me."

Marianne wished she were close enough to kick him under the table. Could he not just accept his daughter's gratitude, and be glad in turn that Nora had shown improvement?

As she expected, that vague reference to his plans for Nora sent Nora back into silence.

"That is too bad, that you must depart, Sir Horace," Mama said, her eyes glittering the way they did when she was fit to bursting with something too delicious to keep to herself. "I was so hoping that you would be here, so I could share anything we learned when we dine with Aylesbury."

Marianne stared at her mother. Uncle Horace did as well. Nora ate her dinner.

"When will this illustrious event occur?" Horace asked.

"In three days. I received the invitation today. By messenger, no less. It will be an informal dinner. His brothers will be there, and their wives. And Marianne and me." Mama said the last triumphantly. "Lord Ywain's wife is hosting, but she assured me, in her private letter written in her own hand—and a very good hand it is—that the duke himself would bring his coach here, and escort us personally."

Uncle Horace's fork had paused midway to his mouth

while he listened to this litany of aristocratic condescension. He set the implement down. "Then I must stay, it appears."

"It is not necessary. The invitation was to me and my daughter."

"I still must stay. To hear all about it, as you said."

"I can write to you."

"It would be rude not to welcome the duke when he calls for you."

"I do not think he plans to sit and chat."

"I *will stay.*"

Mama shrugged. "As you wish. Of course, our new dresses will not be ready in time for this dinner. We will have to buy a few items to update our old ensembles. I know you won't mind. You will want us to do you proud, I am sure, and not look like women from a family of no means."

Uncle Horace's eyes narrowed on Mama. Marianne could almost hear the rude things he thought, and the calculations he made. *There goes another fifty pounds, at least.*

Mama locked her gaze with his, daring him to object. She knew she had him cornered. He did too.

"Just try not to overdo it," he muttered. "I want to see two-thirds of it spent on the girl, not you, too."

Marianne assumed she was the girl. How generous. How fun. How odd.

She returned to her meal, picturing a coveted, expensive headdress that she had denied herself up until now.

CHAPTER 14

"Please do not insist on this."

Lance ignored the request as he hopped out of the coach. If he did not know it was Gareth with him instead of Ives, the words alone would have told him. Ives would not have included the *Please*.

"It is necessary. It is the only way to deal with such ill-formed gossip." He headed into the gambling hall that he knew too well.

Gareth caught up. "It is only that last spring this is where Ives thrashed a man to protect your name. There is too much drink and not enough good sense here. Why not brave it out in your club instead?"

He had already done that. The experience had not been pleasant. No one had said a word to him, but he passed by a low drone of whispers wherever he walked, much like a sailor might be forced to walk a gauntlet.

A firm believer that pain should be endured all at once, rather than suffer a thousand small cuts, he decided he would risk a few sword thrusts this evening, before calling for Marianne and her mother. Hopefully the more stupid of the men would not be foxed yet, and keep their distance.

Alas, it was not to be. No sooner had he walked into the hall than a clutch of men at the faro table noticed him. They watched him, grinning, jabbing each other and mumbling in ways that had them roaring with laughter soon.

"Please do not go over there," Gareth said at his side.

"Of course I won't. Now go ask them not to come near *me*, why don't you?" He took his place at the wheel. The others there eased away, and not out of respect for his station.

As if that were not bad enough, he kept losing. Within a quarter hour he dropped five hundred pounds.

"Are you done?" Gareth asked. He stood back a little and to the side. Lance suspected that position was to try to intercept anyone looking to make trouble.

Unfortunately, the trouble came from the other side, and not the kind either of them expected.

"Aylesbury." The deep voice sounded lowly, and seriously.

He did not look over, but kept his gaze on the wheel and the bets. "Carlsworth. Odd to see you here." The Baron Carlsworth had political ambitions of the sort that were not enhanced by being seen in democratic gaming halls. Especially not at a time when democracy was not popular with those wielding power.

"I accompanied a nephew at his father's request, to keep an eye on the family purse." Carlsworth deigned to place a bet of his own. A very small one.

"You have never met my brother." Still playing, he made the introductions. Carlsworth, a stiff man by nature, got stiffer.

"I would like to have a word with you, Aylesbury. Privately."

"I cannot imagine why. It would be the first such word we have ever had. If you want to complain about my votes on the stupid laws passed in December, I promise you that better men have already burned my ear about it." Few of the lords had liked his vote, or his speech, the only one he had given yet in Parliament. That bill had been the only time he wished he had lived a better life. His opposition might have carried more weight if he had.

"It is in your interest, I promise you." Carlsworth murmured the words right into his ear, like a lover.

He pushed Carlsworth away. "Oh, hell, fine. Gareth, keep an eye on my winnings."

"There are no winnings."

No, there were not. He was down by hundreds more.

He strode off, gesturing for Carlsworth to follow. He found an isolated corner.

He did not dislike Carlsworth. He simply never much noticed him. He did now. Thin and frail and middling in height, Carlsworth's most notable feature was a very large forehead that loomed above eyes a tad too small to carry it. Since his red hair had begun receding, that forehead grew larger by the month.

"I want you to know that I speak as a friend," Carlsworth said. "I hope you will think of me as one. I risk the displeasure of important men by telling you what I am about to reveal."

He wanted something. Lance half expected to hear an overture to blackmail next.

"I have learned—please do not ask me to tell you from whom—that the recent discussions about your brother's death have brought the matter again to the attention of the prime minister and others in high station."

"It is said the king is on his deathbed, and they worry about me? Better they should be planning the transition to a new monarch."

"They worry about the perception of the matter, as it happens, not about you."

He did not like how Carlsworth said that. So seriously. So confidentially. "Go on."

"Liverpool has asked Eldon to consider appointing a lord high steward."

A thickness lodged in Lance's chest. The Lord Eldon was the lord chancellor. He presided over the House of Lords. If a lord high steward were appointed, it would be for a trial of one of the peers. Most likely Eldon would be given that role, too, for the duration.

"Go on."

"He—Liverpool—thinks that the death of a peer should not go unresolved so long. Nor, considering the mood abroad in the land, should it be thought that a peer can escape judgment due to his rank." Carlsworth made a face of both apology and regret, as if he wished he did not bear such unfortunate news.

"Why are you telling me this?"

Carlsworth flustered. "I thought you should know. Once the king dies—that is, soon after, a move may be made."

What do you want in return for warning me? He did not have to ask. Like so many people, Carlsworth wanted a duke as a friend. As a connection. Or, in this case, maybe in his pocket should he catch a cold that only a ducal handkerchief would alleviate.

"Your consideration will not be forgotten." With that, Lance strode back to the roulette table.

"Did you win anything?" he asked Gareth.

"I am not going to gamble with your money."

"You could have gambled with your own." He picked up what was left on the table.

"I have a family now. I don't gamble."

"You don't do lots of things anymore. How can you stand it?"

Gareth just smiled like a man with a secret he would not share.

Lance aimed for the door, and his coach. The pleasant mood he had worn leaving his house this evening deserted him with each step.

He did not know what disheartened him more—that the lord chancellor might begin advocating for a trial in the House of Lords, or whether Gareth Fitzallen, infamous sensualist and curse of aristocratic husbands everywhere, had been thoroughly domesticated.

*   *   *

Lance sat in the library of Radley's hired house, thinking he would not mind getting drunk. Sir Horace sat with him. They awaited the ladies' descent from above after the ladies completed all the things ladies did to prepare themselves.

"I will be returning to Gloucester tomorrow," Radley said.

"To consult with Peterson?"

Radley looked aghast. "What do you mean?"

"According to a Mr. Tewkberry, the coroner thinks the question over my brother's death will be resolved soon."

"Who the hell is this Tewkberry, that is what I'd like to know."

"Not more than I would."

Radley tried an appeasing smile. "I assure you that if Peterson has some intention, he has not informed me of it."

"You said you could influence him. Since it sounds as if he thinks developments are afoot, I simply wondered if you had done so."

"See here. I am a man of my word." He looked at the door to make sure it was closed and no one was about to enter. "I will confess that I wish you had given my niece more attention than one dance at that assembly. However, when I learned of this dinner party—I am not an impatient man, and it appears matters are progressing nicely."

"You may not be impatient, but others are. As for this Tewkberry, he should pray I never meet him." After leaving Gareth at his house to make his own way to the dinner, he had spent the time mentally detailing the indignities he would visit on the troublemaker when he found him.

"The talk will die down. It always does. And once things are settled with my niece—"

The door opened then. The ladies entered.

Mrs. Radley could not be described as anything but handsome. Today she had taken great care with her dress and appearance, most notably in a patterned silk shawl that dripped expensively down her shoulders to her knees, over a dress the color of parchment.

She entered first, obscuring her daughter. Once inside the chamber she stood aside, in a bit of theater, to reveal Marianne.

Even his mood could not defeat his reaction to seeing her. She looked lovely in the same ice blue dress she had worn to the assembly. It had been enhanced with silver trims. A thin wrap hung in a liquid flow on her arms, its color changing from gray to blue as she moved.

His whole being warmed. An arousal simmered, threatening to become more.

He walked forward, and offered one arm to each of the ladies.

Two sons of the old duke had married very interesting women. Marianne guessed that other words were used to describe them in some drawing rooms.

Mr. Fitzallen's wife, Eva, visibly pregnant, refused anyone's attempts to treat her like a fragile decoration or, worse, an invalid. Except for the obvious effects on her silhouette, one would never guess she was well along. She painted, her husband mentioned, and they had even visited Italy so she could study with some famous artist. She still took lessons, despite her condition.

Lord Ywain's wife might be considered odd in every way, although it could not be clearer that her husband adored her. A very tall woman, she did not appear to notice that her unusual stature might be thought unattractive. Indeed, unless Marianne had not seen correctly, she stood taller than normal tonight. Marianne had noticed little heels on her shoes.

Mama commented on Padua's given name before dinner, and received a brief explanation of how her parents had met in that city, and fallen in love, while her mother studied at the university there.

"She wants to do the same thing," Aylesbury said, joining the conversation as he walked by. "You have convinced my brother that it is a splendid idea, haven't you, Padua?"

"As it happened, your brother insisted we go, and that I devote myself this winter to preparing for my studies there." Her dark, glittering eyes did not waver under the duke's gaze. "He even demanded it be part of our marriage settlement."

To conclude they did not like each other would be putting too much weight on such a brief exchange. All the same Marianne sensed a fragile truce between them, as if there had recently been a row.

Aylesbury moved on. Padua shook her head. "He is like a boy sometimes," she said. "He thinks I am taking his brother to the ends of the earth, and he will never have the use of Ives again."

"'Use of him' is a harsh way to put it," Eva said.

"Is it? The duke keeps getting into scraps and Ives keeps getting him out. Or trying to."

"They are comrades as well as brothers. Aylesbury is going to miss him, that is all. He won't admit it, but that is the source of any pique with your plans."

Padua began to say something, looked at Marianne, and thought better of it. "See how informal we are, Miss Radley? We bicker in front of new friends, we are so at ease in each other's company."

"I think it is wonderful. It is rare for me to meet so many new people and have them act so naturally in front of me. I think even a bit of bickering reflects warmth and care."

Just then a melodic laugh drifted to them. They all looked at its source. Mama sat with Mr. Fitzallen, and he had her all aglow with delight.

Eva cast a sidelong look at Padua. They both bit back smiles. Marianne felt her face getting red.

Eva noticed. "Please do not look so embarrassed. He charms ladies without intending to, and ladies respond in the normal way. I certainly did."

"I was not familiar with either of you at the time, but I think it is safe that any charming he did of you was most definitely intentional," Padua said.

Mama had launched into some story. Mr. Fitzallen listened closely, as few men ever did to women. That was part of his charm, Marianne guessed. He actually *listened*.

They went down to dinner. Padua mercifully put Mama at the end of the table away from Marianne. Unfortunately, she found herself sitting right next to Aylesbury.

"What a fascinating family you have," she said.

"You mean my brothers' wives? My mother would not have approved of either one. My father would have raised some objections too. Poor as church mice they both were. Not at all appropriate, but Eros was busy, and here we are."

"Did you object too? Both unions are recent, and you were the duke. I would think your opinion would matter too."

"Someday I will tell you about my parents' marriage. Most appropriate, it was. No one objected. Indeed, machinations were involved to arrange it. Gareth's existence is testament to how well that worked. No, I did not object. Either brother would have ignored me, and possibly broken with me, if I had."

"They were too in love to listen or care, you mean."

"They were both certainly in lust. If there was love, too, I would not recognize it."

Eva, who sat to her left, leaned forward. "Are you gossiping about me, Aylesbury?"

"I was explaining to Miss Radley how you and Gareth were so enthralled by passion that neither one of you would hear the slightest negative about the other." He pretended to whisper to Marianne. "They are still enthralled, by the way. It turns out, I was surprised to learn, that a woman being in the family way does not interfere with—"

"Aylesbury!" Eva glared at him. "Miss Radley is a

guest, not a male friend with whom you have gotten foxed. What will she think of us if you speak of such things at this dinner?"

"She will think I am rude as well as bad, I suppose. My apologies, Miss Radley. And apologies to you, too, Eva." He poured more wine, took a sip, then looked over at Eva. "Didn't you say, upon meeting her tonight, that you saw Miss Radley in the park the other day?"

Eva frowned, perplexed. "No—"

"I am sure I heard you telling Padua that. You were in the park taking some air, and you noticed this attractive woman with a blond girl and a fair gentleman. An officer, I think you said."

"Oh. *Yes.*" Eva gave a half smile. "That is right."

Marianne had to give Eva credit. She was loyal enough to tell a lie if cornered into one by the duke.

"Who was he?" Aylesbury asked Marianne. "The officer."

He obviously knew about that meeting with Vincent. If he did, and Eva had not seen it, that meant *he* had.

Had he followed her? For what purpose? As for his impertinent question—

"He is an old friend. He came up to town for a few days."

"Is that why you came up to town? To see him?"

Eva had turned her attention and conversation to Ives, on her other side. Marianne kept her expression calm, but Aylesbury's inquisitiveness vexed her.

"I do not see how my friends are of any interest to you, sir, let alone cause for such persistent curiosity."

"Your friends are not, but your lovers are. If I am going

to seduce a woman, I prefer she not be in love with another man. That is so complicated."

"Do not trouble yourself about complications. There will be none, since there will be no seduction."

A slow smile. A warm glance. "You know that is not true, pretty flower."

With that he turned his attention to Gareth, across the table.

Seeing Marianne banished the melancholy that Carlsworth's revelation had induced. However, as the night wore on, that dullness seeped back into Lance's spirit like a fog. Damp and gray, it muted his perceptions, and his attention on the others. Only sitting beside Marianne kept it from overtaking him completely.

After dinner, while he and his brothers shared some port before joining the ladies, Ives brought up the health of the monarch.

"The end is near, that is the word out of Windsor," Ives said. "It is said he raved for fifty-eight hours nonstop in December, and then lapsed into his current illness."

"He has been in misery a long time," Gareth said. "Passing may be a blessing. I suppose Prinny will make a decent king."

No one voiced an opinion on that. Lance assumed Ives would not want to, since he had the prince's favor. It is never wise to criticize such a patron, even within the privacy of your family.

"How long?" Lance asked. "After he passes, how long before the government and its actions return to normal?"

Ives shrugged. "It has been so long since a transition occurred, I doubt anyone knows. I would expect it to take at least a month before anything like normal is seen again, and probably a year before Prinny is crowned. The most important matters must be addressed, of course. I expect much will wait, so no one appears so busy it might appear he is not mourning."

A month. Not long. Probably not long enough to find out the truth about Percy. He had made damned little progress so far.

His brothers rose and began the path to the drawing room. Lance followed. The port had only increased the fog. It wanted to settle low on all of him, much as it did on London's streets at night.

In the drawing room, Marianne sat with the other ladies. Their conversation sounded merry, and they all looked happy. His brothers joined them, and Ives and Gareth drew laughs and smiles from Marianne, along with the others.

Lance stood beside the group, watching. Mostly his gaze rested on Marianne. He envied her bright spirit and admired her self-possession. Even as the second son of a duke, women had fawned over him. She had not, even now that he held the title.

He respected that. He liked her. In his dull mood and facing possible humiliation or worse, Sir Horace's proposed bargain did not sound nearly so insolent.

He could do worse. She was not appropriate, but who was he to care about that? She was as poor as his brothers' wives, but that was the least of it. He was rich, after all.

His mother would probably haunt him for it, and even his father's rest might be disturbed. And Percy—well, he could hear what Percy would be snarling from within that ugly mausoleum. The chance to irritate Percy even in death made the idea more appealing.

He enjoyed her company. He wanted her and she might solve a very big problem. At the moment he could not find much to convince himself that the idea was imprudent.

"What do you think, Aylesbury?" It was Eva, trying to draw him into her conversation, and out of himself. She did that a lot. She sensed his moods sometimes. The way she looked at him said she did now.

"About the rumor that a certain countess has already commissioned her gown for the coronation," she explained. "Is that practical, or morbid?"

"Practical. Ruthlessly so." He walked to Marianne. "If the rest of you do not mind, I would like to speak with Miss Radley for a short while. With her mother's permission, of course."

"I—that is—I suppose—" Mrs. Radley stammered out her astonishment. "If it pleases Your Grace, I do not mind, if it is a very short while."

"Thank you." He offered Marianne his hand and helped her stand. Pink spread on her cheeks, but she allowed him to guide her out of the drawing room.

* * *

Everyone watched them go. Silence reigned. Marianne saw a lot of curiosity in the duke's family as he led her away.

As for her reaction to this display of his favor, confusion only named part of it. The last time she had been alone with him, it did not end well. The remnants of a bruise still showed on his face.

Furthermore, he had been reserved all night. Almost melancholic. He had not spoken much. He watched at best, and sometimes she thought his mind was not with them at all.

She should be afraid, perhaps, but she was not. Caution, trepidation, and excitement all mixed together instead. Anticipation teased her, too, affecting every beat of her rapid pulse. Would he kiss her again? Would she allow it? After his declaration about seduction at dinner, she must not. Yet—too much of her hoped he would at least try. Her body started reacting as if he already had.

They did not hide in a garden this time. He took her to the library, and sat down on a sofa, drawing her down beside him. He did kiss her then. She enjoyed a minute of the special vitality he evoked in her, and relished the sensations that increased with his embrace.

Then, with more regret than she should feel, she pushed against his chest, stood up, and sat in a chair that allowed room for only one person.

She had to suffer his silent attention for a long few

minutes. He gazed at her as if judging her ability to resist him for long.

He touched his cheek. Not the one with the scar. "You left me with a bad bruise."

"Should I apologize? If you had not shocked me, I am sure I would have never done it."

"Giving pleasure distresses you far more than taking it, from what I experienced."

His bald statement of the facts surrounding that encounter mortified her. "You are being rude again."

"I am being honest, and only because I am curious. Someday you will marry. Do you intend to only take pleasure then?"

The question left her speechless. However, she suddenly liked him more. He spoke as if he assumed she would marry one day. No one else did anymore. Not even herself.

"That is different." She could only hope her face was not as red as it felt. What a conversation to be having with a duke, in the library of one of his brothers.

"Is he still here in London? Your good friend, I mean. The officer."

"One bold question after another. Did you ask to speak with me privately because you knew such impertinence would pour out soon, and you did not want to impose on the others with it?"

"I only want to know if he is still in London."

"That is all?"

"And if he is indeed only a good friend."

She sighed, defeated by his tenacity on the subject.

What did she care if he knew? "He has left. His ship will
be sailing out of Southampton soon. I doubt I will see
him for many months."

He nodded absently. Falling into thought, he sat there
tapping the fingertips of one hand on his knee.

"This will never do." He stood, came over to her, and
pulled her up into an embrace.

She really shouldn't allow it. She needed to stop the
way he toyed with her, and disabuse him of any idea of—
She looked up into his eyes, and her thought broke off
and disappeared.

It felt good being held in his arms. Wonderful. She
warmed in all kinds of ways. Her breasts became sensitive
to the pressure of his chest. She remembered his hand on
her body. She closed her eyes for the kiss that was coming.

"Open your eyes, Marianne. I am not going to kiss
you. Not yet."

She opened them.

So serious, he appeared. So thoughtful. So . . . dark.
His gaze pierced her, as if he searched for something.

"I have decided to propose," he said.

"Propose what?"

"Marriage. I am asking you to marry me."

What an astounding thing for him to say. "Why?"

"That is not how you are supposed to reply."

"It is the only response I have. After all, you are a duke.
You can marry anyone. And while we have a little friendship of sorts, neither one of us is in love with the other, so
unless there is a good reason why, I have to wonder if you
are toying with me in a different, crueler way."

"I am not that bad, or that unkind. As for why—"

She waited. He did not seem to have an answer.

"You amuse me," he said, proving he had at least one.

"I see."

"We get on well enough too."

"Your requirements are not very high if 'well enough' satisfies you."

"I also desire you. Since you do not mind my advances, I think we will get along well that way too."

She leaned against his embracing arms, back a bit, so she could see his face clearly. "I do not want to sound ungrateful. Such a proposal is beyond the dreams of a woman such as I am. However, I hope you can understand that I find receiving it more than a little . . . strange."

"Now I am strange?"

That had entered her mind. "Not you. This offer. Have you drunk more tonight than is apparent?"

"I am not foxed. I will not awake in the morning, cursing my impulses, if that is what you fear. I must say that your utter lack of enthusiasm is wounding, Marianne. You are supposed to be close to fainting with excitement, not quizzing me about my state of mind and demanding a list of reasons."

"Forgive me. It is all just too—"

"Strange."

"At least odd. Hard to comprehend."

"A duke has just offered for your hand in marriage. You will live in luxury, and have precedence over almost every woman in society. Can you understand that much?"

"Oh, yes. I appreciated that part immediately."

"I think you appreciate this part too." He pulled her closer and kissed her.

She had no trouble understanding the passion he offered. It poured through her now, inciting the special hunger that he knew how to command. Her whole body surrendered to that kiss, and waited impatiently for the caresses that would increase her arousal to a fevered need.

He did not disappoint her. His hands moved over her body, her hips and back and even down to her thighs. His caresses made her feel naked, so completely did they follow her form. His hands' firm warmth penetrated the silk of her dress.

So sweet. So exhilarating. Her senses succumbed gladly, and her heart prayed for more.

Her mind, however, refused to cooperate. Pieces of thought ran through it, nuisances she could not ignore. All the rest of the whys—her lack of fortune—their brief knowledge of each other—Nora.

Gathering what sense and strength she could muster, she broke the kiss. "Stop. Please. The others—"

He complied. He tucked her close against him. With her ear on his chest, she groped for composure.

"So, we are agreed?" he asked.

She listened to his heart. It beat fast, but not as fast as hers. Even in passion he could probably do better.

"No, we are not agreed. I am sorry." She straightened and looked up at him. "I need to think before I give an answer. You would not want me to be reckless, I am sure."

"You should definitely think. Talk to your mother. Seek her advice. And your uncle, if you like. Or anyone else. Your acceptance will make me a happy man, but only if you want me for a husband."

How nice he said that. What a kind smile he gave, to reassure her he was not insulted by her dallying. But of course he probably was.

He turned her in his arm, and walked her to the door. There his embrace dropped away, and they returned to the drawing room.

For the rest of the night, the duke was a different man. He joked with his brothers. He responded with wit to things Eva and Padua said. He laughed.

He acted like a man who had successfully completed a duty that had weighed on him. Marianne had to admit that he had reason to be confident of how it would turn out in the end. She would seek Mama's advice, but she knew, and Aylesbury knew, what any mother would say. *He is a duke, Marianne. A duke.*

CHAPTER 15

Mama threw up her hands and looked to heaven for patience. "Are you mad? Are you so conceited that you think you will do better? As if there even is better! So perverse that you prefer obscurity and poverty to being raised up and living in untold wealth?"

Marianne had finally told Mama about the proposal. Partly she did want Mama's advice, but partly she only wanted to stop Mama from asking what had happened when Aylesbury had her alone.

To say her mother was aghast that she had put off the duke was putting a fine point to it. If Mama had her way, they would march to his house forthwith so she could accept, gratefully and contritely, and pray he did not hold her reluctance against her.

"I am not perverse, thank you. I just needed to think about a few things."

"Are you done thinking yet? Two days now you have thought, daughter. A man like this does not take well any rejection, let alone one that drags out. Certainly not one from such as you, who should be dancing, not pondering whatever makes you frown like this."

She could not explain the way this marriage would betray Nora, and leave her alone and vulnerable. Mama would never accept that as a reason.

Nor could she explain that she had doubts about Aylesbury's character. Not only because of Uncle Horace's story about Nora's illness. There was that matter about his brother. It seemed everyone was talking about it here in London. Even the dressmakers had commented to each other on it. He had admitted not liking his brother at all, and resenting him for his scar and other things. Would it have taken much for him to do something violent, in a fit of anger?

Her heart rebelled at believing that, but she had debated it a lot the last two days. She had seen the best side of him, most likely. If they were married, would there be other sides she found far less appealing?

"Have you filled your head with dreams of a love match?" Mama asked. "If so, I must remind you that marriages among the best people are not decided that way."

"We are not the best people. *You* had a love match. And if it is not a love match, it makes even less sense. Why would a duke, *a duke*, want to marry me, Mama? Do you not find it at all unbelievable?"

Mama looked at her with some sympathy. "Oh, dear. I have been remiss in your education. I am so sorry, my dear. Listen to me now, while I speak of indelicate things. Some men—not your father, my dear, but many others—do not marry for love so much as—how do I say this?—the desire to share a bed with a specific woman."

Marianne wanted to laugh. She managed not to with effort. "Mama. Is there anything about Aylesbury that makes you think his experience regarding women and beds is not vast? I daresay he has had, and will continue to have, many women who are far more beautiful than I am. To suggest he proposed because he could not resist taking me to bed—"

"Really, daughter, you do not have to be crude."

"I am sorry. However, that notion is as unbelievable as any of the other explanations."

Just then a footman arrived to say that Sir Horace would like a word with the ladies in the study. Marianne and her mother climbed the stairs to find him.

Uncle Horace had not left town the day after the dinner as he had planned. Marianne assumed her mother had informed him about the duke's unexpected, and inappropriate, request to speak to her alone. Uncle Horace had been waiting, to learn what had occurred, while Mama tried to wheedle it out.

As soon as they entered the study, Marianne knew that her uncle had decided to wait no longer.

"I have been patient." He sat behind a desk, as if he conducted business or study here. Only the desk in this house he had let was bare and the shelves vacant. "I want you to now confide in me what the duke said to you while he had you alone. Normally such a request for privacy with an unmarried woman is only made for the most serious of reasons, Marianne."

She told him. With each of her words a new spark of glee entered his eyes. He kept looking to Mama with a cunning, bemused expression, as if asking her, *Can you believe this? The duke has probably gone mad, but with luck we will get the knot tied before that is obvious.*

"I assume you accepted," he said when she had finished. "I can see how he may have wanted to keep it a secret for a few days, while he arranges how to announce it, and informs the king's people before it becomes common talk. Dukes do not marry willy-nilly, of course."

Mama glanced askance at Marianne. Marianne looked out the window.

"You did accept, of course." Uncle Horace said it as a certainty, but an unfortunate inflection made it almost a question. A question that hung in the study. Strong emotions began charging the air.

"Tell him," Mama said.

"I did not accept, Uncle. I said I needed to think about it."

His cheeks sunk. His eyes widened. His pale skin started getting red. *"Think about it?"* he boomed. *"You told a duke you wanted to think about whether he is worth marrying?"*

"Sir Horace," Mama began in a soothing tone.

"Leave us," he commanded her. *"Leave.* I will talk to my niece alone, and make sure she and I have a right understanding."

Mama left. Uncle Horace stood. He breathed deeply and closed his eyes. "See what you have done, you ungrateful wretch. I am halfway to death." He breathed deeply again, deliberately. He seemed to calm.

He looked at her. "You will marry him. If he will still have you, that is. You will marry him, and bring renown to your family."

"Nora—"

"If you do not marry him, she will be sent away, so do not sacrifice yourself for her. And if you do not marry him, you and your mother are dead to me. Expect nothing from me, not a shilling. If you will not be a duchess, you will be a beggar."

He meant it. She could tell he did. In his cold fury he did not exaggerate.

She stood, so she would not feel so small in front of him.

"He took advantage of your own daughter," she said desperately. "Ruined her, as you said yourself. How could you want to be tied to him so closely now?"

"Because it is all I will ever get. There are all kinds of ways to pay for one's sins."

"I am your niece. The daughter of your brother. Aylesbury may be a murderer. Would you have me marry him, if there is a chance of that?"

He thought about that, for about ten seconds. "It is not known what happened that night. I would not deprive you of this chance on the basis of open questions."

"But I am not sure that I want this."

His eyebrows met over his glare. "Then allow me to

say that differently. I will not allow you to deprive *us* of
this chance. I speak for myself, your mother, my daughter, and all the generations to follow. Make yourself sure,
soon. I am going to write and ask him to call this evening. You will give him your answer then."

He turned his back on her. Close to tears, she ran
from the study, and up to her chamber. Her mother was
waiting for her there, and not to comfort her.

The sons of dukes do not expect to be put off when
they propose marriage to a woman. Dukes themselves certainly do not. Therefore, a good deal of annoy-
ance, justified to his mind, had accumulated by the time
Lance received a note from Radley, asking him to call
in the evening.

He went, not convinced that Marianne would accept
his offer when he got there. Since he did not like being
uncertain about much of anything, let alone this, his
mood had not improved by the time he arrived.

The whole family, even Nora, waited for him in the
drawing room. After greetings, Sir Horace smiled broadly.
"My niece has something to say to you. Don't you,
Marianne?"

Lance had no intention of doing this with an audience.
Since Marianne was not smiling, there was no guarantee
how it would go. "Leave us. I will speak with her alone."

Surprised by the summary dismissal, Sir Horace herded
the others out of the drawing room. Lance closed the doors

behind them. No doubt Sir Horace and Mrs. Radley would not go far from its other side.

He returned to Marianne. He sat and took her hand. "Did he beat you?"

She smiled then. Finally. "I am too old to beat. He would not dare anyway."

"So he knows how hard you can punch, then?"

She even laughed a little at that. Then she looked down at her hand, nestled between his. "It was kind of you to make a little joke. That helped. Are you always kind?"

It was a fair question under the circumstances. "No. I will try to be, but I can make no promises."

"My uncle plans to take advantage of you if we marry. Will you not find that a nuisance?"

"All of my life, people have done that. I am skilled at making sure I give no advantage unless I choose to."

She nodded. "Will you mind if I still see my cousin Nora?"

"Why should I mind?"

She gave him an odd look.

"Do you have any other questions, Marianne?"

"I want you to tell me just how bad you have been. I think it odd that everyone knows things I do not."

"Since I was perhaps fifteen years of age, I have sometimes—no, I have often—found myself in trouble, often situations of my own making. Fights. Duels. That sort of thing."

"Drunkenness?"

"That, too, at times."

"Indiscriminate fornication?" She blushed at that question, as well she might.

"*Indiscriminate* is perhaps too strong a word." He searched for a better one, but found himself at a loss.

"Did you ever kill a man in a duel?"

"I did not." This felt too much like being led through a confession.

"Do you expect to continue finding yourself in such situations in the future?"

"I cannot promise I will not. It seems to be in my nature. Do you have any other questions?"

"Just one. Forgive me, but I must ask it."

"You are forgiven in advance, whatever it is."

She avoided his gaze for a long pause. Then a bit of determination entered her eyes. "Did you kill your brother?"

He had hoped she did not need to ask. That was probably an unrealistic expectation. Their knowledge of each other had been brief, and not very deep.

"No."

She believed him, apparently. Her expression lightened and the sun entered her mood and her eyes. "Then I accept your offer, if it still stands. I will marry you."

He stood and leaned over her. He took her face in his hands and kissed her. "I will call your uncle and mother in, and we will tell them. We will also arrange for the wedding. I would prefer one very soon, if you do not mind."

He walked toward the doors.

"His name is Vincent," she said to his back. "The officer. My old friend. He is Nora's brother by their mother's first marriage."

Truly an old friend, then. She did not have to explain Vincent now, but he was glad she did. Jealousy was a new emotion for him, and he had not been spared its insidious gnawing since he saw her with that blond naval officer in the park.

"You must introduce him to me someday." With that, he strode forward and opened the doors abruptly. Mrs. Radley and Sir Horace almost fell into his arms as their ears lost the support to which they had been pressed.

W hen he left Radley's house, Lance found himself ill inclined to return to his home. He therefore went instead to a different house.

"I am glad you have not yet retired," he said when he entered the library.

"It is only ten o'clock," Gareth said.

"Yes, well, what with your marriage and such . . ." Lance threw himself into an upholstered chair. "Is Eva about?"

"She *has* retired. Her condition requires rest." Gareth rose and went to the decanters. He returned with two glasses.

"Whiskey, thank God," Lance said after a sip. "I was about to demand it, so you did not hand me sherry or some other sweet nonsense."

"I thought whiskey would be appropriate." He sat down again.

Lance looked at the account books and correspondence littering the floor near Gareth's chair. "I have interrupted you."

"For which I thank you. If this is a simple visit, I am glad to have your company. If it is something more, I am flattered."

Lance stared into his glass. "The oddest thing just happened, and I thought I should share it with someone. I became engaged to Miss Radley."

Gareth merely smiled, angelically. "I am doubly flattered now."

"Is that all you have to say? No exclamations of shock? No hooded glances of disapproval?"

"She seems a fine woman. Why should I be shocked? As for approval, I am the last person whose approval you need."

Lance relaxed in the chair. "I knew you would react thus. It is why I am here. If I had gone to Ives, he would have bored me with a long explanation about how this is not necessary, how we would do this or that to fix everything, how I need only be patient, et cetera, et cetera." He took a long swallow of the spirits. "I always said Ives could talk with the best of them."

Gareth was not a man to fill silences with small talk. They sat and drank together in companionable quiet.

Gareth finally spoke. "Is there a particular reason you concluded you could *not* be patient? Why you have given up your plan?"

He told Gareth about Carlsworth's revelation. "I will still investigate the truth about Percy's death, but I cannot count on learning anything fast enough. I need to take Radley up on his bargain, is how I see it."

Gareth's expression reflected concern now. "They would not dare make a move to try you. It isn't done on such flimsy evidence."

"Because I am a duke? I doubt most of the peers even see me that way yet. Nor have I endeared myself to them, have I? No, if they start down that path, and the lying informant is found—" He pictured it, as he had for several days now. "I do not choose to be the leading man in the public theater it would create. I will not risk it. Furthermore, I want to be done with this. The effects on my mind are not healthy."

"I will not cajole you to think again, Lance. I hope, however, that you have some true affection for Miss Radley. You are choosing a lifetime with her."

"I like what I know of her. As for a lifetime, your existence is proof that for a man, and especially for a duke, that need not be an unrelieved burden, should it become a burden at all."

"Of course. Since I am fortunate to know better in my match than my father did in his, I assumed you had hoped for better, too, that is all."

Had he? He could not remember forming any expectations. Like most dukes, his father had married an appropriate daughter of an appropriate peer, a girl recommended to him by his parents. It was how such things came about then. How they still came about. If the daily living of that marriage had soon proven impossible, if what little affection that existed died within a few years, if his father's bride had proven herself vain and selfish and unkind—that was not unusual either.

"I had formed no hopes at all. Not before I inherited, and certainly not since. Miss Radley will suit me well enough."

Gareth raised his glass. "Then I congratulate you on your engagement, Lance, and hope that fate surprises you with more than well enough."

CHAPTER 16

Marianne stood utterly still while the servants fastened her wedding dress. Mama had gone immediately to the modiste and demanded the best of the new wardrobe be finished within two days. On hearing some of the garments would be worn at a duke's wedding at week's end, the modiste had put all of her seamstresses on the chore.

Now the dress, creamy and lacy and luscious to see and touch, all beribboned and embroidered, flowed down her body.

"You look like a princess," Nora said from her chair in the dressing room.

Nora's willingness to share this ritual touched Marianne. Her cousin refused to attend the wedding, however. Nor had Nora expressed true happiness about the engagement. She had not said anything at all, if truth be told. Since Marianne had feared the news would send Nora into one of her turbulent spells, Nora's blank acceptance had reassured her.

At least she was here. She served as a reminder, however, that this marriage would start under more than one cloud. Although Marianne no longer felt that she betrayed Nora through her relationship with Aylesbury, his history with Nora was never too far from her mind.

She sat at her dressing table, so the final touches could be done with her hair and her headdress could be attached. In the glass's reflection, she saw Mama enter the dressing room, resplendent in her own ensemble.

Mama came over to inspect her hair, then handed over a little box. "This just came by messenger. From Aylesbury."

The box contained a beautiful and expensive necklace. Carefully worked gold links formed a chain from which was suspended one exquisite diamond in a simple rope setting. A note was tucked beneath the stone.

A diamond of the first water, for a woman who matches its clarity, purity, and worth.

Aylesbury

Mama exclaimed over its beauty and cost. Nora barely took a look at it.

"Such a lovely note too," Mama said. "And to think you were inclined to reject his offer."

Marianne hoped to one day forget the argument with Mama after she left Uncle Horace. They had both been in tears by the end of it. *Abject poverty, that is what we face. Do not doubt he will cast us out, daughter. Would you do that to me?*

"If she does not want to marry him, she should not have to." Nora voiced the opinion in a dull, bland voice. "Men are so crude and cruel by nature, it is a wonder any woman wants to marry. Except Vincent, of course. He is not like that."

Mama turned to her. "A lot you know about any of it, Nora. You should keep your ignorant opinions to yourself."

That dragged Nora out of her private reverie. "I know more than you think. I think you and Papa browbeat Marianne into this, for the money. Look at her. She appears terrified, not happy. And well she might be, being forced to give herself to such a wicked man." A spark of panic entered Nora's eyes. The spark that often heralded one of her fits.

"I am not terrified, darling," Marianne lied. The truth was she feared she might throw up. "It is normal for a bride to be nervous. Isn't it, Mama?"

"Indeed it is. Nora, you should leave us now. I want to speak with my daughter alone."

The maids needed no such instruction. They departed with Nora, and closed the door.

Mama fastened the necklace, then made an inspection of Marianne's appearance. "Perfect. Beautiful. No daughter of the ton would surpass you."

"You exaggerate." She did feel beautiful, though. Expensive, perfectly fitted dresses did that to a woman. The diamond now hanging below her chin did not hurt either.

"Now, before we go down to the coach, I need to explain a few things to you, regarding your behavior as a wife."

Marianne could not suppress a laugh. "I am not a girl. I will not be shocked when it comes to the marriage bed."

"*Really*, daughter. To think I would speak aloud of such things! I was going to explain how to manage your pin money, and how to wheedle more funds out of him."

"Ah." She stood and draped the strip of silk that would serve as her wrap, then picked up her silk and lace reticule. "That is something I do need to learn. You can share your considerable expertise on the topic while we ride to St. George's."

The wedding proved less small than planned. Word had spread. Even before Marianne took her place for the ceremony, the nave of St. George's had filled with attendees besides those invited. The stream of people only caused curious passersby to wander in too. Right up front, having procured the best views, three men watched and scribbled, much the way Marianne did when she attended events as Elijah Tewkberry. She assumed they were from newspapers or scandal sheets.

Aylesbury took his place at her side, and suddenly the crowd distracted her no longer. The rector approached in his vestments. Panic shook down her center, like a plucked harp string sounding a loud note.

She glanced over her shoulder, at the crowd and at her mother and Uncle Horace. And at the door, heaven help her, to see if she could dart out before anyone caught her.

"Do not look at them. Ignore them," Aylesbury's voice came low and soothing. "They are all mere observers. Only you and I matter."

He did not appear at all nervous, or worried. He definitely did not look like he wanted to run away. No doubt he had fortified himself the way men were allowed to do, with a quick gulp of spirits. It really was not fair that women were denied that solace.

Then the ceremony began, and to her surprise it really did become only about them. She forgot about her family and the onlookers, and even about those men scribbling right behind her. She did not hear much of the ceremony, either, however. A daze descended on her like a sparkling cloud.

It heightened her perceptions of all the wrong things. Of the texture of the rector's garments, and the timbre of his voice. Of the stones in the church's walls, and the dust dancing in the light flowing in the windows. Of Aylesbury standing beside her, of his height and strength and mostly of his sheer presence.

He overwhelmed her in every way. Yet, as they stood side by side within the daze, and said the words that bound them, she found some peace because he was there. His strength supported as well as dominated. She wanted to believe he willed that to happen, in order to help her.

Then it was over, and he was kissing her. The bright

fog disappeared, leaving her in front of a crowd of strangers being kissed by a duke who was, unbelievably, her husband.

"At least Tewkberry wasn't here," Ives muttered as they walked out.

Marianne's head snapped in Ives's direction. "Tewkberry?"

"A correspondent to the *Times* from Gloucestershire," Lance explained. "One of his letters caused a stir for me here in town, that is all."

She frowned. "What kind of stir?"

How charming. His new, little wife already displayed loyalty on his behalf. "Renewed gossip about my brother's death. Do not concern yourself."

Her mother came over to embrace her then. Sir Horace took the opportunity to catch Lance's eye and give a big wink.

Lance took that to mean that with the bribe now paid, Sir Horace would complete the bargain.

The wedding breakfast lasted hours, through most of the afternoon. Lance enjoyed the company more than he had in memory. When not chatting with the others, he watched Marianne. Her poise impressed him. He thought she looked lovely, and happy enough. She would indeed suit him well enough.

Happy enough. Well enough. Those were the foundations of this marriage. He supposed it was all most couples had. Whether enough was enough *for him* remained to be seen. At the moment he was not inclined to wonder about it. Mostly because he wanted her. Not just enough, but a lot.

Marianne found herself wishing her mother had given more advice than how to spend Aylesbury's fortune for him.

After the breakfast ended, close to dinnertime, she retired. The housekeeper brought her upstairs and gave her a tour of her new home. The duchess's apartment consisted of five chambers. In addition to one for her bed and another for her dressing, there was a private drawing room, a withdrawing room, and an entire chamber just for her wardrobe.

Her trunks had been delivered already, and they awaited her attendance. The household provided a maid, but she intended to call for Katy to join her if they stayed in town long.

The housekeeper behaved with unwavering deference. All the servants treated her like—like a duchess, she realized. Because she was one. Only she did not feel like one. She felt out of place, and lost in that apartment, and terrified—yes, Nora had been correct in that word— terrified of her marriage night.

"Would you like to rest, Your Grace, while we unpack for you?" One of the servants asked the question while she began to turn down the coverlet on the enormous bed.

Was she supposed to rest? She had no idea. When she

saw Mama again, she intended to scold her for neglecting to explain all the rituals.

They helped her out of her dress and into the bed. She stared up at the drapery of the tufted silk canopy. From the adjoining dressing room, she heard the servants dealing with her wardrobe.

Was she supposed to just lie here until it was night and Aylesbury joined her? It could be a few hours still.

Exasperated, she rose from the bed and walked over to the dressing room door. "Have you unpacked the yellow muslin yet? The one with long sleeves? I want to wear it now."

They found the muslin. One of them got her into it. She stuck her feet into shoes, and left the apartment to explore the house. From the looks the maids gave her, she guessed she was not expected to do that, but she needed to do *something*, or she would go mad.

It was a very big house. It had two drawing rooms, one very big and one not so much, and a library that could swallow the cottage in Cherhill several times over. She thought the public rooms old-fashioned in their decorations, all full of gilt and heavy fabrics.

They had eaten the wedding meal in a nice-sized dining room. She discovered it was not the only one when she found the official dining room. She had never seen a table so big. She did not know such tables even existed.

"What do you think of it?"

She pivoted to the voice. Aylesbury stood just inside the door. Dark, handsome, and intently interested, he watched her. In that instant, the reality of the day cleaved through the festive theatrics created out of lace and silk and ceremony. Even speaking the vows had not made the change in her life so starkly real.

Married. His. Forever.

What had she done?

"It is very large," she stammered. "This could be a ballroom."

"The ballroom is much bigger." He gazed around. "There will be dinner parties that fill this table. Or there are supposed to be."

She tried to imagine herself hosting a party here.

"Does it frighten you, Marianne?"

"I feel more a trespasser right now than I ever felt that day we met, when I truly trespassed."

"You will rise to it. I do not doubt that. I would not have married you if I questioned it at all. It will be strange at first, and then it no longer will be." They strolled around the large chamber. "If you have questions, ask me."

"You know how to be a duchess?"

"I barely know how to be a duke. I can find someone for you who does know, however."

She calmed from the way he reassured her. Perhaps the first few times she got it wrong and made a fool of herself, he would not be angry with her.

Why? The word had been nudging at her again while she took this house tour. It would be nice if she were so vain that she did not know there had to be a why, and a good one, for her to find herself mistress of this mansion.

He drew her into his arms and kissed her, as if answering the question. Before passion clouded her mind, two truths asserted themselves. First, desire, though strong, was not the reason why, and second, this was not the day to press for the real answer.

His arm holding her close, he guided her to the big staircase. "Go tell your maids that you want to retire. I will join you soon."

Twilight had come early and so, apparently, had the rest of this day's ceremonies. He kissed her again, then released her. She walked up the stairs, not daring to look back at him.

The maids left her alone, in bed, in a nightdress with more lace than five dresses needed. The modiste had shown Mama this ready-made garment upon hearing about the wedding. *Très jolie*, she had said while she unfolded the dress like it were made of gold. *Très elegante*.

Also *très* transparent, being made of the thinnest lawn. Its rows and flounces of lace were not placed where one would choose if modesty were the goal. Mama must not have noticed that.

She kept her gaze on the door of the dressing room. He would come that way. A maid had pointed out the door at the far end of that room that offered access to His Grace's apartment. And vice versa.

Her nerves had her close to nauseous. She felt foolish, in this bed, her back propped on pillows, awaiting her deflowering. Surely there had to be a better way—

Suddenly Aylesbury stood in her chamber. He did not emerge through the dressing room after all. He appeared inside the doorway to where her bedchamber connected to her sitting room.

The illumination from the small lamp left near that door washed over his tall form. He wore a long robe. She could not see the top of a nightshirt at his neck.

"You look surprised. Were you expecting someone else?" he asked.

"I thought . . ." She pointed to the dressing room, since her voice would not cooperate.

He walked over. "I do not use the duke's apartment."

Why?

He began unbuttoning that robe. "Close your eyes, if you are likely to be shocked."

"I am not a child."

"Of course not. Forgive me for insulting you."

His robe parted more with each button he worked. His naked chest showed, then his whole torso, then—

She did close her eyes. She would be sophisticated another day.

Bedclothes moved. A weight suppressed the mattress. She opened one eye a crack to see him lying on his back beside her, looking up at the drapery, with the sheet up to his waist.

He turned, and rose up on one arm. "I am not practiced at doing this with an innocent. You must tell me if I hurt you. When I do, if I do."

She nodded, dumbly. Nerves no longer afflicted her. Raw panic did. "I think you should kiss me," she said, "or—"

"Or?"

"Or I may lose my wedding breakfast."

"I have never had such an unusual invitation, Marianne."

"I thought I should warn you."

He gave her a sweet, long kiss. "Better?"

She nodded. Sensations other than nausea took over. She ventured a touch on the skin of his shoulder, then tiptoed her fingers down his back. Then a bit lower. He was indeed naked. Completely.

He kissed her again. Her body did not mind. Pleasure scurried around inside her, like a joyful imp lighting little fires as it moved.

He looked down at her nightdress. After a bit of study, he found a button buried beneath a layer of lace near her neck. Her unfastened it, then sought the next one. She watched that male hand, dark and experienced, doing that which he had probably done many times in the past.

He looked up at her. His hand paused. "Do you mind?"

"I do not know. I will admit that it is—" *Exciting. Naughty and titillating and—*

He stopped, and instead kissed her while he caressed down her body. The thin lawn of her dress did little to interfere with the sensation of being claimed by that hand. His handling of her drew her toward the delirium she had experienced in the garden.

Another kiss. Deep and invasive and shocking. At the same time his caress lined up her side, then onto her breasts. The intense pleasure defeated her shyness. Her body had been waiting for that all day, maybe even since that night in the garden.

He had no experience with innocents, he said, but he had much experience with women. Even she could tell that, from the way he knew just how to drive her mad. When his caresses became quick and focused on the hard tips of her breasts, arrow after arrow of intense thrills shot through her. They aroused her low and deeply, and awakened erotic hungers that got worse and worse.

Then his hand moved to between her breasts and rested there. She almost cried when he stopped. She opened her eyes to see him looking down at her. Passion firmed his jaw and mouth. It added new depths to his eyes.

His hand played with one of the buttons.

"Do you mind?" This time he did not sound so solicitous. Nor did he appear so.

She shook her head. She would agree to anything if it meant he did not stop.

His fingertip traveled back to her breast's tip. He gently teased at it. "You do it. I am preoccupied."

She fumbled with the buttons, one by one, until she could reach no more. All the while he aroused her and watched what it did to her.

He ran his fingertip down the small gap between the sides of the dress, where her skin had been exposed. "Show me how lovely you are."

She understood what he meant. In the very small world in which they both dwelled together now, she just felt his meaning.

She pulled the dress open, so it fell on either side of her body and exposed her breasts and more. The chamber's cool air licked at her, arousing her even more. Her breasts rose high and firm and heavy, their tips hard, revealing how desire affected her.

He knew, of course. She would have no secrets from this man, not about this. He deliberately skimmed his fingers across her nipples, again and again, ever so slightly touching them, until she fought not to groan.

Another kiss, controlled but fevered. His mouth lowered to her breasts, and he kissed them. Then, he used his tongue to do what his fingers had been doing.

She lost any claim to control. She could hardly bear the intense desire of the demanding, needy pleasure streaking through her. Shame became something that belonged to a world she abandoned in her crazed need.

With a few deft moves he had her completely naked. His embrace encompassed her so she felt his skin against hers. Shock after wonderful shock stole her breath when his hands moved freely over all of her. He deprived her of the remnants of modesty. Each relinquishment of privacy spun a denser cocoon of furious pleasure. Inside it she experienced an intimacy that awed her.

Even her mound did not escape his controlling touch. A caress there made her squirm. With one leg thrust over her left thigh, its knee pressing her right one, he prevented her from clamping her legs together the way she tried, to escape the sharp and insistent sensation he forced on her. An anguish of discontentment permeated her, as if her whole being cried for something it could not have.

Instead of relieving her, he made it worse. Wonderfully worse, until she did cry out her frustration. His mouth teased and sucked on her breast until she groaned aloud from the tension racking her. His other hand explored her mound, and deeper. Strokes against the moist pulsing flesh sent her to a delirium where nothing existed in her except a high-pitched, overwhelming urge to find release from the torture of ever more intense desire.

He came over her. She clawed at his back in her desperation. A fullness pressed against her, then into her. At first it felt wonderful.

Then it hurt.

"Now," she managed to say after a gasp.

It hurt more. Enough that the need and pleasure became a shadow to the pain that tore through her.

"Now." She hit his shoulder. "You said to tell you if you hurt me, and when I do you ignore me."

He rose up enough to look down at her. "I thought you were saying you were ready."

"You did not tell me to tell you that, did you?"

He dipped his head and kissed her cheek. "At least the worst is over, I think."

"You *think*?"

"I am sure. Almost."

She had to admit that she no longer felt real pain, only a fullness her body did not want to accommodate, and a raw soreness. She could see and feel the tight rein he had on himself.

"You should probably finish it," she said.

"I do not mind waiting. This is . . . pleasant."

In other words, he felt no pain. How nice that one of them enjoyed this. "No, no. Go ahead. I will not mind."

"How brave you are."

He moved in her. Not painfully, but . . . she could not name what it did to her. She felt too sore for pleasure, but . . . her body responded in ways that implied it could be very pleasant, another time.

The effects on her spirit astonished her, however. This act renewed the stark awareness of reality that she experienced when he found her in the dining room. *His. Forever.* She could not deny he had controlled her body, her mind, and a good part of her soul from the first kiss tonight. She sensed how he strained now to avoid hurting her, and imagined his power when he no longer had that concern.

His passion drew her in so she was not separate from it. Kisses to her neck, shoulders, and breasts revived some of her euphoria. Pleasure allowed her body to accept him better, and made the fullness more welcome. In the moment of his completion, as the final pleasure shuddered through him, and his need made him almost vulnerable, she experienced a most peculiar reaction. Joy.

He dropped on his back afterward. The passion and intimacy gave way to the world, and the drapery above her bed, and the reality of the man beside her.

"Why don't you use the duke's apartment?" she asked in a quiet voice. The night seemed to demand quiet tones.

"Because he lived there." He stood and reached for his robe. She watched his body move out of the corner of her eye. Lean and muscular, his muscles corded as he donned the garment, covering himself from her view.

He turned and looked down at her. She waited for him to speak, if that was his intention. When he did not, she did.

"It is not always like that, is it?"

"I will not hurt you like that again."

"I did not mean— It is not always so polite and careful, is it? I should not expect it to be, should I?"

He reached down and traced his fingertips along the side of her face. "No."

He left then.

She had not needed to ask. She had sensed the power in him, much like she felt when riding a horse that is forced to trot when it wants to gallop. Nora's words came to her, about men being bestial and crude and cruel.

Thinking about Nora tinted her mood with sadness and misgivings. It would have been horrible to face this night ignorant, and to have known only pain and fear. The shock might never pass.

Lance returned to his apartment sated, but aware he had not acquitted himself very well in this ritual.

He should have sought advice from one of his brothers. Probably Gareth. Eva had undoubtedly been a virgin when she met Gareth, while Lance was fairly certain Padua had not been when she met Ives.

At least he had not brutalized Marianne, despite the overwhelming urge to take her fast and hard. He had not lost sight of who she was, or what she was. He may not have given her much contentment, but except for that one unfortunate moment of misunderstanding—an honest mistake on his part, but, he admitted, one he welcomed because he held on to control by the thinnest of tethers—except for that, he trusted it had not been too bad for her.

No, his deficiencies had been more social than physical. He should have seduced and cajoled, flattered and teased. He should perhaps have pretended he loved her. She had not been raised to be a peer's wife and part of a political and dynastic match. She probably expected more than carnal satisfaction at best.

Not that he had even given her that either.

Unable to consider sleep at the moment, he left the apartment and walked back toward her chambers. Instead of entering her door, he let himself in another one near it.

He did not come here much after his father died. Not at all in the last year. If he visited London, it was to forget the ghost who lived here, not entertain him.

The vague moonlight that leaked into the sitting room did not permit more than dark forms to reveal themselves, but he knew every item and where it was. The decanters on the table by the wall. The books, so rarely read, in their case nearby. The sofa and chairs. Percy's scent still pervaded the place, as if it had not been aired since his last visit to town.

He had not killed his brother, but God help him, he definitely did not mourn his passing. The unholy relief he experienced on learning of his brother's demise had been short-lived. As if in punishment for his lack of grief, fortune made certain Percy could not be forgotten quickly.

Now he had made a marriage in an effort to banish that oppressive shadow. How Percy must be laughing. At least it had been Marianne. It could have been someone as malevolent as Percy himself.

He left the apartment. As he passed the duchess's door, he thought of Marianne inside. Her family had surely pressed her hard to accept his proposal. Radley might have threatened to cast her out if she refused.

He had left her thinking she might face violence in the marriage bed, or far worse than she had known tonight. Gareth, renowned for his charm with the ladies as well as his skill, would be appalled with him on many counts tonight.

Hell, he had been an ass.

He pressed the latch and retraced his steps to the bedchamber. Marianne had put her nightdress back on, all buttoned and beribboned up to her neck. She looked to be sleeping under that canopy.

Her eyes opened. He could not see her expression well, but he could imagine what she assumed.

"You look very small there, Marianne."

She rose on her elbows and looked at the bed. "I am not so small. It is the bed that is huge."

"You also look very alone."

Did she wipe sleep from her eye, or a tear? "More strange than alone. Foreign. And more different than I expected, in so many ways. Does that make any sense?"

"I understand completely."

"They should warn us that marriage does that. It is not fair that we are not prepared better."

He lay down beside her. "I assumed you would want me to go, but I will stay for a while now, if you do not mind. Perhaps you will not feel so foreign then." Gareth's

voice whispered in his head. He repeated his bastard
brother's prompt. "Do not worry. I will not impose on you
again tonight. Sleep now."

Her body relaxed. She yawned and snuggled deeper
under the bedclothes. "You should cover yourself. You
will get cold otherwise."

He rose, pulled back the bedclothes, and slid under
them. She turned and tucked the sheet and coverlet up
higher on him. No one had done that to him since he was
a child.

She rolled onto her other side. She began falling asleep,
so perhaps she felt better.

He looked at her back move with her deepening breaths.
He found himself smiling.

Even when she was unconscious, she managed to
lighten his mood.

CHAPTER 17

Mama, Nora, and Uncle Horace called the next day, on their way out of town. They were returning to Gloucestershire, their carriage laden with trunks carrying new wardrobes. Everyone made small talk in the drawing room for fifteen minutes, pretending they had no idea what had occurred in this house the night before.

She and Aylesbury showed them out. Her husband and uncle spoke a few private words before Uncle Horace climbed up beside the coachman.

Aylesbury chose not to leave London yet. That delighted Marianne. She wanted to see the sights she had not had time to tour already. In the afternoon they rode horses in the park, then visited the shops. If she looked at anything for long, he bought it for her. She soon owned an enviable collection of kid gloves, an etched crystal box, a headdress that would do a princess proud, two new bonnets, and an ermine muff.

He took her to St. James Palace and old cathedral the next day, and in the evening they attended the theater. The Duke of Aylesbury owned a yacht, with a small crew at the ready, and the day after they donned warm clothing and sailed down the Thames and into the sea.

The fourth day Eva wrote, asking them to call. She had a guest visiting from Coventry, her letter explained, and she wanted Marianne to meet her. Could she and Aylesbury interrupt their new marital bliss for a brief visit?

"Their guest is Gareth's mother, Mrs. Johnson," he explained while they ate breakfast in the morning room. "She was my father's mistress for decades. He took up with her when I was a young child."

"I know that is common, but your mother must not have liked it."

"I do not think she minded too much. She and my father were not a good match. She had given him three sons by then. They had little to do with each other after Ives was born." He spoke absently while he flipped through his mail. "He told me years later, not long before he died, that she lacked loyalty in every way. He could not trust her, and quickly came not to like her."

"Did you not find it hard to hear that said of your mother?"

He set a letter aside. "A little, but not much more than that. Percy was my mother's favorite, of course. She had little time for me. I was the spare, not the heir."

How sad that he said this with so little emotion, as if

that distance were to be expected. What an unhappy family his must have been. It was a wonder he had not grown up malformed in character.

Then again, perhaps he had. His reputation in the county spoke of trouble and rebellion when he was a youth. And more recently.

"Mrs. Johnson rarely comes up to town," he said. "I assume her visit has to do with the approaching birth of her grandchild. We will go. I would like to see her."

That afternoon Marianne dressed in what she called her duchess clothes. When she went below, Aylesbury assessed the pale green wool dress. "You look lovely."

"It is part of the excess Mama enjoyed inflicting on Uncle Horace's purse. I am sure he is happy to be rid of the keep of at least one of us."

"You will need to visit the dressmakers again soon," he said as they settled in the coach. "Find several you trust. You will need a gown to be presented at court, and there will probably be a coronation before the year is out."

"Are you commanding me to spend a fortune on new dresses? Such drudgery you require of me!"

He took her hand and kissed it. "Work your wiles artfully, and you can probably enjoy as much such drudgery as you want."

That kiss reminded her of the first one he had given her, in that little boat, before Nora— She stopped her mind from traveling through that entire afternoon. More to the moment, she suspected that kiss meant he would come to her chamber again tonight. He had not since their wedding night.

Eva had suddenly entered that stage in pregnancy when a female appears uncomfortable. She sat in the drawing room with an older woman of impressive appearance. Mrs. Johnson's dark eyes and hair and angular face marked her as handsome more than beautiful. Her son Gareth looked much like her in certain features. If one were critical, one might say the similarities enhanced him beyond fairness, while they gave her a vaguely strict visage.

Marianne could not deny that Mrs. Johnson looked very interesting, however. Also very distinctive. She could see how the old duke found a young Mrs. Johnson to his liking.

Eva introduced them, adding, lest Aylesbury had forgotten to explain, that Mrs. Johnson was Gareth's mother.

"If you are thoroughly confused, my son was given a surname that reflected he was the bastard of a noble father," Mrs. Johnson said. "Nor was I born Amanda Johnson. There was a very brief white marriage to Captain Johnson, so the duke did not take up with someone officially an innocent."

"As you can see, my mother does not stand on ceremony regarding her history," Gareth said, amused.

"To do so would be the worst hypocrisy," his mother said.

"Do you plan to stay until the child is born?" Marianne asked.

"I have asked her to," Eva said. "She declined. I think she believes she would be in the way. Don't you, Amanda?"

Mrs. Johnson assumed a serene expression. "If I know

one thing, it is that it is not good to have two mistresses of one house. You think I will not intrude or impose my views, Eva. In truth, I probably would."

"Your advice would be welcomed."

"Would it?" Mrs. Johnson stood, walked to a large footstool, brought it back, and set it down. "Then put your feet up, as I told you twice already."

Eva glanced at Marianne, bit back a smile, and dutifully rested her feet on the footstool.

Then she took them right down. "I promise to use that as soon as I return. I want to take Marianne and show her something in the garden." She stood, took Marianne's hand, and urged her to follow.

"Put on your heavy wool pelisse," Mrs. Johnson called after her. "And your half boots. Those shoes are little more than slippers."

Eva ignored both bits of advice. She did grab a cloak and wrap herself before they stepped outside.

"I lied when I said I had something to show you," Eva said while they walked down from the terrace. "Gareth wants his mother to talk with Aylesbury, and he with her. The conversation might be more forthcoming if we are not present."

"He said he has known her most of his life. He would want some privacy for them."

"Of more significance is she knew that household at Merrywood for most of *her* life. Her father was a butler there. She has kept in touch with some of the servants. And the whole time she was the duke's mistress, she lived close to Merrywood, in Cheltenham. If Lance is determined to learn what really happened to his brother, he would do well to start by talking to her."

He was determined to learn that? He was investigating? She tried not to show her surprise at hearing this.

"Now, let us talk about you." Eva smiled slyly and slipped her arm through Marianne's. "How do you like being married?"

"It has been a long time, Lance." Mrs. Johnson took his measure. "You do not mind if I address you like that still, do you? Your Grace seems too formal for someone I scolded when he was a boy, and Aylesbury—well, to me, there will only be one Aylesbury."

He sat beside her. "I do not mind. Is all well with you in Coventry? Do you have everything you need?" His father had provided well for Mrs. Johnson, in ways that Percy could not touch. Times were hard, however, and it might not be enough now.

"Is that an offer to improve my situation if I ask? That is kind of you. Percy would have been happy to see me starve."

"I am not Percy."

"No. You never were. You were a bad boy, and still are from what I hear, but I preferred your honest disobedience to his sly and false compliance. One knew where one stood with you. With Percy, one felt the need to cover one's back."

A more succinct and accurate depiction of Percy's

character as a boy would be hard to find. Mrs. Johnson did not seem to expect anyone to come to Percy's defense.

"Mother, Lance is looking into the events of the night Percy died," Gareth said. "I thought you might have some idea of who in the household can't be trusted to be loyal, and perhaps even be the kind of person who might lie if the price were right."

"I suppose if we are going to talk about this, it would also help to know if there was anyone there who hated Percy," Lance said. "If he was indeed poisoned, someone had to do it."

Mrs. Johnson frowned while she pondered. "To the first question, I cannot help you. Every person probably has a price, when one gets down to it. Not to commit murder or treason, perhaps, but a lie? If I were you, I would assume each one of them has potential."

What she said was probably true, but not good news.

"However, you might speak with Stuart. He is the old footman. The lame one. He is given light duties now, and often sits by the door. He has been there forever, and knows them all personally."

"Thank you. That is helpful."

"As to the second question. Stuart wrote to me that Percy's valet, Mr. Playne, was pensioned off. You should talk to him. He served Percy for years. He would know if Percy had been especially cruel to someone, or if a servant had taken serious offense for some action or words."

"Would he not have come forward and said something if he suspected someone?" Gareth asked.

"You are assuming that he is loyal to his master even

now, after that master is dead and he is no longer in service," Lance said. "Your mother is right. Playne might know something he did not want to share with the justices. Perhaps he did not mourn Percy much either."

"Then we must talk to him. Where is he?"

"He left before I even realized it. The pension was part of Percy's testament. I have no idea where he went. Perhaps one of the other servants does."

"Kent," Mrs. Johnson said. "He went to live with his daughter in Kent. Stuart wrote and told me." She held up her hands. "Beyond that, I do not think I am of much use to you."

"You have been very helpful," Lance said. "Are you sure there is nothing you need?"

"A new pair," Gareth said. "One of her horses has gone lame."

"Gareth, *really*."

"Mother, *really*," he mimicked. "It is a little late to be getting embarrassed about gifts from a Duke of Aylesbury."

Mrs. Johnson thought about that. "He has a point."

"Indeed he does," Lance said.

"White," she said. "I have always fancied a pure white pair for my carriage."

Lance seemed subdued as they rode back to the house. He remained so through their dinner. Only after it did he come out of his thoughts. He looked at her in an odd way, as if wondering what she was still doing there.

"Mrs. Johnson is a lovely woman," she said, lest they just look at each other in an awkward silence. "Very forthright too."

"I expect it was one of her appeals. My mother, you see, never said what she meant or meant what she said."

"What did you and Mrs. Johnson talk about? Old times?"

"Didn't Eva tell you?"

He had caught her in her first attempt at dissembling with him. "She did say something about your looking into your brother's death."

"Gareth concluded his mother might be able to help. That is what we talked about."

"After all this time, you think to discover what really happened? Why now, and not nine months ago?"

"Nine months ago, even six or four, I believed that by now this would all be in the past. The coroner would come to his senses and accept that Percy's death was natural. Not only has that not happened, but recently a few things have transpired to make me realize, finally, that I cannot expect it to ever be in the past unless I find a way to put it there."

"What kind of things?"

He contemplated that question as if it were far more complex than she thought it. "One thing will seem so small as to be ridiculous, but it has created new difficulties for me. A letter was published in the *Times* by one of its correspondents. It described my attendance at that assembly, and made oblique reference to the sword still hanging over my head. The author, a Mr. Tewkberry, no doubt thought his letter benign, but it revived all the gossip, all the speculation, here in town."

Nothing in the way he spoke suggested he knew Tewk-berry's identity. She felt sick. She could not believe she had caused him trouble when she wrote that letter.

No, that was not true. Now she dissembled with herself. She had written it after he went too far in that garden. She had written it with Nora on her mind. She had known that repeating what the coroner had said about new developments could be taken two ways. She had not wanted to cause big trouble for him, but she had not cared too much if she caused a little.

At the time, she had no idea she would end up married to him, of course.

"Perhaps this time it will die down fast. Everyone has feasted on this before, and it can't hold anyone's interest for long again."

"Normally I would agree. However, members of the government who have no love for me have now taken an interest like they did not before." He took her hand. "You are not to worry, so stop frowning. The worst that will happen is I will be publicly embarrassed, and even that will be hard to manage with a duke."

"How would you be embarrassed?"

He shrugged as if it mattered not to him, but his eyes held depths that made her wonder if it would in fact matter a good deal. "A trial in the House of Lords," he said. "I do not think the other peers will allow it, when there is no evidence."

Public embarrassment did not do justice to the kind

of humiliation he described. She did not think any man could remain nonchalant about that prospect. Not even a duke.

Her astonishment gave way to more curiosity. Evidence made all the difference, of course, in any trial. If there was none, why was he investigating the whole business? Did he see more danger than he claimed?

Another thought slithered into the others. He proposed soon after he came up to town this time. A coincidence? Or did the one relate to the other—

He squeezed the hand he held, drawing her attention. His eyes no longer held shadowed depths, but bright ones. "You are recovered?"

"Recovered? *Oh*. Yes, I am . . . well recovered."

"Then come with me." He stood with her hand still in his. He led her out of the dining room and up the stairs.

A maid waited in her apartment to assist her when she retired. Aylesbury walked in with her in tow and, with a vague gesture, sent the maid scurrying out the door.

He turned and swung her into his embrace. Kisses and caresses submerged her under an onslaught of pleasure. She did not even realize he had her dress unfastened until the sleeves sagged on her shoulders.

She glanced askance at one of them. He took the opportunity to push it farther down.

"You do that with aplomb," she said. "I expect practice helped you develop the skill."

"Lots of it." He eased his hold of her, so the whole bodice could drop. Then the whole dress, until it puddled at her feet. "I have my preferences. Short corsets like this one, that lace in front, for example." His fingers deftly worked at unlacing that garment.

"My maid could have done this."

"Only if I were prepared to wait a moment longer." He displayed no impatience, but that corset abandoned her body with alarming speed.

"It was good of you. To allow me to . . . recover."

"You should wait until the morning before you conclude I am good." A deep kiss distracted her from thinking much on that veiled warning, but not from the way her chemise drifted down to join her dress.

His hands moved over her naked body, arousing her, claiming her. She thrilled at his possessive touch. Her vulnerability excited her. Her breasts turned heavy, and sly desire titillated where she had "recovered."

When he set her back and looked at her, she was too immersed in pleasure to know much shame. She looked, too, down at her body's pale skin and dark, hard nipples. She still wore her hose. She wondered if she was supposed to remove them herself.

He began untying his cravat. "Get on the bed, Marianne."

She obeyed, climbing onto the huge bed, pushing aside the bedclothes. She lay there while he undressed. His gaze never left her. She turned her head when he stripped off his lower clothes.

"That will not do, Marianne."

She glanced to see him standing right next to her.

"I am going to show you how to receive pleasure, and

also how to give it. I do not want you merely willing but too shy to participate. So, look at me now."

She turned her head at the tone of command. He stood naked, a mere arm's length away. He was lean and muscular. His chest commanded most of her attention. His shoulders and arms reflected activity in their hard and taut lines.

He waited, and she knew why. Finally she lowered her gaze to his erection. It did not appear nearly as odd as she expected.

"That is because of you," he said. "That is my desire for you." He reached for her hand, and placed it on the evidence of that desire.

It did not feel how she expected either. It moved under her touch. Enlarged, unless she was mistaken. She drifted her fingertips along it, fascinated by the reaction she evoked.

"You like that," she said. "It is why in the garden . . ."

"Yes."

She looked up at him, but continued her light touch. "And if I had allowed it?"

"I would have ravished you."

"It is a good thing I punched you, then."

"A firm *no* would have sufficed." He gestured for her to move over, and joined her on the bed.

"Are you going to ravish me now?"

"It is not my intention."

"But you are not sure?"

He spoke between kisses on her neck. "I thought to wait a few weeks for a true ravishment, but one never knows these things."

"Will you warn me when you intend that?"

"I doubt it."

She wondered if being ravished included the delicious way he now caressed her breast and the maddening fervor taking control of her.

He wove a sensual cloak over the bed, and she soon ached. Pleasure made her crave yet more pleasure. Her whole essence waited and urged and grasped for more.

His mouth closed on one breast. His fingers played at the other. The combined sensations sent her mind crying from the beauty of it, and from the urges building. She relinquished any pretense of restraint. Despite her dazed sense of time and place, she found one thread of sense and moved her arm so she could touch him again, to share the pleasure. To participate.

That changed their passion more than she expected. A new tension entered him. Their kisses turned frenzied and impatient. She vaguely realized they both expressed their arousals in that fervor, she as well as him.

He caressed lower, at first carefully, then less so. All of her consciousness lowered, too, until the need pulsing there dominated her body and mind.

"Now," she gasped, the lesson from the last time coming to her in her anguish.

"Not yet." With expert, ruthless touches he drove her further into her oblivion of need.

She could not bear it. She thought she would die. She released her painful frustration by clawing at his shoulder.

"Allow the release your body wants, Marianne. You have to permit it."

That made no sense. Then it did. Something in her understood. She took a step without knowing she could. The tension that tortured her shattered in a glorious release of exquisite pleasure and fulfillment.

Her awe detached her from everything else, even her awareness of him. Even as he came over her and pressed into her, even as she filled her arms with his strength, she dwelled in astonishment as waves of perfection eddied through her.

She hardly recovered, but slowly the world intruded. He was in her totally, looking down at her.

"What was that?" She blinked hard as reality reasserted itself.

"The scientific word is *orgasm*. Perhaps that is what is meant by marital bliss, however."

"*Bliss* is a good word. I don't think that is what women mean when they say that, however."

"Probably not, since many wives never experience it." He reached down and bent her knees. He hooked one over his hip. She knew to do the same with the other.

The rest was not like the last time either. He was not as restrained. She had not totally recovered, but she did not mind the sensation of his thrusts. Her body accommodated them in its own way. Her excitement revived. The feel of him teased at her, intimating she might know that bliss again if he kept at it very long.

His finish came hard, in her and in him. Not so kind. Not so considerate. She felt the break in his tension and sensed his own release crash through him.

She did nothing to interfere with how he lost himself.

Even after he rolled off her, she did not speak, but drifted
in the rare intimacy she felt with him. Finally he stirred,
and kissed her.

"I do not know why you said I should wait until morning before saying you were good," she murmured. "You
did nothing to shock me, except in the best way."

She felt his smile against her cheek. "It is not morning yet."

I t was a wonder he had not taken her right there on the
table.

Dinner had been two hours of hunger that the food
could not satisfy. It was all he could do to pay attention
to their conversation. It had been months since he
wanted a woman so much. Years.

Now he lay with Marianne in his arms. He enjoyed that
more than was normal too. Perhaps this ill-advised marriage would actually be pleasant, at least for a while. One
could never be sure from the first weeks and months. New
pleasure had a way of obscuring the truth about a match,
as his father's experience had proven.

Right now, contentment reigned. With her, and with
himself. At least he had showed her how pleasurable
pleasure could be. He had not left her incomplete again.

"How did you learn how to do that?" Marianne, ever
curious, asked.

He did not mind, but her curiosity had the potential
for being a problem at some point. It was not the normal
sort. She had an unfortunate talent for seeing matters

too clearly and from all angles. Her questions could be incisive to a fault, and inconvenient.

"My father sent me to a very polite brothel in my youth. The older women there had a tendency to school green boys in certain things. I believe they thought it their duty to our future wives to explain that bliss should go both ways. Or perhaps they wanted payment in more than coin."

"Had he not sent you there, would you have never known?"

He shrugged. "Men do not discuss much about whether their women know contentment in bed. The talk is much cruder than that."

"I imagine so."

He doubted she could come close to imagining it. Just as well.

He rose up on his arm and looked down at her. She had not covered herself much, and her smooth body looked lovely in the glow from the two lamps left by the maid. He smoothed his hand down her softness. Her skin felt cool and silky.

She looked up at him with an impish light in her eyes. "What are your intentions, sir?"

He responded by putting his hand to her mound, and stroking deeper into her cleft. She startled at the immediate intensity. Her lids lowered and lips parted.

He brought her along slowly, luring her back to the unguarded passion she had displayed. He watched her flex to the throes as they claimed her, until she abandoned any pretense of controlling what he did to her. She would probably permit him anything now, but he would not be too bad.

She caressed him, too, and sought to give him pleasure. That charmed him. He restrained his impulses and allowed it, even if he was already inside her in his mind.

"Someday I will do this with my mouth, Marianne." He slid his finger around her lips, then tantalized her with short penetrations.

She blinked several times and looked at him. Confused. Curious. He teased at her until thought left her again.

He could wait no longer. Nor did he want to. He pulled over a pillow and flipped her, so she hugged the mattress and her bottom rose. She showed more confusion, until he kneeled behind her and put his hand to her again. She lay one cheek on the mattress and watched him out of the corner of her other eye.

Her erotic position pushed him to the edge of his control. He caressed her bottom. Round. Soft. Waiting. Her lower back dipped even more as she offered herself. He waited until she moaned, and the pleasure overwhelmed her.

He entered her slowly, holding his passion back while he enjoyed the feel of her. Erotic fury built fast, however, and soon it howled in him. He took her hard then, until pleasure exploded and cast him into a place of pure sensation.

He collapsed beside her, his arm thrust possessively over her back. Their heavy breaths matched each other's, meeting in the space between their heads on the pillow. Slowly he calmed, and appeared to be drifting to sleep. Only instead that arm moved, and a caress traced down her back and up the hill of her bottom, and to where her hidden flesh still pulsed.

One touch sent her back to the height of her passion. She clutched the sheet under her hands. She closed her eyes and let it happen.

She almost wept before it ended. She screamed when it finally did. Even then he did not stop, but sent echoes of the ecstasy shuddering through her.

He did sleep then. She wondered if he intended to stay in this bed. Perhaps he thought to do this yet again, a different way. She did not mind his presence beside her. She thought it cozy and intimate.

She could not sleep at once, so she lay there as he held her. Her thoughts traveled drowsily over the day's events. Eva's revelation came to her, that Aylesbury now looked into his brother's death. After all this time . . . right when he chose to wed . . . After all this time . . . right when the government showed renewed interest . . . After all this time . . . even as he finally took a wife. An inappropriate wife with no fortune or rank, whom he did not love . . . After all this time . . .

She must have slept because suddenly she jolted awake. She found Aylesbury sitting upright in bed, wiping his eyes. In the distance a pounding sounded and a voice yelled. Then that stopped, but soon after the pounding resumed, right on her door.

Aylesbury rose and, naked still, opened the door. Marianne grabbed at the sheet and covered herself.

His valet stood there, his back to the threshold so he would not see in. "Milord, there is a man below, a messenger from Windsor." He thrust his hand behind his back. A banyan dangled from it.

Aylesbury pulled on the banyan and walked out while he buttoned it. The servant managed to close the door without turning his head.

Ten minutes later, Aylesbury returned, appearing subdued.

"What is it?" she asked.

"A private courtesy message, sent from Windsor because of my station. The king died tonight at half an hour past eight o'clock."

Soon after he finished speaking, the big bell of St. Paul's Cathedral began tolling.

CHAPTER 18

"We will stay here in town until the king's funeral." Aylesbury explained the plans to Marianne over dinner two days later. "He will lie in state on the fifteenth, and be interred the next day. You will need to press your dressmaker for appropriate garments. As my duchess, you will have very high precedence in the procession."

Marianne appeared much subdued. Far more than he expected after the night they had just shared. He might be itemizing their duties for her, but half of his mind saw her wild and naked, rising above him while she rode him in her frenzy. That image of her had not left him all day.

He was enjoying their time in town, and was not sorry that they had to stay. Still, he kept waiting for news from Gloucestershire. In particular he expected a letter from Sir Horace, informing him that the coroner had finally issued a verdict of death by natural causes for Percy. If one did not arrive by tomorrow, he would write to Sir Horace and inquire about the delay.

Marianne no longer ate. She just looked at her plate and wineglass, distracted.

"What is wrong?" he asked.

"Putting myself in an appropriate garment will hardly make me pass muster. I have no idea at all what I am supposed to do. You speak of a procession, but I have not even seen one. And how am I to know what an appropriate garment even is?"

"I will arrange for someone to explain it all, as I promised, and to help you with the dress. You will also wear traditional state garments at the coronation that is coming. I will have those shown to you, so you become accustomed to them." He reached for her hand. "Do not look so glum, pretty flower. It is not the ideal way to first meet your equals, but it cannot be avoided and you will dazzle them all."

How easily those flatteries dribbled out. He was not a man given to such things, so he impressed himself. He realized it mattered to him that she not be so worried. He truly wanted to reassure her.

A spark of humor entered her eyes. "I doubt I will dazzle. I do not think anyone's eyes will be on me. Have you learned anything else about the ceremony?"

"Only what the papers report." He returned to his meal.

That had been a lie. He knew all the details. In particular he knew which dukes would be pallbearers. His own name was not on the list.

There were many explanations for that. He was newly invested in the title. The king had not been his friend, or even of similar age.

However, he did not miss that as the royal servants and government officials made their arrangements, the Duke of Aylesbury had been given no role. Since there were not many dukes, and even fewer nonroyal ones, the slight appeared deliberate.

It might all have to do with that revelation Carlsworth had shared with him. It most likely did. He really did not give a damn if he had a place in a ceremony. He very much cared if the notion of trying him had gained any supporters.

"Now you are the one looking worried," Marianne said. "I daresay it is more than garments and protocol that concern you."

"Perhaps that is all it is. It will be my first ceremony as a duke, after all."

She laughed, and squeezed his hand. "I hope I can judge character enough to know that such things do not make you frown. You will do it like you have already done it a hundred times. Something else troubles you, I think. I will not pry, however."

He wished he could tell her. Odd that he wanted to, but there it was. Only if he did, she might realize she had her answer to her big *why?* about his proposal. He never wanted her to know about that bargain with her uncle. She would not, either, if he had any say in it.

Their meal had not ended, but he stood and drew her up by her hand. "The days weigh heavily with talk of the

king and his funeral and his past. Wherever one goes, that
is all one hears. I am not immune to the melancholy
abroad in the realm. The nights, however—they are about
life and pleasure and the present. Come to bed with me
now. You will see no frowns there."

"Nor will you, if you use your best skills."

He embraced her with one arm and guided her from
the dining room. "Which are my best skills?"

"Don't you know? Can't you tell?"

"As it happens, you have not yet experienced what I
consider my best skills, so I am confused."

At the stairs, she extricated herself from his hold.
"Allow me to go and prepare, but come to me soon." She
started up the stairs, then paused and looked back. "I
know great pleasure from all your skills, Aylesbury. But
I think no matter what else happens, it will always be the
best for me when you allow me to hold you close in the
peace afterward. I am old-fashioned, I suppose."

She continued walking upward, leaving him astonished and unexpectedly moved.

The king was dead. The proclamation of the next
king was delayed one day, because January 30 was
the anniversary of the execution of Charles II.

The day after that, Lance received a letter from Merrywood's steward. He read it, put it in his pocket, and
left the house for a morning ride in the park with Ives
and Gareth.

"The town is filling," Ives reported. "Even in the High

Season we do not see such a collection of peers. The Strand is jammed with coaches."

"Two weeks hence, they will all jam the road to Windsor," Lance said. "I assume our new king is distraught at his father's demise?"

"So it is reported," Ives said. "He has taken ill. A malady of the lungs. He is very ill, I have heard. So ill that some fear there may be a double funeral."

Since Ives had a friendship with the new king, he probably heard right when he heard about Prinny.

They continued walking their mounts at a sedate pace. Everyone in the park who was astride did the same. Galloping would appear too joyful in light of current events. It would be insulting to the Crown to publicly enjoy oneself right now.

"He is a robust man, even if more corpulent than is healthy," Gareth said of the new king. "He will pull through."

Lance did not know if his brothers offered prayers in the silence that followed. His own mind calculated. Two weeks until the funeral. No one would think of anything else during that time. Then another fortnight at least while the practicalities of the transition occurred. He had a month more or less to have his problem settled so no one bothered with it when life began getting back to normal.

"Is your bride overwhelmed while she prepares herself for her first public court ceremony? It must be a daunting notion for her," Gareth said.

"She is at the dressmaker today, with Lady Kniveton as her advisor. The viscountess has agreed to shepherd her through the preparations, and explain where she must go and what she must do."

Gareth glanced over, surprised. Ives grinned.

"An odd choice of advisor," Ives said.

"She was very happy to do it. Delighted. She has taken to the task with enthusiasm."

Ives laughed aloud. That drew a few scowls from others in the park. Including Gareth.

"Did you limit your list of possible advisors to Gareth's old lovers, or were there others considered?" Ives asked.

"She was not really my lover," Gareth muttered. "It was a very brief fascination."

"On your part."

"I did not limit my choices to our brother's conquests, for lack of a more accurate word," Lance said. "I merely realized one of them would be most likely to agree in these most busy and trying times."

Gareth did not like it at all. "If you so much as intimated to her that I might attend on Lady Kniveton while she advised, I am going to thrash you."

"I intimated nothing." Lance smiled. "I cannot be held responsible for any hopes the lady may have, however."

"If she expects a little attention, you can surely give it," Ives said. "For Lance. For his duchess. For the family. For England, by Zeus!"

"The hell I will."

"You speak like it takes great effort on your part to charm ladies," Lance said. "It comes to you as naturally as breathing. No one will expect you to compromise yourself or your love of Eva. However, if Lady Kniveton gets peevish, it might help if you smile once or twice when in her company. Flatter a tad. Et cetera, et cetera . . ."

"I keep telling you there will be *no 'et cetera.'* Nor will I ever be in her company."

"He gets very piqued when we mention his past, doesn't he?" Lance asked Ives. "Oh, how the mighty fall when vanquished by a woman."

"Let that be a lesson to you, Lance, lest marital delight cause you to abandon good sense. If a man is not careful, a woman will make him sentimental and doting," Ives lectured.

"I should follow your example instead, you mean. Remain in command of both my woman and myself."

"Exactly."

They plodded along the path. Lance looked over at Ives, just in time to see Gareth doing the same. Gareth smiled slowly, and shook his head in amazement.

Ives gazed straight ahead, confident in his illusion that marriage had not changed him in the slightest.

L ance soon peeled away from his brothers, and aimed his horse southwest through Middlesex. Once he had left London's environs behind, he stopped and took out the letter the steward had sent him. It contained an address and a few directions.

A half hour later he walked his horse up a country lane to a cottage surrounded by a garden. A young woman and a girl sat beneath a tree beyond the house, amid shrubbery. The girl saw him, spoke to the woman, and ran into the house.

By the time Lance reached the door, it had opened. A short man, bald and bespectacled, stood there pulling on his coat. "Your Grace! When my grandniece said a gentleman approached, I never imagined it would be you."

"Mr. Payne. It is good to see you so well."

Payne looked behind himself, then smiled weakly. "Would you like to come in?"

Lance did not want to impose the way a duke's visit inevitably would. "The day is fair. If you can spare a few minutes, we can chat out here."

"Time is what I've plenty of these days." He closed the door. Together they paced back up the lane.

"I was neglectful in not seeing you before you left Merrywood," Lance said. "I should have done so, to thank you for your long service to the family."

"I took no mind of that, Your Grace. It was a confusing time."

"You are living with your daughter here, I am told."

"She was good enough to have me. Her husband is a farmer. My situation suits me. The air is fresh, and the neighbors are honest. Do a bit of gardening, I do now. I have a knack for it. Who would have guessed?"

From up the lane, they could see the gardens again. The girl had returned to the woman. "I am happy to hear you are contented."

"Thank you, Your Grace."

"I did not only come about that, though."

"I did not think so. I expect you'll be wanting to ask about him." Payne appeared bland, even resigned.

"You may have known him better than anyone else. I am not asking you to be disloyal—"

"I knew someone might ask me about him eventually. What with how he died— I have thought hard about loyalty, and what I may owe him. He settled a good sum on me, didn't he? More than I expected." Payne made a face of consternation. "I decided not to see it as a bribe, Your Grace. A man has struck a bargain when he accepts a bribe, hasn't he?"

"A clear bargain, with two parties in agreement."

"That is how I see it."

Lance allowed that conclusion to sit there a few moments before broaching his question. "My brothers and I have believed he died naturally. However, I have decided to see if perhaps the suspicion it was not natural may have some credence. I must now be more disloyal to him than you could ever be, when I ask you if you were aware of any reason why someone might do this?"

"Kill him, you mean. Murder him. Most definitely."

Not only the admission surprised Lance, but also the plain, flat way Payne said it.

"Was he unkind to any of the servants at Merry-wood? To you?"

Payne's gaze turned flinty. He looked Lance right in the eyes. "Does a man kill another because of unkindness? He does not. Does he even kill him over one dastardly act of cruelty? Did you kill him because of that scar? Oh, yes, I knew about that. He told me, the little—"

He caught himself. He took out a handkerchief and wiped his brow. "Forgive me, Your Grace. I forgot myself. That was uncalled for."

"Was it? I am thinking not."

Payne composed himself. "A man does not kill so easily because of slights to himself, but those that might kill could have had good reason to do him in. What I am trying to say is that a man might be moved to murder to protect those dear to him. A man not given to violence might well entertain such notions then."

Lance said nothing. Payne would either confide, or not. Damned if he was going to badger the man on such a topic. It entered his mind that he should have brought Ives, for whom badgering witnesses was a profession.

Payne stopped walking. He looked back at the cottage. "He had a part of him no one saw, except me and those bloods he found to ride the countryside with. You know what I am talking about." He glanced again at the scar. "He had a taste for young girls, for example. Sweet girls, from farmers' families and such. I could tell when he went hunting, so to speak. He had a look to him then." He sighed heavily, and shook his head. "Forgive me, but he was not a good man, and that is the truth of it. Sneaky he was too. Sly. The kind that might embrace you as a friend, in order to slide the dagger between your ribs from the back."

He spoke like he relieved himself of something that had needed saying for years.

"The steward gave me the names of three servants

there that night, who have since left Merrywood. Cooper, Young, and Sharp. Did you know them?" Lance asked.

"I knew them enough to believe you waste your time with them. Cooper was a timid man. Young had little contact with His Grace, being as how his situation did not involve serving the duke. Sharp was a footman. A more mild-mannered man you would never meet."

"Can you think of anyone else I should consider?"

"I have no name for you. I am sorry. I am not sure I would give it even if I did. Can you understand that?"

He could. Better suspicion fall on a duke than some servant who might find his neck in a noose without sufficient evidence.

"I have one other question. Can you think of someone there who might be amenable to a bribe? Who would perjure himself, for a price?"

"It would have to be a big one, from someone who could guarantee it would never come to light, wouldn't it? I cannot say I know of such a man."

"If some name comes to mind later, I hope that you will write to me."

"Is someone lying about that night? Bold, if you ask me. I am not sure there is a price large enough to get most men tangled into such a thing. Who knows where it might lead, and who might get angry enough to strike back."

"Who indeed."

They strolled back to the cottage. He took his leave of Payne, mounted his horse, and rode back to town with Payne's revelations repeating in his head.

                              *   *   *

Aylesbury had retreated into his own head. Marianne did not think he was melancholic, although one might interpret his distraction that way. Rather she sensed deep thought in him.

He had come back from that ride in the country preoccupied. Even while she described her activities with Lady Kniveton, and how the lady kept asking about Gareth, all the time she expressed her reassurance about the procession in two days, only half of his mind listened, at best.

His mood touched their passion too. Did he seek her out hoping pleasure could obscure what weighed on him? She thought it did, for a while. Afterward, as she lay in his arms, her ear against his chest and the comforting warmth encompassing her, she sensed the thoughts claiming him again.

"After the funeral, we will go to Merrywood," he said.

"Should I have the maids pack up everything? Or will we first return here?"

"Pack. I do not think we will stay long, but I do not know."

She turned so she could look at his face. She ran her fingertips along the firm line of his mouth. "You are distant. Almost gone from me. You hold me, but you are not really here."

He smiled, as if to prove she was wrong. He lifted his head and kissed her. "I learned something today that did not surprise me as much as it should have. I am trying to convince myself that I was not deliberately blind."

"I am sure you were not."

"I am not sure. Not at all."

"And when you go to Merrywood, you will know?"

"Possibly."

She snuggled back down. "I will be happy to return. I miss my mother and Nora. I think I may even miss Uncle Horace a little."

His hand trailed up and down her back. "Have you received any news from him?"

"News? He does not write to me. He leaves that to my mother."

"But he is well? Not ill, or overwhelmed with duties?"

"My mother did not say he was. Why do you ask?"

"I wrote to him two days ago. I have not received a reply."

Aylesbury had written to Uncle Horace? Perhaps it had been a kindness, to make it clear their connection was now one of family. If so, Uncle Horace should have been delighted.

"I am surprised he did not reply. Perhaps he *is* ill."

"I am sure we will find him busy, but otherwise in fine form."

She drifted, cocooned in the contentment she experienced when they lay like this together. Sometimes she thought he relished it too. Not from anything said or done. Her soul simply reacted as if it knew that another soul embraced it.

CHAPTER 19

L ance entered Merrywood with a short list of things to do without delay. One he loathed. The other he hoped would change everything.

Marianne had been relieved to have the state funeral over. She had looked beautiful despite her mourning ensemble, and correct in every way. He would have to find a way to thank Lady Kniveton. He doubted she would find his gratitude sufficient. She had taken up the tutoring of Marianne with one hope in mind—that she would see Gareth, and he would be so overcome with desire he would forsake his new wife.

Of course that had not happened. Lance wondered if some pearls would salve any hurt feelings.

He left his apartment at Merrywood and strode to the

one he was supposed to be using, that of the duke. He walked in and looked around. Nothing had been changed since Percy died here. Payne had left before orders could be given to clear out Percy's belongings. Nor had Lance thought about issuing such a command. Without it, no one had done anything except dust.

Percy's presence pervaded this space even worse than the apartment in town. This had been his real home. His lair. Battling his distaste for the reminders of his brother's life and death, Lance looked around. He opened the wardrobe in the dressing room, and the drawers in the writing table. He perused Percy's diary, and flipped through the letters received that last day.

He was not sure what he hoped to find. Not direct evidence of who, if anyone, killed Percy. Rather he wondered if some indications of his brother's misdeeds might at least provide a possibility or two regarding who might have a motive.

When he was done, he stood in the middle of the sitting room, accepting failure. There would be no quick resolution, the way he hoped. No damning letter, or written confidence. He had two weeks to settle this, and Merrywood contained nothing revealing.

His thoughts broke. He realized he was not alone. He pivoted. Marianne stood at the doorway to the sitting room, watching him.

She turned her attention to the chamber itself. "I expected it to be grander. More ducal."

"My father was not given to grandeur."

"With the grave marker he has, I expect he was not." She strolled in, and stuck her head into the bedchamber. "You speak as if your brother changed little when he inherited. Perhaps he thought living as your father had might make him more like your father."

It was an interesting notion. Lance had never attributed Percy's preference for leaving the properties as they had been to that kind of sentiment. "I never thought he felt inadequate to his inheritance."

"He scarred you, didn't he? That sounds like the act of a boy who guessed his younger brother fit the role of duke better than he did."

She slipped into the bedchamber to get a better view. Then the dressing room. "There is little to tell me about him in any part of this apartment. I suppose that is how it is with such men. Their valets and servants keep their lives so tidy that they leave little of themselves behind."

He wandered around in her wake, hearing her observations. She saw more clearly than he did. Her reactions to the sites they visited in town and along the river had been similar. In seeing with fresh eyes, she both enlightened and impressed him.

"What were you doing here?" She lifted and flipped through Percy's last day's mail, and what had come in the days right after his death. "Seeking information about his demise?"

"I had hoped there would be something. Anything. Instead—" He gestured around, and shrugged.

She walked back to the bedchamber. "Are your chambers so devoid of you? When your father lived here, were his? I find the utter lack of personal effects increasingly peculiar, and chilling."

"There had been many personal effects when my father lived here. I even took a little statue he had bought, as a remembrance of him. There were other things. His favorite books, bits of his life since he was a boy—"

"It appears your brother was a blank, however. Or else he never became comfortable here." She returned to the sitting room, and its doorway. "I did not mean to intrude. I came looking for you to say that Mama has written to ask us to join them for dinner tomorrow night. Do you mind if we accept? I could go alone if you prefer not to—"

"We will both go."

She favored him with that smile that could light up the world. She came back and embraced him. "Thank you. I know that you must fear they will be a nuisance. I promise to make sure that my mother does not become one."

"I fear nothing of the kind."

"Then you are better than I am. Because I *do* fear just that." She went back to the door, and left.

The invitation to dinner ensured the second thing he had to do would be accomplished quickly. Glad for that, he returned his attention to the apartment.

Marianne had been correct. There was little of Percy here. Nothing really. This may have been his home, but it had not been his lair at all.

Which meant that lair lay elsewhere.

He was almost certain he knew where to find it.

*   *   *

Nora did not join them for dinner. Mama appeared happy she remained in her chamber, and with a whisper promised to tell Marianne why once they were alone.

The dinner progressed well enough. Mama asked lots of questions about the funeral, and Marianne's role. Uncle Horace quizzed Lance on how the government would accommodate this most rare situation. All in all the meal was pleasant, if somewhat formal for a family affair.

The pleasant part changed when she and Mama left the gentlemen alone and went to the drawing room.

"Your cousin has shown an unhealthy interest in the entire proceedings regarding the king's death," Mama reported as soon as they sat down. "She pores over the newspapers. She talks about it far too much. The news has raised a morbid element in her character that is most disconcerting."

"I will go and see her before I leave. I will encourage her to be less morbid."

"I simply do not have the time to coddle her as you used to do, daughter. My life has become far too busy now. I receive callers almost every day, except the days when I return the calls. Why, even Lady Barnell paid a visit last week. I am close to exhaustion, I tell you."

"I regret that my marriage has put such strain on you. Had we but known, I might not have married at all."

Mama's gaze sharpened at the sarcasm. "Are you unhappy that you followed my advice? Do you wish you were not a duchess, and did not take high precedence in the procession at Windsor?"

"I am not unhappy, but my contentment is not due to the things you enumerate."

Mama did not miss the implications of that, nor, Marianne feared, the blush she felt warming her face.

"That is good news, daughter. My one concern was he might prove to be a brute when you were alone with him. Although, I suppose if he had as many conquests as is rumored, he has to know what he is about in that regard."

"Let us talk about other things. Is there any good gossip in the region? Has Uncle Horace regaled you with humorous doings at the petty sessions?"

Mama told a funny story about one of the minor offenses brought before the magistrates at the sessions. It was just the kind of story Elijah Tewkberry was known to retell well. All the while, however, Marianne sensed that her mother swallowed another tale, and had been doing so all night.

"You still have not told me the local gossip. Surely something worth whispering about has transpired during my absence."

Her mother took an intent interest in the buttons on her sleeve. "Nothing much."

"I am sure to hear whatever it is you resist sharing."

Her mother primped at the curls around her head-dress. "I resist sharing nothing."

"Then I am all ears."

A deep flush rose from her mother's chest to her

neckline. "You are sure to hear, that is true. Perhaps it is better coming from me." She rested her hand on Marianne's. "There is talk about your marriage. Scurrilous, slanderous talk."

"I hope it is not assumed he got me in the family way. If so, that will be disproved with time."

"I wish it were that. I truly do. Marianne, there are those who—and let me say they are horrible people whom I will never receive if I learn their names—have put it about that Aylesbury married you so that your uncle would not send forward a magistrate's report calling for a trial. I speak of that matter of the last duke's death and the idle talk about Aylesbury's character that resulted."

Marianne thought her heart might stop beating, this news so appalled her. Even worse was how it gave voice to something she had tried hard not to wonder herself. "Who told you this? It is not the sort of thing to be spoken of openly."

"Mrs. Wigglesworth, of course. That meddling old woman has never heard a bad word about a person that she was not eager to repeat. She enjoyed revealing it to me, as you can imagine. Oh, she almost cried because she felt so terrible, she claimed, but that kind will explode if they cannot spread such tidings far and wide."

"You and I listened often enough. I suppose I should not bear her ill will if I now get what so often I was willing to give."

"This is different. So very different. This gossip is without merit. Completely made up by some malevolent minds. I only hope Mr. Tewkberry does not hear of it. I have lived in a state of fear for three days now that he might. I read the *Times* with trepidation, and will continue to do so for a year."

"I would not fear that too much. He has not corresponded to the *Times* for over a fortnight."

"Only because he has been ill."

"He has been ill?"

"According to Mrs. Wigglesworth, a bad fever claimed him, but he is on the mend."

"Does she know him?"

"Not personally. She knows a woman whose brother claims to have met him, however. Mr. Tewkberry has let chambers in Cheltenham, while he takes the waters at the spa. Gout is his enemy." Mama wrung her hands. "Oh, daughter, I am plagued by worry. What if he hears of this, and shares it? I can just imagine how he will do it too. No names, but enough that everyone will know it is you."

She patted her mother's hand. "I do not think Mr. Tewkberry is so rash as to do battle with a duke. Do not let this rumor distress you either. Such nonsense is for fools."

Even as she comforted her mother, Marianne experienced a good deal of dismay herself. The coincidence of timing had tried to garner her attention for days now. She could not deny that this rumor lived because the explanation of her marriage was so plausible.

"Let us speak of better things. Tell me all about the reaction of Mrs. Wigglesworth and others to your new wardrobe."

Enjoying the description of other women's envy took

Mama's mind off her worry. She spent the rest of their time alone gloating.

"The port is acceptable?" Sir Horace asked after they had both sipped.

"More than acceptable. It is finer than what I have at Merrywood."

Sir Horace beamed. "I brought it back from town. I wanted something very fine when friends called to toast my niece's marriage."

"You have been enjoying the attention, then. I am glad. Dukes are so rarely useful to their fellow men. It is good to know I have brought you some benefit."

Sir Horace laughed, but the sound died a slow death as he met Lance's gaze. He coughed a bit, then forced a weak smile. "I did receive your letter."

"I assumed you did. The lack of a reply did not please me."

Sir Horace's tone turned beseeching. "It has become complicated. I swear I spoke to Peterson. Within days of my return I went to him. See here, I said, nine months is too long. It is time to end this, and you have no proof of anything except natural causes. Be done with it. Those were my exact words. And, by Zeus, he agreed."

"And yet, here we sit, with no coroner's final verdict."

He coughed again. "Quite. Quite. As it happened, two days later, he wrote to me. To issue his verdict so quickly on the heels of your wedding to my niece would

look bad, he wrote. There were rumors afoot of a quid
pro—quid quoe quid—"

"*Quid pro quo*. It is what we have agreed to. It means
I do this, and you do that."

"Quite. Quite. Anyway, he put me off."

"Then go and speak with him again, and have him
put you on. I cannot undo my part of our quid pro quo,
so you must complete your side of it."

Radley rubbed his deep frown with one bony hand.
"Here is the thing. There has been talk about it. Speculation your marriage was contingent upon my standing down
on your brother's death. Peterson surely heard the rumor."

Lance found his patience thinning fast. "Did you think
there would be no speculation? It was inevitable. However, as a peer I can never come in front of you as a magistrate. It is not as if I married Peterson's relative."

"He does have his principles."

"Find a way for him to see his way clear on it. You said
you could. You even said he was inclined to anyway."

"Yes. Quite. Quite. Only I think someone else has become involved. I am not sure of it, but I think— He said
something about those higher up taking an interest in
his deliberations. He received some kind of letter."

Irritation with Radley gave way to deep interest in this
revelation. "Tell me exactly what he said. Was it from a
government official?"

"I think so. Someone in Whitehall. I could not imagine what interest there would be in a vague case here in
this county." Radley's eyes brightened. "Perhaps this

letter told him to settle the whole matter quickly, that the realm can ill afford to have one of its dukes under such a cloud. Perhaps he will do so, and it will all be over, without my pressing him."

Unlikely. From the sounds of it, the letter did not come from the lord chancellor, however, or one of his people. Lance began enumerating the other members of the government who might bear him ill will.

Foremost on the list was Viscount Sidmouth, the home secretary. That business last autumn with Ives and Padua had probably left Sidmouth hungry for revenge regarding his humiliation during the denouement of that episode. He had no authority regarding legal proceedings in Gloucestershire, but men enjoying unchecked power often ignored such details.

He cursed himself for not seeing sooner how Sidmouth might be exploiting this situation. He may have even put the notion of a trial in the prime minister's ear. *You helped humiliate me. Now I will help humiliate you.*

"I am truly sorry," Radley said, trying a smile. "I will do what I can, of course. I was sure I could influence the coroner, but I do not control him."

Lance could barely contain his anger. It filled him, an ugly fury longing for release. He stood. "That witness you claimed to have is a part of the quid pro quo that you do control. If you are a man of honor, you will not allow this person to repeat those lies to Peterson, or anyone else."

Radley had the gall to take umbrage at the insinuation. "Are you suggesting I am not a man of honor?"

"The question is open at this point."

Radley stood. "How *dare* you, sir. I have acted in good faith."

"The hell you have. You have acted in your own interest. Not mine and not Marianne's."

"I must insist you take that back, sir!"

"I will do so when you have completed what you promised. If you do not, I will question your honor publicly and you can either call me out, or live with the result." Lance advanced until he stood mere inches from Radley's lanky body. "Damnation, right now I almost hope it comes to a duel."

Radley stared, his expression one of shock.

Lance strode to the door. "I will be in the carriage. Send your niece out to me."

CHAPTER 20

Marianne resented the way Uncle Horace sent her away. *Aylesbury awaits you outside. He chooses to leave now.* She disliked even more the way Aylesbury had ended this visit so rudely. She had not even had time to see Nora.

She carried her pique to the carriage, and into it. Once seated across from Aylesbury, however, it drained away at once.

She had never seen him like this. The lamps on the portico carved his face in harsh highlights and shadows. His eyes blazed. His gaze pierced her. She might have been a thief who tried to pick his pocket.

"Did you and Uncle Horace have an argument?"

"We shared some excellent port while we discussed various things."

That was not the same as saying there had been no argument. Perhaps her uncle had shared the same rumor that her mother had shared. That might explain his dark mood. The way he regarded her made her wonder if he somehow blamed her for the malicious talk. The news of it had certainly dampened her own spirits. A man, and a duke at that, most likely would take such gossip far worse.

They rode back to Merrywood in silence. By the time they arrived, she felt as though she sat across from a stranger. One with a jagged, dangerous streak in him, much like the scar on his face.

She went to her apartment at once, after a brief goodnight. He aimed for the library.

Katy helped her undress. She sat at her dressing table while Katy brushed her hair out. She averted her gaze from her looking glass. Each time she glimpsed herself in it, a thought seemed to repeat in her head, one she wanted to avoid. *What if it is not just a rumor? What if that is the why?*

The idea sickened her heart. She was not so childish as to expect love to blossom between them, but she had begun to think that perhaps theirs could be a decent marriage, one with intimacy at least, and humor and joy. That optimism could not survive in her reflection, where truth wanted to assert itself.

If that is the reason he married you, you are nothing to him. A convenience at best. A woman purchased with his honor at worst.

Suddenly, Kay ceased brushing. The air in the dressing room instantly grew heavier. Marianne did not have to look to know Aylesbury had entered. He had brought his darkness to her.

Katy put the brush on the dressing table. She left. Aylesbury's robe appeared behind Marianne in the looking glass's reflection. His hands slid up her shoulders and around her neck in a peculiar caress.

She forced herself to speak. "You are displeased about something."

"Most displeased."

"Did I do something to cause this?"

"No. And yet, you are at the heart of it all the same."

"My uncle told you about the talk abroad regarding our marriage, didn't he?"

"He did. I would have learned soon anyway."

She turned and looked up at him. "It is true, isn't it? You married me so he would remove the suspicions about your brother's death."

He just looked at her. She had her answer then. She knew. She just knew. She wanted to both weep and apologize at the same time. Instead she held on to her composure, barely.

"There had to be a good reason, of course. I knew that. I must conclude something went wrong with the plan, if you are so angry. A bit of gossip would not be enough for what happened after dinner."

"You are not only curious, but clever, pretty flower. I believe you were unaware of your uncle's plot, but of course I will never know."

"Of course I was unaware. I am indignant that you would think otherwise."

He smiled, not kindly. "Indignant, are you? You do not know true indignation. Imagine mine. You are my duchess and my wife due to a bargain gone bad. At most I will get half a loaf. Other than the use of you, I received little secure benefit." He took her hand and bade her to stand. "I find myself inclined to make the most of my situation. Can you understand that?"

She guessed what he meant. A tremor shook through her. Fear, to be sure, but also excitement colored that response. His sensuality had become palpable. The way he looked at her reflected no interest in polite love play. He appeared as bad as everyone said he was.

The danger in him should not arouse her, but it did. Not so much that she did not worry, however.

He saw it in her. "I am not going to hurt you. If you allow yourself, you will even know great pleasure."

She nodded. Speech had become impossible.

He sank onto the divan in the dressing room. That left her standing before him. "Open that frothy thing you are wearing. I want to remind myself what I got in return for my imprudence."

She looked down at the froth. She pulled the ends of four ribbons to untie the bows. Her fingers trembled while they sought the buttons buried under tiers of lace. She glanced at him once, but his attention terrified her so she did not look again.

The sides of the undressing gown fell apart, leaving her nakedness visible.

"More."

She eased the sides apart farther, so her breasts and mound showed.

"Take it off."

She obeyed. The lace fell to her feet, leaving her naked.

He left her standing like that. She felt awkward. Vulnerable. Allowing him to gaze upon her like this charged the air in the chamber with an undeniable eroticism. Despite her nervousness, a sly arousal began spinning its insistent lure.

He stood. His own robe floated to the floor. "Look at me," he commanded. "I do not want you shy. I have told you that."

She forced her vision to him. He stood as naked as she. Hard. Sculpted. Stern.

He will not hurt me. He is not like that. And he promised. Yet much had changed since that promise, and he appeared harsh enough that she might be too trusting. A small part of her, the primal part, found his dominating disposition thrilling, however, and her vulnerability almost delicious.

He came to her, so close that her breasts touched him and his arousal touched her. That made her feel small as well as naked. She should not like that, but—

"Kiss me."

She had to go up on her toes to do so. She had to hold on to him for balance. His shoulders felt hard beneath her fingertips. She pressed her lips to his.

"Kiss me the way I kiss you, Marianne."

Feeling more foolish than bold, she let her tongue

invade his mouth. She had to hold his head for it to work. That brought her closer to his body, until she pressed his warmth. His arm surrounded her waist, holding her closer yet.

She was not sure she even did it right, but he did not correct her at least. His embrace lifted her so her toes barely touched the floor. He took over, and his own invasion proved far more aggressive than hers. That and the strained energy his body contained gave her an inkling of how it would be.

He released her. He took her hand and led her to the bed. "Sit."

"Will it be like this all night? With your commands, and my obedience?"

He looked at her the way a king might look at an audacious rebel. "Yes."

She sat.

He stood in front of her. "Kiss me again."

She looked up. She could not kiss him unless he bent to her.

He did not bend, but only looked down at her.

She stared at the torso in front of her face. Tentatively, she leaned forward and kissed it. The taste of him fascinated her. Soft skin over hard body. A little salty. Spicy, perhaps. She kissed again. And again. The action ceased being a strange novelty. She held his hips and kissed more, using her mouth, finally venturing her tongue along his ribs.

He pressed closer, between her legs, until his erection teased at her breasts. His hands did, too, reaching below her arms to caress her nipples until she forgot his mood, and the reason for it, and the way this had started.

Then he reminded her again. One hand went to her crown. Subtly, unmistakably, he pressed her head down and encouraged her kisses lower. She realized what he wanted. Thoroughly aroused now, already anticipating the bliss to come, she did not know shock so much as ignorance. She stroked the length of his shaft with her fingertips, then ventured a kiss on the tip.

He did not demand more, or even wait for it. Instead he pushed her away, and down, so that she fell back on the bed.

"You first." He went to his knees.

She watched in a daze. Watched and felt his hand demand her passion. Deliberately, ruthlessly, he coaxed her arousal higher and higher. When she was moaning and frantic, his head dipped and new sensations assaulted her. Too intense to bear, they forced her eyes closed while her mind contracted until it knew nothing else but erotic pleasure and need. Wicked caresses teased her until she wanted to scream. Then she did scream as the release exploded in her.

She emerged from her stupor to see him standing again. Jaw tight, eyes narrowed and fury raging, he reached for her hand and pulled her up again. *You first*. His words repeated in her head. She knew what he expected. She grasped his erection and lowered her head.

He told her what to do. His words came to her through the daze in which she still floated. She liked how he reacted, how she tortured him as he did her so often. She sensed the fury tightening in him, and his pleasure at her command for a change.

Something in him changed. Snapped. She found herself on her back again. He lifted her knees to his hips and entered her hard, with one forceful thrust. He withdrew and did it again. And again. Each time he closed his eyes, as if to contain or savor what it did to him. Five times he did that. Then he withdrew, reached for her, and flipped her. Hands grasping her hips, raising them high, he continued his thrusts, furious and hard, until after a long while a violent release claimed him.

He collapsed on the bed, spent and sated. Not satisfied, however. Not at peace.

Marianne did not move for a long while. She remained as he had left her, bottom high, her pose erotic to him even now. Then she rolled onto her back, and pushed herself up the bed so her legs did not dangle. The action made her grimace a little.

Hell.

"I hurt you."

She closed her eyes. "Not really. Although I thought you might reach the bottom of my throat if you kept it up."

Damn. "I did not mean to."

"I think you did. I think you meant to have use of the woman you had received in a bad bargain, and courtesy be damned. At least now I know what being ravished means."

He should feel guilty. Only he didn't. Not nearly enough.

She opened her eyes and looked at him directly. "I think I like being ravished."

"That is good to know." Very good to know. A relief to know, he had to admit.

"Not all the time, of course. If that is your intention, you will find me unwilling. I still know how to punch when I have to."

He had no idea what his intention was. He had not yet completely conquered the fury born of discovering he had been Horace Radley's fool.

He turned on his back, too, and waited for his body to replenish some strength.

"What happened between you and my uncle?" she asked. "I think I have a right to know. I have earned that right."

He told her, because she did have a right to know. She listened without comment.

"I had guessed part of it. Not about this witness he claimed to have. The rest, however. I suspected that for a long while. It was the only why that made any sense."

He reached for her hand, and pressed it to his lips. "If I had not liked you, and not had affection for you, there would have been no proposal. It was very easy for me to do, you see." Too easy. She had earned the right to know that too.

"Thank you for that." She gently extricated her hand from his. "Do you mind leaving now? It has been a long day, and a startling night. I would like to sleep."

"Of course." He left the bed, retrieved his robe from the dressing room, and let himself out. Chaos still churned inside him, but not like before. The ugly anger had diminished at least.

Of course it had. He had relieved himself of its ragged edge by turning it on Marianne. She had no blame in this, but he had treated her as if she had.

She had never requested that he leave before. He suspected she would do so frequently in the future. *It will always be the best for me when you allow me to hold you close in the peace afterward.* That had ended tonight, probably forever.

The next morning Marianne called for a bath soon after dawn. Then she dressed and went below. She asked for Calliope to be saddled. Once astride she rode directly to her uncle's house, and barged in while he was eating his breakfast.

Her mother sat there too. And Nora. They all looked at her. Mama's mouth fell open.

Marianne had no interest in anyone except the one man at the table. "I would speak with you, Uncle. In the library, if you do not mind."

He sat back in his chair. His eyes got that steely glint he liked to use at the petty sessions. "Perhaps I do mind."

She grasped the back of a chair so she did not spew forth right there and then. "Hear me well, sir. If you want to have any chance of being received by me in the future, if you do not want me to publicly repudiate our relationship, you will be in the library in three minutes." She turned and strode out of the chamber to the library.

Uncle Horace arrived in two minutes. He pulled himself to his full height and waved his long arms in dramatic indignation. "How dare you enter this house and speak to me like that in front of my daughter."

"How dare *you* barter my life for your own purposes. How dare you coerce a man into a marriage by threatening his good name and very life."

"He told you? Bold of him. Stupid too. Better if you never knew. I assumed he would have more courtesy than to rub your nose in the circumstances."

"After his meeting with you last night, there was no reason for him to pretend with me, and extend the courtesy he had before."

Her uncle sank into an upholstered chair and glared at her over his high knees. "You are a duchess, aren't you? What complaints can you have? What do you care about the negotiations that led to that proposal?"

"Do you think status and jewels can replace happiness? Excuse me. That was a stupid question. Of course you do. You had better finish it as you began, Uncle, or you will have gained nothing from your cleverness."

He laughed aloud so hard his eyes showed tears. "You are an ignorant provincial, Marianne. You know nothing about it. I already gained from it. I will continue to, even if you or he never speak to me again." He brought his hand down on his knee, hard, and suddenly laughed no more. "I have been repaid for the insult to my daughter and myself. Finally. I will be repaid more, again and again, in the years ahead. Enjoy your jewels and silks,

Marianne. Make the most of it, as I will. I have done you a great favor."

She could not control her fury. He spoke of her marriage as if it were nothing more than a sly fraud, with her as an accomplice. He spoke as if a lifetime bound to another person could be endured, even enjoyed, if she received luxuries and highborn friends. It mattered not to him that his scheme meant her husband saw her as a bad bargain at best.

"You told him you had a witness, Uncle. Who is this witness?"

"That is for me alone to know."

"Is this witness reliable?"

"Anyone who swears information such as this man will is reliable enough when it comes to murder."

"Perhaps it is only a man who bears some resentment toward Aylesbury. A man willing to lie. Have you considered that?"

Her uncle pursed his lips. "Of course. I happen to know this person holds no ill will against the duke. Rather the opposite. That is why he is willing to hold his tongue if I demand it."

"Yet he told you. No doubt he thought you a good man when he did. A person who could advise him honestly."

"I do not care for your tone."

"You will have to excuse me for that. I find that one thought will not leave me whenever I look at you."

"What might that be?"

"You believed Aylesbury to be a murderer when you

plotted to marry Nora to him, then me. What kind of man would do such a thing to a female relative?"

He stared at her while his face turned red. He unfolded his body and stood, then walked to the door. He turned back to her before he left, and a snarling smile slowly formed. "Think what you like, but I said I had a witness who would lay down information. I never said I believed him to have actually done the murder."

CHAPTER 21

The day had a bite in the air that heralded snow. Lance rode out anyway, and not to hunt. Instead he aimed his horse to a place he had avoided for months now.

He approached an unoccupied cottage, one of the few not collected together in the little hamlet some earlier duke had arranged. It was the one his steward pressed him to let to a tenant. The one Ives suggested he tear down if he did not want it, so vagrants and poachers did not make use of it.

He had been here once before. He discovered it while helping Gareth and Ives find some missing paintings soon after Percy died. He had not stayed long. As soon as he stepped inside, he knew his older brother had made use of the cottage. He had not only seen some evidence of that. He had felt it, as surely as if Percy's ghost lived there, and woke with the intrusion.

This, then, not the apartment at Merrywood, was the last duke's lair.

He tied his horse and threw open the door, then hesitated. He had not looked much the last time, or stayed long, because he knew, just knew, he might learn things he would rather not know. Ignorance had ceased to be a luxury he could enjoy, however.

He stepped inside. A chill entered him. The cottage had gone long without heat from a fire. Its windows faced north, so little sunlight entered. Yet he could not shake the sense that once more Percy resented the intrusion.

The evidence of use remained. Nothing had been moved. The bed still showed hard use, and that edge of a stain he had glimpsed last time. He flipped back the bedclothes. The stain revealed itself more fully. Blood, it appeared to be.

A row of bottles lined the mantel over the fireplace. Wine, spirits, sherry, and port. Three were empty. The sherry and port still contained liquid.

He pictured his brother here, perhaps with friends. Oh, yes, Percy had friends, youngbloods from this county and others nearby. He probably brought them here to drink. Lance glanced at the bed. And for other things.

He began a methodical examination of the premises. A wardrobe stood next to the fireplace. Odd to have one in the sitting room. He opened it, and found an assortment of weapons. Not only swords, muskets, and pistols. Also a teamster's whip and a cane such as was used to punish boys at school. Heaped below them lay a pile of used, soiled cravats. He lifted one. It had never graced a neck. The ends showed the results of having been tied together.

A high chest of drawers almost filled the wall facing the fireplace. He opened the drawers, one by one, and lifted the contents out. Clothing. Women's garments. Two chemises, showing soiling. A corset, its lacings cut as if a knife sliced them while still tied. Hose. Lots of hose.

Finished, he stood in that chamber, wishing he could avoid the conclusion forming but knowing he could not. He had suspected it, after all. Even before he found this cottage was used by Percy. His brother possessed a cruel and ugly character as a boy. His own scar proved that. Apparently he had not outgrown it.

He pivoted and left the building. He threw himself onto his mount and rode hard. Two questions repeated over and over in his head, keeping pace with the beating of his horse's hooves: Who had known? And whom had his brother harmed?

Marianne could not bring herself to return to the house. She sat in the garden, under a barren tree, wrapped in an old cloak that she had worn for years in Wiltshire. There were fur mantelets inside the house, and exquisite wool pelisses that her fingers loved to stroke. She had taken this cloak instead. It fitted her. She belonged in it.

Aylesbury had been gone when she returned from her

uncle's house, but he was back now. She had heard the grooms leading his horse to the stables. She lacked the courage to face him. Not because of last night. She simply did not know what to say to him, or how to go forward in this marriage, knowing what she did now.

She felt foolish. Stupid. She had lied to herself that this marriage could be anything more than the peculiar union it was. She had imagined the intimacy she thought they shared. Her optimism had betrayed her better sense.

The late afternoon sun gave some warmth to her bench, but soon it would not. She could hardly remain out here forever. Still, she did not move.

A figure appeared on the terrace. She squinted against the bright, low sun, to see who it was. Aylesbury. He stood by the terrace balustrade, not moving. He held a glass in his hand. Spirits, she guessed. He looked deep in thought. Perhaps he would remain distracted, and not notice her.

Fortune refused to smile on her, even in this one small thing. He walked over to the stairs, then came through the garden toward her. Without greeting, he sat beside her, set his head against the tree trunk behind, and closed his eyes.

He did not truly rest there, however. She sensed that darkness in him, and chaos. Both poured out of him, far worse than yesterday.

"Has something happened?" She asked mostly because the silence turned awkward, but also because she worried for him. She did not know why she did. He was a duke. A man at the top of the world even when he faced adversity. A person so confident and in command of himself that it inspired one to seek sanctuary with him or from him, but not for him.

He did not reply. He did not appear to have heard. She left him to his thoughts, and retreated into her own, the ones that had occupied her the last hour. She wondered again if, as a duke, he could end the marriage due to having been hoodwinked. If he could, it would be best if he did.

"I discovered something today." He spoke unexpectedly. "Something I should have known before. Or guessed. Or at least had the courage to discover sooner."

"From your tone, it was not pleasant."

He actually smiled. To her surprise, he took her hand in his and held it. He did not open his eyes, though. His face still angled toward the setting sun.

"Not pleasant, pretty flower. Far from it."

If he was unhappy, there was no point in seeking her out. She was only the source of more unhappiness.

"There is a cottage that my brother used for his own purposes. He indulged himself there in ways he never could in the house. I think—no, that is the coward in me, or the man trying to spare his family name—I am sure he brought women there. Girls sometimes, from the size of the garments I found. I do not think his tastes were of the normal kind either." He paused. "I saw evidence of violence. Nor do I think he always acted alone."

Her mind pieced through his words rationally, but her heart understood at once. Her breathing came hard for a few moments, as if her lungs ceased functioning. When her mind grasped it all, one thought, and one alone, yelled silently inside her. *Nora.*

"I have been wondering how long he had this habit," Aylesbury said. "I have tried hard to believe neither of my parents knew. However . . . " He shrugged.

"Would they not have stopped it?"

"My mother had ready excuses for him." He touched his scar. "For this. For the time he tried to kill Gareth. Oh, yes, he did. Neither Ives nor I doubted Gareth's story. As for my father—I believe he knew what he had in Percy, even if he arranged to never learn the worst of it. Like me, he probably turned a blind eye when he could."

Nora. "What will you do?"

He finally opened his eyes. He turned his head and looked right into hers. "I will learn to live with the suspicion that had I been at all vigilant, I might have spared someone a great deal of pain."

Nora. "I meant about him. About what you found."

"Nothing. He is dead. Unfortunately, there may have been more than a few people who wanted to see that. Those women and girls had families, didn't they?" He looked at the house. "I wonder how hard it is to get in there in the evening, if one had a mind to poison a duke's food."

"Perhaps you should find out."

He closed his eyes again. "Maybe I should."

He still held her hand. It touched her that he had confided in her.

She watched his profile, and the subtle frown he wore. She touched his cheek, then leaned toward him and kissed it. "I think you are blaming yourself. You must not. He had little to do with you, and you with him, once you were grown. Nor could you have stopped him. He was a duke's heir, then a duke, and he believed he answered to no one, least of all you."

He rested his forehead against hers, and slid his arm around her shoulders. He stayed like that a moment, then lifted his head. The frown was gone. He appeared more himself.

"You have a talent for lightening my life, pretty flower. You always have." He stood. "You have been out here a good while, I think. Your nose is cold. Come inside."

They shared a quiet dinner, then read by the fire in the library. All the while Marianne's mind examined the day's conversations, first from one side, then the other. She was right about Nora. She would learn for certain tomorrow.

She looked over the top of her book at Aylesbury. He appeared lost in whatever he read. An emotion swelled in her chest. She had held a part of herself back from the sentiments he evoked in her. Whenever they wanted to take her too far, she thought of Nora. Now that barrier fell like the straw wall it had always been. Her heart no longer had even that defense.

Theirs was a marriage built on the worst deceptions and game. She doubted the brief intimacy they had known could revive, or grow. To love him would be a mistake, and offer only pain. And yet . . .

A heart does not understand such practicalities, she realized. It turned toward love if given any chance at all. And she could no longer deny that hers had done just that.

*   *   *

"You again." Uncle Horace muttered the dismissal after turning to see who had brought a horse alongside his.

"Yes, me again," Marianne said. "It was fortuitous to find you out riding. I feared I would have to ask you while we were in the house. That might be awkward."

"Ask me what?"

"I would like you to tell me exactly what Nora said while she was ill, that made you blame Aylesbury for her condition."

He waved at her, as if pushing her away. "I do not choose to talk about it."

"I must insist that you do. I no longer trust your judgment, on this or anything else. Tell me, so I can find my own conclusion."

He stopped his horse. He sighed heavily. "She was raving from the fever. Talking nonsense mostly. I sat with her sometimes. One night, in her mumblings, she began pleading. Begging him to stop." He looked away, then closed his eyes. "Hemingford, she would mutter. Hemingford. Well, that made it clear enough."

"It does not sound very clear to me."

"There were three sons. The first was the duke, Percival. Not known as Hemingford then, but Aylesbury, and well respected and a good man. The third was an upstanding barrister in London, on whom ill repute never fell. Well, not until that business with the woman he married and her father. The middle one, Sir Lancelot *Heming-*

ford at that time, was a seducing scoundrel known far and wide as a man without scruples when it came to women. Is that clear enough now?"

"Has no one ever referred to a duke by his family name? It is how relatives and neighbors knew him for his whole life before he inherited. It was what Nora would have heard him called most of her life too. In fact, I think I have heard you refer to the current duke as Hemingford."

"Friends from boyhood might still address a peer the way they did for years. Friends he caroused with. Siblings. His mother. No one else would address him that way."

"She was a young girl. She was hardly in the condition to stand on ceremony regarding forms of address."

He looked at his saddle. Then at the field. Then at her. "Are you done? If so, I will continue my ride."

She turned Calliope so there were no farewells. Her uncle galloped off in one direction, and she in the other.

N ora ran over and threw her arms around Marianne. "I am so glad you came. Your mother said you had to leave their dinner early. I was so sad not to see you." She pulled Marianne toward the window. "Look at my friends. I have so many now."

Her plant collection had grown. A dozen little pots formed a circle on a table now placed near the window.

"You do not talk to them, do you?"

"Of course I do. I think it helps them grow better too." She petted one plant's leaves. "Mr. Llewellyn said this one may flower before winter is out, if I keep it warm. I wonder what color the flower will be."

Marianne admired the plants. She watched her cousin, noting her good color and how she did not appear so blank now. Perhaps she should leave well enough alone where Nora was concerned. Then again, perhaps the truth would help everyone, Nora included.

Of two minds, and hardly secure in the wisdom of her actions, she encouraged Nora to sit beside her on the bed. "I want to ask you something. I hope you will try to answer me, even if it is difficult."

Nora slipped her arm around Marianne's back. Marianne did the same, so they sat next to each other in a half embrace.

"Ask what you want. I do not mind. I have no secrets."

"It is about the day they found you out in the storm."

Nora stilled. "Oh. That."

"Where had you been? I think you met someone earlier. A beau perhaps."

Nora shook her head. "I met no beau."

"A man who flattered you? Someone who lured you to an assignation?"

"No."

"Maybe instead you came upon him while you rode."

"No." Her voice rang with the frantic note that heralded nothing good.

"Who was it, Nora? Tell me who it was, and what happened."

"No one. Nothing happened." Nora tried to extricate herself from the embrace. A wildness entered her eyes.

"On our way here that first day back, you became emotional and wild when we rode near the Duke of Aylesbury's estate. Do you remember? We were right near some of the farmhouses that the tenants use. During your fever, you begged someone to stop hurting you. Your father heard you one night. You called him—"

"Stop it. *Stop it.*" Nora clawed free of Marianne's hold. She jumped off the bed and strode around the chamber like a caged animal, holding her ears.

Marianne went to her. She forced the hands away so Nora could hear her. "What happened that day, Nora? You keep it deep inside yourself, but I think you remember very well."

Nora broke her hands free and began hitting Marianne about the face and shoulders. Tears puddled in her eyes, then flowed down her cheeks. "I don't want to. *I don't want*—" She ran to her dressing table, crying so hard she moaned. She pulled over the looking glass. It crashed to the floor and shattered.

Marianne pulled her away from the shards, then embraced her firmly. "I am here, darling. I am here. But tell me now. I do not like to cause you distress, but it is time you told someone. You cannot live like this, with such a horror inside you."

Nora screamed and moaned at the same time. Marianne got her to the bed, and sat with her in a tight embrace. And amidst the crying and screaming, a story came out in bits and pieces. A terrible story, of Nora coming upon Hemingford while she rode, and riding with him, flattered that he even noticed her. Of being lured to a cottage where he said he had to bring something to a tenant. Of being pulled off her horse by another man, and dragged inside, and held down while they and another hurt her and ripped her dress and chemise and hit her when she bit one of them. Of being left there alone afterward, and trying to get home in a downpour.

Her frenzy broke halfway through. After that she only cried, finishing the horrible memory between gulps of air.

Marianne held her all through it, and cried, too, as she imagined frail little Nora being so misused, and so frightened.

Afterward they just sat there while Nora calmed. Only then did Marianne speak. "Was it the brother who is now the duke? Was it that Hemingford son?"

Nora shook her head. "The other one. The shorter one. The eldest. They all watched each other do it. They kept saying things, laughing while he—like it was a horse race. Round the bend now, Hemingford. Nearing the finish line I think, Hemingford. It was a joke to them. They made fun of me when I pleaded for them to stop." She covered her eyes with her hands. "I am so embarrassed. I feared someone would learn of it. What would anyone think? He was the duke then. The duke." She buried her face in Marianne's shoulder and cried again.

Marianne held her and soothed her. She stayed for hours even after the tears stopped. She prayed her insistence had helped Nora, not damaged her more. That would be too high a price to confirm her suspicion that her uncle had taken his revenge on the wrong brother.

She had one more thing to do. Then she could let Aylesbury live his life as his legacy required.

"Y̶ou have been riding a lot recently." Lance poured more wine into Marianne's glass and his own.

"I enjoy the cold air. It is good for one's complexion." She looked toward a third glass on the table. "Your brother must agree, to leave right at the end of dinner for a ride at night when it is frigid."

Ives had arrived today, at Lance's request. His ride tonight was not an idle one. "He came down in the carriage. That always leaves him yearning for some exercise."

"I see."

She appeared lovely tonight. In honor of Ives's company, she had donned one of her duchess dresses, as she called them. Its pale green hue favored her. The candlelight brought out the more fiery tones in her copper hair.

He had enjoyed her company the last few days, when she graced him with it. Theirs had become a periodic friendship, shared at odd moments and meals. She amused him with stories from the village, and light banter. He always felt calmer, happier, afterward.

There had been nothing else, however. No passion. No pleasure. Half his mind was always on the time passing, and the need to have Peterson issue a verdict.

"I have something to tell you," she said. "I was sworn to secrecy, I suppose. However, I have decided you need to know."

He did not like the frown knitting her brow, or the

way her humor became subdued. He could feel the way she marshaled her courage while she fingered one of the unused spoons in front of her.

"I am trusting you will not blame me, and not bring me your anger," she added quietly.

Hell. That was another reason he had not visited her bed. She did not hold what had happened against him. Not the acts and not the ravishment, at least. How it had happened, and why, mattered, however. She had known what was in his head from the way he treated her.

He had no defense. No excuse. He wished he did. Even claiming drunkenness would be a help. Only he had been totally sober. Sober and burning and furious.

"I promise I will not."

She let that statement sit there a moment.

"I need to explain why my uncle did all he did." She said much more then, about her cousin and her illness, and how she had been violated on the day she was found out in a storm. "While she was ill, she named the man he thought was her seducer. Hemingford. He told me it was you."

"I swear it was not."

"No, it was not. It was Percy. And it was not a seduction, but a violent act. He was not alone either. When you confided about him, I suspected at once. I made her tell me. She did not want to. She did not go into that lake because of you, but because the very idea of suffering that again with any man, in any marriage, revolted her."

Her revelations made him numb. Sick.

"I wrote to my uncle yesterday. He knows the truth now. He was taking his revenge ever since your brother died. He encouraged the suspicions about you." She lowered her gaze. Her face flushed. "Even I was part of it, of course. He wanted the relationship, so he could take advantage of you. But you already know that part."

"Your cousin. Having told you, will she— Will it help her?"

"I have been visiting every day since. That is where I go when I ride. I think I see improvement. Perhaps speaking of it served like a purge."

"If it would help her to name him publicly, she is to do it, Marianne. I will not ask you to protect his name. Not from something this criminal."

She sniffed, and wiped her eyes. "Thank you for that. I do not think she or my uncle have it in them to be so bold, however, no matter what your reassurances."

Boot steps sounded, coming toward the dining room. Ives appeared in the doorway. He caught Lance's eye, then walked away.

Marianne noticed. "I will retire, so the two of you can talk in privacy."

He stood and offered his hand. "Stay. Please do. We are in this together, and you have a right to hear everything."

She took his hand.

"At this hour, there is only one way in, through the kitchen." Ives gave his report in the library. He sat in a deep armchair, with muddy boots propped on a footstool. Marianne and Lance sat together on a sofa. "I tried every door."

"I expect the kitchen is busy still," she said. Ives had come down from London to investigate access to the house in the evening and night. He had indeed gone riding, but circled back to approach the house like a criminal might.

"Very busy, as it has been since at least three o'clock, according to the butler," Lance said. "So it had to be someone here. If it was anyone at all."

They kept adding that last part, she noticed. They both hoped to discover that Percy died of natural causes. She had given up on that possibility after hearing Nora's tale.

A man does not do such a thing one time. There were fathers abroad in this county, perhaps in nearby ones, who might know about the last duke. The victims themselves might seek revenge. Poison was an easy weapon that required no strength, only stealth.

God forgive her, but she clung with relief to the knowledge that Nora had not even been in this county the night the last duke died.

"I said there was only one way in, other than past the footman at the front door," Ives repeated. "I did not say I think coming in was impossible. The activity in the kitchen does not encourage vigilance on that entry. Servants come and go. Provisions are dropped off by tradesmen's workers. Someone might slip in. Once inside, there are places to lurk until the way is clear to the stairs."

"Did you try to enter that way?" Lance asked.

"I did. I was noticed at once."

"You are not a tradesman's worker, or a servant," Marianne said. "You are known here and, if I may say so, are a prominent presence in any chamber. Of course they would notice *you*. But a man in rustic clothing, or servant's garb, perhaps not."

"Unfortunately, even if we accept it was possible, we are no closer to learning who it was."

"Nor do we need to," she said to Lance. "I understand the desire to learn the truth. However, all you really need is to ensure no one officially points a finger at you."

"That is what we assumed for the last nine months," Ives said. "Yet, here we are, with your uncle dangling the possibility of revealing a witness who will provide enough evidence for that finger to point."

"I do not think he will do that now. Not after what I told you in the dining room, Aylesbury."

Ives looked at Lance, quizzically. "Has the plot thickened, and I do not know it?"

"She is probably correct. Radley is unlikely to produce that witness."

"Yet that witness may produce himself. Dare we leave that to chance, and not have an answer ready that proves him false?"

"You can see the conundrum, Marianne."

She could see it. However . . . "I betray my uncle in saying this. I have thought long on it. I am not convinced he has a witness who saw anything."

Silence.

"Again, do we chance that?" Ives said. "And would he wield such an empty threat? He risked much if he did."

"I did not think his threat is empty," Lance said. "He spoke with overweening confidence that day. He had me well cornered and he knew it."

"I am not saying there is no witness," Marianne said. "I am saying whoever it is may not have really seen anything. Let us acknowledge that my uncle's character is not the best. Also that he had reasons to corner you, he thought. Might he not have found someone to bear false witness, if necessary?"

"He might," Lance said. "I would not like to wonder forever, however, whether that is the case, and whether this person will do it even without your uncle's encouragement."

"I do not think he will," she said.

"You are more optimistic about human nature than I am," Ives said. "I regret to say that I have seen it done, out of spite or anger, with devastating consequences."

"I do not think he will," she repeated, "because I do not think it was his idea. I think my uncle coerced him into the role." *Much as he coerced me.* "I think I know who it might be."

She could tell Ives wanted to argue. Aylesbury held out a hand, stopping him. "If she thinks she knows, there is a good chance she does. Whom do you have in mind, Marianne?"

"If I am wrong, it is easy enough to find out. If I am right, you must promise not to hold it against him."

He nodded. "Who?"

"Jeremiah Stone."

Ives retired first, after they laid plans. Soon after Marianne and Lance went up. They mounted the stairs together.

"You have a good memory," he said. "I had all but forgotten how your uncle let Stone off when Langreth laid down information about catching him that day."

"Is such generosity common to my uncle in his role as magistrate?"

"Hardly. Even without my testimony, or my steward's, normally Mr. Stone would have been convicted."

"That is why I thought it might be him. You cannot coerce a man unless you have some threat to his well-being. Or something he wants. You know that better than most."

"As a poacher, he would have a plausible explanation for how he was on the property, and even near the house. Would he have admitted to trespassing in the house, however?"

"It is a far less serious crime than poaching. And my uncle would preside on the petty session where he would be brought, if anyone bothered to do so."

They reached the level with her apartment. She looked down the passageway. "You should take possession of the duke's chambers. Have the servants clear them all out. Bring in workers to change the paint and paper, and buy a new bed. You have never really accepted the title, it seems to me. One would think you did not want it."

"Perhaps I did not. Events since then have hardly made me warm to it either. However, if you change that apartment as you suggest, if you bring in those workers, I will consider claiming it as my own."

He gave her a brief kiss on the cheek, then walked away. She stayed at her door, watching him.

Thirty feet away, he stopped, then turned. He must have noticed the lack of sounds from the door. "Is something wrong?"

"You know there is."

"I am sorry, Marianne. My thoughts are never at peace now. You have asked that I not bring my anger to you, and I cannot promise that right now."

"I have decided that I would rather have half of your mind, and all of your anger, to nothing at all, Aylesbury. I understand if what you have learned about my uncle's scheming has made you not want me, however."

"Not want you?" He came back toward her. "Is that what you think?"

"Under the circumstances, it is understandable. I was part of a trick. One built on misunderstanding and bad motives."

He cupped the side of her face with his hand. "You did not know what he was doing."

"I knew there had to be a why. I should have found out what it was."

His thumb slowly meandered down her cheek, until it reached her lips. He stroked them so they tingled. "Rather suddenly, I am not compelled to explain your innocence in your uncle's scheme. I am more interested in the decision you just shared with me. Did you mean it? Are you sure?"

She nodded, although she was not really sure. Her heart trembled, reminding her of the cost now, and in the future. She wanted to know the best that pleasure could be, however, even if he did not join her in intimacy's full potential.

He took her face in both his hands and kissed her. She

still felt the absence of part of him, and the churn of his thoughts. She wanted to soothe that, if she could. Even if he only knew a moment's peace, she would be happy for it.

She reached behind and pushed down the latch on her door. In a slow dance of steps they crossed into her sitting room, and on to the bed.

He tried very hard to bring none of the anger to that bed, and all of himself. She felt the effort his spirit made. He handled her with great care, slowly giving her pleasure and not allowing her to do more than receive it.

She allowed him to do as he wanted, although she yearned to instead care for him. She wanted to soothe and distract him from his hard thoughts and dark mood. She tried to absorb all of that into herself, through the way she held him and by the way she opened her heart to whatever he was willing to share.

It was not at all like the last time. Even at the end, the kisses and caresses mattered more than the release. To her, at least. Perhaps to him too.

Did she imagine that the last kiss he gave her before falling asleep was one of gratitude? She held him all night, while asleep and when awake. She kept him close, so he would know she was there, and so her heart could indulge its love as long as possible.

CHAPTER 22

The scarlet coat grew larger, until its rider came into view.

"I told you to tell him he did not have to come," Lance said.

"So I explained in my letter. It appears he came anyway," Ives said.

They stood in the portico of Merrywood, dressed for riding, while they awaited their mounts. Gareth galloped up the drive, then pulled in his horse. He paced the steed forward, smiling.

"Are those pistols I see there? Only two, Lance?"

"I trust they will be enough, if any are needed at all. The goal is a conversation."

"It is a good thing I came, then. Should you require

one shot to encourage a chat, I will hit his hat while you might blow off his head."

"At least I will not shoot his ass, like Ives here."

Ives sniffed dismissively. "Pistols are cowardly weapons. I prefer swords, and could slice off a lock of his hair if required."

"We would have to get damned close for that. Do you expect him to just stand there while we walk up and you give him a haircut?" Gareth asked, dismounting.

"No, he will hurl a law book at him, and bring him to his knees from a distance," Lance said. "What are you doing here, Gareth? Shouldn't you be with your wife, awaiting the glorious event?"

"It is months away yet, Lance. She does not require my constant attendance. Don't let your wife know I told you that, in case she has other ideas when you are in my shoes."

Lance had no idea what attendance such events required, or when. While having an heir was the whole point of marrying, he had not even considered that eventuality. Until the last few nights. Rather suddenly it had struck him that with all the etcetera going on between them, he and Marianne might have a child soon.

He would like to say that the idea left him happy. Instead it terrorized him. Even good men sometimes made a shamble of being fathers. And, as he kept explaining to Marianne, he was not even good.

A boy from the stables rounded the house. He positioned himself out of hearing of their little group. He just stood there, looking nervous.

"What is it, boy? Why is it taking so long with the horses?"

"I was told by the others to tell you that the two were all set to go when the late request for the third came down. She is almost saddled now, and all will be here shortly."

"We do not need a third. See, he already has one, and there are only two of us. There must have been a misunderstanding."

"The lady called for the third, milord. Just a bit ago."

Lance sent the boy off. His brothers' jaws shifted as they tried not to smirk.

"She is not coming, of course," he said, in response to those burgeoning grins.

"Of course not," Gareth said, then chuckled.

"Damn it, I won't have it."

"Don't get all ducal with *us*. *We* were invited," Ives said.

"I will not need to get ducal. I will explain she is not coming, and that will be that."

"Of course," Gareth said again, nodding sagely. "Perhaps you want to waylay her inside, and explain that to her there?"

"Why?"

Ives shook his head in disbelief. "Hell, you are green. Explain it to him, Gareth."

Gareth clamped his hand on Lance's shoulder. "It could be in your interest not to annoy her by issuing commands in front of us, especially ones she is not likely to welcome. Women are not happy when involved in a scene, even if the audience is composed of friends."

"*Especially* in front of friends," Ives said.

"What shit." Lance turned to the door. "Marianne is not willful like your wife, Ives, nor queen of all she surveys like yours, Gareth. She is reasonable and accommodating. However, I will explain it to her inside, and be out forthwith after we reach a fast and right understanding."

He entered the reception hall just as Marianne descended the stairs, wearing one of the new riding habits her mother had soaked out of Radley. A handsome sapphire color, with military embellishments, it complemented both her form and her color. The former quality captivated him, and as she came down that staircase the habit dropped away in his mind, until she reached the last step naked.

She pulled on her gloves, then grasped her riding crop. "I am ready. We should be off. You said that poachers usually do their work in the early morning, and it is almost nine o'clock."

"You are not coming."

"Of course I am. I will not hold you back. I can ride with the best of you."

"You ride splendidly, but you are still not coming."

She looked up at him with a rebellious glint in her eyes. "It was my idea. I want to be there. I need to hear what he says, especially if I am right."

So much for accommodating. "You knew I would not permit it. If you thought I would, you would have asked me, or mentioned it before this. Last night, when I confided our plan, for example."

"I was preoccupied last night with other things, or have you forgotten already?"

As if he ever would. Her mention of it raised memories, none of which strengthened his spine.

He sliced his hand, to indicate finality. "I forbid it. He will be armed. It could be dangerous. We will be riding cross-country and through forests and brush. It is no place for you."

She stepped closer. Very close. Close enough that the servants in the reception hall and adjoining spaces disappeared with a shuffle of quick steps.

She looked up at him with those doe eyes pleading. And seducing. "I very much want to do this. It is unfair of you to try to deny me. I will stay well back, and not put myself in danger. He may be armed, but I doubt he has ever turned his musket on a person, from how you have described him."

He liked that "*try* to deny me" part. Even in petitioning the lord, she let it be known that she might lead an uprising. Hell, he was glad he wasn't outside. Ives would be howling with laughter by now.

"No." He tried to sound firm, but it did not sound like he succeeded. His cock had risen to salute her, and that affected his voice.

She pouted. "Are you sure?"

"Ah—yes."

She slid her hand under his coat and gave him a very different look. "Very, very sure?"

A good part of his mind wondered how late poachers poach, and whether he might tell Gareth and Ives to wait a half hour while he dragged her upstairs.

Whatever her gaze saw in his eyes, it was not *his* victory. She rose on her toes and pressed a kiss on his lips and her breasts on his body. "I knew you would be reasonable."

She turned, and strode to the door.

She was already halfway down the steps by the time he reached the portico. Gareth and Ives stood like sentries on either side of the steps and she marched down between them. Then both turned their eyes on him.

Marianne accepted the groom's help in mounting Calliope. Lance joined his brothers.

"She will stay far behind," he said.

"Oh, good." Ives did nothing to subdue his sardonic inflection. "I am glad you reached that right understanding with her."

"Stone probably has never used his firearm on a person. Only game and fowl," Lance added.

"True. True," Gareth said.

"She rides very well too. She should not hold us back at all." Lance decided it would be a good time to lead them to the horses.

Ives mounted. Gareth did too. Marianne paced her horse over. They waited.

He looked at his horse. And the saddle. Gritting his teeth, he swung himself up, then lowered himself, very carefully. They turned their horses and began walking them away. He fell in.

There were, he decided, few worse ways to start a day than riding in a saddle with an erection. He looked forward to exacting a suitable revenge, but thinking about that now would only make it worse.

* * *

M r. Stone saw them while he was still two hundred yards away. He turned and ran deeper into the woods.

Aylesbury led the chase. Marianne brought up the rear, as she had promised. Mr. Stone was too smart to stay on the rough path. He darted into the undergrowth when they had gained half the distance.

To her surprise, Aylesbury did not pursue their quarry. Instead he gestured for them to follow him, and galloped harder. In the blur that followed, it seemed to Marianne that the path took a circuitous route through the trees.

They jumped three fallen trunks and one broad stream. Low-lying branches snapped at her. She tucked herself low over Calliope's neck and hoped for the best. A branch caught her new hat. She glanced back to see its sapphire brim dangling above the path.

Suddenly the forest broke away and they were on a field. A lane wound a short distance beyond. Aylesbury raised his hand, and led them along the edge of the woods, then stopped.

Marianne cocked her head, and listened. She heard sounds, like an animal approached through the woods, still at some distance, but coming closer. She paced up beside Aylesbury.

"Is that him?"

"I hope so. If not, we will be doing this again in a few days." He leveled a forbidding look at her. "Without you."

"How did you guess he would come this way?"

"I played in these woods for years. I know them better

than he, and he knows them very well. The direction he took aims at that lane there, which is not on my property."

Of course. Mr. Stone believed them to be after him for his poaching. He would want to get off the duke's lands as fast as he could.

The sounds came closer. Then a body thrashed its way free of the undergrowth and darted across the field.

They gave chase. Mr. Stone looked back, horrified to see them closing on him. He almost reached the lane before they caught up. Ives and Gareth circled him so he could run no farther.

Aylesbury looked down on the poacher. Marianne noted Mr. Stone appeared to be little more than a youth. He could not be older than twenty.

He hung his straw-haired head, dejected. In one hand he held his musket. From the other hung two hares.

Aylesbury dismounted and walked over to him. He took the musket, and threw it to Gareth. "Bold of you to come back here, Stone, after being caught so recently."

Mr. Stone gazed at the ground, looking miserable.

"Did Radley promise to let you off again should you go up before him, if you did him that favor he wanted?"

Stone looked up, shocked. He glanced back at the others, with desperation in his eyes. Then he sank to the ground, crossed his arms over his knees, and cried.

"I cannot believe that you let him keep the hares," Ives said. They were almost back at the house before anyone spoke. Ives had looked fit to burst the whole way, and now he finally did. "He admits that he was prepared to lie and say he saw you poisoning the food, and you give him his stolen game."

"What was I going to do with it? I can only eat so much rabbit stew."

"That is not the point. He steals with impunity, and you let him. Encourage him. Then you learn he was willing to name you as a murderer, falsely, and you reward him. Society cannot thrive with such generosity, Lance. The rule of law is suborned by how you overlook too much."

"I think it was a nice gesture," Marianne said with emotion. Mr. Stone's story of being tempted and coerced by her uncle had left her close to tears. "And Mr. Stone showed great remorse, not that you can blame a man for accepting a way out of being transported, or worse. It was a devil's bargain, and not of his making."

Lance reached over to pat her hand. She saw the best in people. The truth was that while Jeremiah Stone poached to feed his family, he was by nature a thief. Since she wanted to sympathize, he would not explain that, however.

She looked disheveled from their chase and flushed from the cold. Locks of hair fell about her face. One epaulet on her habit hung, ripped loose by a branch. She had lost her pert little hat.

He thought she appeared beautiful and fresh.

Ives looked to heaven in his exasperation over their inability to see the bigger picture.

"He told us what I wanted to know," Lance said, before the lawyer started in again with his lessons. "It is safe to say that with three witnesses to his confession, he will not try to do it now, no matter what. Nor would he have, once Radley saw the error of his ways."

"At least you know now," Gareth said. "You will not have to wonder who the witness was, and whether he might come forward with his tale."

He did know, thanks to Marianne. If she had not overheard that argument with Langreth while she had her nose to the shop window that day, if she had not remembered what she heard about Mr. Stone's trial, and her uncle's unusual magnanimity, if she had not looked at all of it this way, then that, as was her mind's method of working, he might never have known.

As for Radley's use of Mr. Stone—that would be handled later. He could not excuse it because of what Radley thought Lance had done to Nora. He knew Marianne did not think so either.

They handed over their horses at the portico. Lance led the way inside. "It is early, but I say this calls for celebratory cheer."

He aimed toward the library. Marianne aimed to the stairs.

"Where are you going?" he asked.

"Above."

"The hell you are. If you ride with the devils, you can drink with them." He held out his hand. After a small hesitation, she came and took it.

Ives threw himself onto a sofa in the library. Gareth leaned against a table. Marianne sat on a wooden chair.

"Nothing for me," she said. "I do not care for ratafia."

Lance carried over a glass. "It isn't ratafia. I would not insult you with that today."

She peered into it. "What is it?"

"Whiskey. The best Scotland can make." He handed glasses to his brothers too.

Marianne kept peering into her glass. "I have always been curious about its taste and fascination to men. I suppose a bit won't hurt."

Gareth raised his glass. "A few more details, and it is over."

Ives raised his. "To the life you once knew, Lance, and will now have again."

They took long swallows of the spirits. Before he joined them, Lance raised his glass to Marianne as well.

Marianne watched, then gamely took a gulp of her own. For a two count she remained serene. Then the whiskey's effects hit her. Her eyes widened. Her face turned red. She coughed hard, then inhaled like she wanted to blow out a flame.

Hand to her mouth, she stood. "I will leave you now, so you can discuss those details while you celebrate," she said. "I dare not stay for more such cheer. It might kill me."

Lance walked with her to the door. There she leaned close. "Promise you will come to me tonight," she whispered. Then she was gone.

Celebrate they did. Marianne did not go down to dinner, but had it brought to her. Laughter came to her from below at times. The brothers were enjoying

Aylesbury's freedom from the prison in which he had been confined for almost a year.

She saw the difference in him as soon as Jeremiah Stone finished his story. She loved the man she knew already, but she suspected the real Lancelot Hemingford would dazzle her silly. Even on the ride back, the fullness of his spirit, now released in all its self-assured, arrogant independence, almost overwhelmed her.

His aura stretched as they rode, and assumed a stance that dared anyone to interfere with him, or object to his behavior, or deny him his due. The man on the horse next to hers transformed into a man she had only met on occasion before, and then mostly during the passion they shared.

It had all been in him all along, however, only obscured by shadows and at times lost in darkness. This Lancelot had been the source of her excitement. Her soul had known him all along. She had always thrilled to the wicked possibilities he offered without saying a word.

She expected the brothers also sorted out the details. How to confront her uncle would be high on the list. Demands on the coroner would be second. She suspected that would all be settled within the next few days. She would have to tell Mama to let her know as soon as a verdict came from Mr. Peterson.

As night fell, she did some arranging in her dressing room, then sent Katy away. She sat at her writing desk and penned a few letters. She sealed them, but did not prepare them for posting. Instead she tucked them into the table's drawer.

Then, with her heart so full of emotion she could barely breathe, she waited for her lover to come to her.

L ance entered Marianne's chambers in high spirits. What waited for him there changed his mood. Thoughts of the day's victory, of his life's return to normal, flew from his mind when he saw her.

She lay on the bed, already naked. She had built up the fire so she might stay warm, and its amber glow moved over her skin as the flames danced. Her copper hair flowed on the pillows. Her breasts showed she was already aroused.

She rose on one arm, creating an erotic, sinuous line from her shoulders to her toes. "Oh, good. You are already undressed. I did not want to have to wait," she said.

His blood was already high from the day's events. Her words only sent it higher. He went to the bed.

"Are you drunk?" she asked.

"Not even half so."

"That is good too. I did not want you drunk."

He cast off his robe. "You have a list of what you did not want, it seems. Is there another one of what you do want?"

She kneeled and faced him. Her arms encircled his neck. "Yes. I want everything."

"Everything could take a long time."

"It is fortunate that there are long nights in winter, then."

She kissed his chest, slowly and carefully. Her hands glossed his body with soft caresses. He reached to embrace her, but she angled away.

"No. Let me—" She kissed his lips, then used her tongue aggressively. "I want to do this." She tugged gently on his hand, inviting him onto the bed. She pressed his shoulders until he lay down, then straddled him and lowered her head to kiss again.

His hunger rebelled against the passive role she put him in. The earnest, sweet pleasure she gave lured him to compliance. She kissed him and touched him as if she savored the feel of him. Of everything. His body accepted the luxury of her ministration. His consciousness focused on each warmth and titillation she created.

Her own arousal showed. She expressed its steady rise with her mouth and hands. Soon she required more of him. She leaned forward, positioning her breasts near his mouth. He teased her with his tongue and mouth. Soon she was moaning, and rocking gently so her vulva tantalized his cock.

She rocked back on her heels so his cock nestled in her damp warmth. With her expression transformed beautifully by pleasure, she caressed his body, then leaned forward, lower now, to kiss his chest and torso.

She shifted ever lower, now straddling his thighs so she could caress and kiss his erection. Undone now, beyond sense or thought or any awareness except the erotic vision of her hand and mouth, insane from anticipation and urges too wild to control, he waited with a command and a plea for more yelling in his head.

She flipped her body so her back faced him as she sought better purchase. Her mouth enclosed him. He closed his eyes and submitted to her torture, glad that in her everything she had started with this. He gritted his teeth and rode the pleasure higher and higher, forcing some control so it would last.

She did not end it that way, nor did he care. With quick moves she swung and faced him, and lowered herself so her tight passage replaced her mouth. She took her pleasure then, with moves subtle or hard, fast or slow as she chose. He watched what it did to her until neither of them could wait any longer. Grabbing her hips he held her firmly, and released the ferocity she had incited in his body and soul.

M arianne did not sleep that night. There was no time. When she spoke of everything, he had taken her at her word. Three times, then four they explored erotic games, the last time with her spread-eagle at the fireplace, her arms wide and grasping the mantel and her body bowed to him.

Between each time, while they embraced each other in rest, she memorized all that she could of what had happened. The sensations, his body, her ecstasy—she made new memories so she might keep the night alive forever. She savored the love filling her all night. It changed the pleasure and made it better. It wrung more intensity from the intimacy by wrapping it in emotions more blissful than any physical release could express on its own. She even grasped at the poignant ache beneath it all, the burgeoning nostalgia and the danger of pain.

She thought he was with her in some of that, at times.

She could not tell. He was with her otherwise, however. In the pleasure and the bliss. He had brought all of himself to her tonight. No shadows burdened his spirit and no anger made him dangerous. After her initial game of control, his full spirit took command, and she thrilled at how he handled her with both dominance and care.

When the barest light showed out her windows, she turned in his arms so she faced him and his breath tickled her face. He had been sleeping, but her movements woke him. He pulled her closer as he stirred. She kissed his face, then his shoulders with a heart so full she could not contain it.

His lids rose. "Is it your intention to kill me with pleasure tonight, Marianne?"

"I do not seek to impose on you again. I think we have tried everything."

He smiled. "Hardly, but perhaps enough for now."

She studied his face hard. His mouth and his scar and the dark eyes watching her. "What will you do today?"

"We will settle some of those details. Without you, in case you thought to come with us."

"I did not think to do that. I will be glad when it is all over, though."

"I am already glad, because it is all over in my mind. And damn, it feels good."

She laughed and kissed his chest. "I know."

"Was it that obvious?"

"Oh, yes." She kissed again. "You are probably planning on how to raise some hell."

He laughed. "How did you know?"

"That is who you are, isn't it?"

He grabbed her and playfully threw her down on her back. A different joy entered him.

It had not been enough for now, after all.

CHAPTER 23

The next day, Lance, Ives, and Gareth called on Thaddeus Peterson while he took his coffee. Lance let Ives do the talking.

Ives used a most reasonable tone of voice. One that lured and cajoled, that even flattered and dissembled. By the time he was done, Peterson's face had turned to stone.

Lance assumed that Ives's several uses of the words *slander* and *criminal libel* had something to do with Peterson's expression. Ives had neither threatened nor accused. He had merely expressed profound sympathy for the difficulties in Peterson's duties, and the vulnerabilities it created if he, through inaction or false judgment, smeared a good man's name.

His brothers chose to ride on to Cheltenham for a few hours after that. Lance returned home in high spirits. Once Radley pressed Peterson more directly—and after the letter Lance had sent Radley this morning, some hard pressing should transpire very soon—Percy's death would be ruled as by natural causes.

Heady with a rare intoxication, he went looking for Marianne so he could share his joy with her again. In a few days they would go back up to London. There were still many things he wanted to show her there. She should be thinking about her wardrobe for the coronation too.

She had left her apartment, and her maid only shrugged when he asked where she had gone. Down below, he learned that once more she had visited her cousin, this time in the coach. While the butler explained this, a footman nearby began looking as guilty as hell and nervous about something. Lance called him over.

"Is there something about the lady's visit that I should know?" he asked.

"She departed soon after you did, Your Grace," the footman said. An unmistakable defensive note rang in his voice. "Called for the coach and came out at once."

"Then why are you all but shitting in your breeches, boy?"

The footman wiped his nose. His gaze darted left and right, like he sought an escape path. "She gave me a command, she did."

"What was it?"

"That was the command. To tell no one about—" He broke off.

"I now command you to tell me what she commanded you not to tell me," Lance said. "When there are two such commands, I win."

"Yes, Your Grace."

"Tell him," the butler snapped.

"She took a trunk, Your Grace. And the coach is not likely to return today either, from what I heard. She is having it take her someplace after she visits her family."

The butler's face turned red. "You knew this, and did not inform me?"

"She commanded my silence," he pleaded.

Lance walked away, and back up the stairs, while the two of them bickered. He did not want to understand what he had just heard, but he did. All too well.

She had left. Gone. After a night when he felt her essence inside him, touching his own, she had abandoned him.

He returned to her apartment. The maid Katy was nowhere to be found. Of course not. She did not want to betray her mistress either.

In the dressing room he found the duchess clothes, but none of the others. In her sitting room, propped on her writing desk, he saw the letter with *Aylesbury* scrawled large on it. He tore it open.

My dear Lancelot,

How does one address a man who is both duke and husband? Not like this, I suspect. However, as I began this letter, writing Aylesbury *felt too formal, especially this morning. I do not pen a state document, do I?*

I think you know why I have left. Not because of anything you said or did. Not because I lack affection for you. Rather you were terribly used by my uncle, blackmailed into the marriage for all intents and purposes, and that is wrong.

Yesterday, Ives toasted to your having your life back, the one you were intended to live. I am not a part of that life. I never can be, not really. I too want you to have your full legacy, and sons by a woman whose stature is worthy of you and them. The truth is, except for my uncle's scheme, you would have never married me.

You were defrauded by him. Surely Ives can find a way to argue the marriage was a fraud too. Do not worry about my uncle's reputation, or mine, as you pursue your freedom. I am an insignificant person in your world, and none of those people will even remember my name in five years.

I am sure I will see you again. I will look forward to that, and in the meantime I will cherish many memories.

Marianne Radley

It was a sensible letter, well thought out and rational. Anyone who knew their situation would agree with her in all that she said.

She assumed he would be grateful for her understanding, and glad she was so noble and good. She took it for granted that he wanted this too. She thought he would be happy.

Instead he was furious, and wounded more deeply than he had thought ever possible.

CHAPTER 24

To the editor of the Times of London, *from Cheltenham, Gloucestershire:*

The recent coroner's final verdict regarding the cause of death of the last duke of Aylesbury has no doubt been reported in your paper. I write, however, with details unlikely to reach London by other means.

Mr. Thaddeus Peterson made verbal comments after issuing his findings, words that did not make it into the official document. He expressed heartfelt regret at the length of time he had deliberated the matter, and further regrets for any unfounded and disgraceful suspicions that his delay may have visited on innocent persons. Although he partly blamed the physician's initial letter for the long consideration, he admitted he had perhaps been too diligent when in fact no evidence existed of anything other than a natural death.

He then made a most unexpected statement, to the effect that he has issued the verdict in light of all evidence, and that he was in no way influenced by individuals either in the county or outside it, and that should outsiders interfere with this county matter, he would feel obligated to be forthcoming regarding a letter sent to him that did in fact seek to interfere to the detriment of fair and timely justice.

The citizens of the county are all talking about this last part of the day's events, and much speculation has spread on just who dared such interference, and in what way and to what reason. The general belief is that politics raised its hot and irrational head at some point, with the coroner being pressed to act in one way or another.

There having been at least one innocent victim who suffered much unfounded suspicion, there are those who have advised talk simply cease, and the last duke be left to rest in peace, lest this much aggrieved individual now decide to clear his name of the remnants of slanderous musings the old-fashioned way, on the field of honor.

With this I finish my last letter from Gloucestershire, as I end my visit here soon, the waters at Cheltenham spa having done wonders for my health,

*far more than I hear they ever did for our recently
departed and much-loved monarch.*

Elijah Tewkberry, Gloucestershire

Ives tossed aside the paper after reading the letter. "He
writes well. If I ever meet that man, I will both compliment and thank him."

"He is probably trying to make amends for that letter
that set the stew boiling again," Lance muttered. "Maybe
now I will not call for his head on a platter, though."

"I liked the subtle threat at the end," Gareth said.
"Good of him to report that advice, if indeed there is any
such advice abroad. It will make men think twice."

"I expect we will still have to thrash one or two," Lance
said.

He sat playing a lazy few hands of vingt-et-un in his
favorite gaming hall. Ives and Gareth, unaccustomed to
allowing him out on the town without nursemaids, had
followed in his wake by habit. It was his first visit to
London since the denouement of the Percival Mystery,
as he had come to think of it. The first since Marianne
left ten days ago. Not that he was counting.

The last three days had been filled with trying to indeed
pick up his old life. He was coming to the conclusion that it
no longer fit him well. Every morning he donned its coats
and went on his way, trying to ignore that the sleeves were
too short and the shoulders too tight.

Ives watched his handling of the cards from where he

sat beside him, his back to the table. "You do not seem to be enjoying yourself much."

"Nonsense. If you were not here, I would be burning up the town."

"He is still snarling," Ives said to Gareth. "Surly."

"I wonder why?" Gareth said.

"You two are boring me, that is why."

Ives sighed dramatically. "Why don't you just admit that you miss her? In fact, why don't you go and get her? She is your wife, damn it."

"She chooses to have some time away. Can you blame her, after learning the truth about our marriage? Her pride is hurt, and she needs to retreat while she—does whatever women do when their pride is hurt. As for getting her, or missing her, you are wrong. Unlike you two, I was not sewn to my wife's side on my wedding day, nor she to mine."

That was a lie. He did miss her. She had been foisted on him, only to make him grow accustomed to her brightness, her smile, her passion. Nor did he think she intended merely some time away, much as he lied to himself about that too.

He managed to distract himself, until alone at night. Then thoughts and memories would haunt him, of Marianne, of things said and done, of Percy and of the revelations of the last few weeks. The next day he would pursue escape from it all again.

He had fenced with Ives and boxed with Gareth. He had ridden too fast in all directions. He had visited a brothel for five minutes, only to depart in disgust. He had even gotten roaring drunk with some old friends last night.

A mistake, that. On returning home, and missing her badly, and too drunk to have any dignity, he had staggered to her bed and slept there, as if some remnant of her might be with him. The servants had found him there this morning, to his eternal embarrassment.

She had ruined him. Made him unfit for the life he knew. She was why the damned sleeves were too short. Worse, she had turned him into a sentimental idiot, then *left him*.

"There is nothing wrong with missing her." Gareth used a soothing voice one would employ with a child. "It is very normal."

"Not for me."

"Only because you have never loved before."

Normally if a man accused him of such a thing, he would make very clear that man was in error. This time he just called for another card because, from the looks of it, Gareth might be right.

He did not warm to that possibility. Love turned men into asses. That he was far along in that metamorphosis was evidence enough that maybe Gareth was correct.

"Did Peterson hear from anyone in Whitehall since he issued his determination?" Ives asked, changing the subject pointedly.

"You would know better than I would," Lance said. "I am not the one who is a friend of the new king."

"I did ask around about that, discreetly."

"Discretion is your name. It is why you are so useful."

"I am not at liberty to say what I learned, unfortunately, since I am so discreet. I have reason to think the undue attention that whole matter garnered was the work of one man, who has stood down."

"You must mean Sidmouth." Lance looked over from his cards to see Ives's surprise. "He is the only one with a score to settle. Plus, he is a snake."

"I do not know why I spend days ferreting out information on your behalf if you already have it," Ives said. "In the future, could you spare me the courtesy of telling me you figured it all out?"

"If you insist, but you so like ferreting that I will do you a disservice."

Ives and Gareth turned the conversation to a horse auction, a topic that bored Lance. Except that Marianne liked to ride, so that started him thinking about her. He continued his play, his mind wandering through memories. Those images and loose thoughts began to nudge at him. Rather suddenly, as he received a card that gave his current hand exactly twenty-one, several of them lined up in a new way.

He called for a new hand. "He *was* murdered, by the way."

Ives and Gareth stopped talking. He felt them looking at him.

"What makes you say so?" Gareth asked.

"Mostly because he deserved being murdered. Trust me, he really did." He threw in the cards and turned to them.

Ives reached over and grasped his arm. He leaned toward him. "Let it lie, Lance. No matter what you think you know, leave it alone."

Ives looked so serious and earnest. So worried and, as always, so loyal.

"Of course, Ives. I will be sure to follow your advice on that."

The smallest dusting of snow showed on the shaded side of the house, the remnants of a winter storm that had blown through the night before. Lance walked his horse up to the door, dismounted, and rapped on the wooden panels.

A girl opened the door. Fifteen, maybe sixteen years old, she was a lovely child with golden hair and big brown eyes.

"Your Grace!" A man's voice boomed behind her.

Lance looked past the girl to where Mr. Payne had entered the sitting room from a chamber beyond. Fixing his spectacles better on his nose, Payne came over. "You go to your mother now," he said to the girl. "Tell her I have a visitor and must be left alone here."

The girl skipped off. Payne invited Lance in. "Too cold to chat outside today, Your Grace. It makes my bones ache."

Cozy and domestic, the cottage offered comfortable chairs near the fireplace. Lance and Payne sat there. Payne first dug into a cupboard and produced an old bottle. He offered some of the sweet sherry it held.

Lance accepted to be polite, and to encourage Payne to have some, so maybe he would not mind too much the conversation coming.

"The matter of my brother's death is finally settled," he said. "Death by natural causes."

"So I read. Took that coroner long enough to decide the truth of it."

"Well, now, he decided the official truth. Not the real truth. I think you know that."

Payne's expression turned stoical. He stared at the low flames licking the fuel in front of him.

"I have learned what you meant that day, when you said he was not a good man. I know about his worst sins, at least, and exactly where his taste for sweet girls led him. I found the evidence of it, and know of one particular case. If one of his victims sought justice, or a member of her family did, I am not inclined to pass judgment."

Payne tried to maintain his composure, but his lips trembled and his lids lowered. "Do you have someone in mind, Your Grace?"

"As you said, he settled an uncommonly large amount on you in his testament. Was he perhaps not bribing you for your silence, but instead paying reparations for a crime?"

"That is bold of you, Your Grace. Bold, but possibly true. It was not something he explained, or told me about."

"What was the crime?"

"You will be thinking I killed him if I tell you. I did not. I wanted to, however. I thought about it a very long time." He shook his head. "I came close."

Lance said nothing.

Payne's gaze turned flinty. He looked Lance right in the eyes. "My daughter and granddaughter visited me two years ago. They had a holiday in Cheltenham, but came to

Merrywood to visit the gardens. He saw them. Met them. Invited them back. How flattered I was at first—" He inhaled deeply. "They came one day when he had duties for me, so they enjoyed the gardens while they waited. He got the girl alone. When I realized his interest in her, I sent them away at once, but—not soon enough, I learned later. I cursed myself for putting her in harm's way. I was a fool to think that my long service would mean something to such a scoundrel. So I plotted how to kill him."

"Yet you did not."

"I did not have it in me. Even in my anger, I did not. Nor would it have changed anything for her. Yet I regretted I did not have the fortitude."

"You did not have it in you, but perhaps someone else did."

Payne rose and went to the fire. He spent a good deal of time adding fuel, and moving it around with the poker. When he turned back to the chairs, he appeared resolute.

"If you learn who did it, do you intend to see him hang, Your Grace?"

"I doubt there is even any evidence. I want to know so that I can move beyond the last year, that is all."

"Then wait here. I will be back." Payne left the sitting room. He returned shortly with a small folded brown paper in his hand. He eased himself back into the chair, wincing as his bones took the new position.

"A gift was delivered that evening," he said. "A bottle of wine. Very rare wine, from France. An old friend had sent it, someone he had known in his youth. They had fallen out, and this man was trying to make amends.

When he took ill, it struck me that perhaps that wine had been . . . tainted."

"Poisoned, you mean."

"Either. There is no way to know for sure."

Maybe not, but they both did know.

"What happened to that bottle? Did the physician not take it to test in some way?"

Payne flushed. "I got rid of it. I assure you it is well gone, Your Grace. Because if it had been tainted, I did not want that person to swing for it when he had given me the only justice I would know."

"Do you remember who sent it?"

"I do. I have prayed for the man every night, I have. Prayers of thanks, if you will forgive me. I hope it was poisoned. I hope someone had the courage that I did not have, you see."

Lance did see, too well. "Are you going to give me his name?"

"It had an odd second label on it. A label with a hand-written note. Very private that note was. I soaked it off. It is the worse for that, but still legible." He handed over the crinkled, folded paper. "You may want to think hard before looking inside. He was not a good man, but he was your brother. Blood runs thick, as they say. Perhaps it is best to believe what the coroner said."

Lance tucked the paper into his coat. "I will think long and hard, I promise you."

CHAPTER 25

John Potter, lean and wiry and thirty years of age, stood to speak for himself. The magistrates settled back to hear his story.

"She is a shrew," he said. "No man should have to live with such a woman. If you had to, you would a sold yourself into slavery to escape her."

One magistrate leaned forward. "Mr. Potter, did you or did you not try to sell your wife in the market last week, rather than yourself? That is the only question you need to answer."

"I was just explaining that I had good cause. I was defending myself. If she drinks a bit she starts yelling and cursing and—and—and taking the Lord's name in vain." He brightened, as a new thought illuminated him. "She was sure to get my soul damned. A man has a right to save his soul, doesn't he?"

"Not by trying to sell his wife for five shillings. We do not do that here in England."

"I heard of it. It is done. I heard of a blacksmith up on Yorkshire who done it. Everyone knows it can be done," Potter protested.

"That blacksmith should have been brought before magistrates, too, then. So, you did try to sell her, correct?"

"In a manner of speaking."

It went on like that for several more minutes. Fortunately for Mr. Potter, he had not succeeded in selling his wife. Perhaps out of sympathy for what he faced when he went home, the magistrates fined him only one shilling and sent him away.

Marianne hurried outside and scribbled with her pencil on the paper she had brought. This was just the kind of humorous proceeding that the *Times*'s purchasers liked to read about. Elijah Tewkberry had enough to finish his letter now. She would take care of that as soon as she returned home. The beginning of the letter waited on her writing table in the sitting room there.

She stopped at the grocer to buy a few provisions, before aiming to the edge of the village. Friends waved and greeted her as she passed. No one asked about her reasons for taking residence here again. All of those questions had already come her way, many times over.

The story she had given, that she visited to close up the house, would serve for now. When Aylesbury found his way out of their marriage, she would simply admit the truth to everyone, that the duke had obtained an annulment. She did not think any of the folk here would find it at all odd, especially if sometimes men sold their wives in the marketplace. What they did find odd was that the duke had married her in the first place.

Didn't everyone?

Aylesbury. She tried not to think about him. She had taken up her correspondence again to occupy her days and her mind, so she might not mourn too much. It helped a little. At night, however, she grieved badly. Her heart just kept breaking.

He had written her two letters. One came three days after she arrived here. *Come back.* That was all it said. She had responded more fully, telling him he would realize she was right, and that she was sorry if her action had wounded his pride.

The other came a few days later. Almost as terse, he wrote he was going up to London. *Come with me.* She had not responded to that letter yet.

She pictured him in London, enjoying that life he was born to lead. She wondered what story he had concocted about her absence. Not for his family. He probably told them the truth. He would have to tell Ives at least, so Ives could begin finding the best way out. She wondered if all of them secretly were glad she had taken this decision. She suspected his brothers might be, since they knew most of the story behind the marriage.

She tried hard to put all of those thoughts out of her

head. That was her eternal struggle, but she managed now by composing the rest of her letter in her head as she walked to her home on the outskirts of the village.

She entered the cottage deep in thought on the matter. Her cloak was off and her bonnet untied before she realized something was wrong. Altered. A shiver danced up her spine. She was not alone in the house.

The sitting room was empty. She heard some sounds, however. Subtle movements. She grabbed a poker propped near the fireplace. As if drawn by a magnet, she walked softly toward the kitchen in the rear of the building. Grasping the poker like a sword, she entered.

A glorious, wonderful rush of emotion swept her. She would pay for this, oh she would pay, but she could not resist surrendering to the happiness.

Aylesbury sat at the kitchen worktable. He had helped himself to some cheese and bread. He glanced over, then back to the cheese that he cut. "I don't know why you bothered with a weapon when you are so good with your fists, Marianne." He gestured to another chair. "Join me. I can cut cheese for two as well as one."

She set down the poker. "You are lucky I did not swing it as soon as I saw my intruder."

"You are lucky I did not throw you on the divan and take you as soon as you walked in the door."

She accepted some cheese and munched. He looked very dashing, although he had started that beard again. Stubble shaded his face. She thought it made him look like a pirate or highwayman.

"Why are you here?" she asked.

"I came to bring you home."

"This is my home now."

"Actually, it is my home. It was given to you by Radley, at your request, as part of the wedding settlement, but as your husband I have the use of it while we are married."

"Which, if you have any sense, and if Ives is half as good as you say, will not be for long."

He folded his arms over his chest. His gaze pierced her. "I should have followed my inclinations and just thrown you on that divan and settled this the easiest way."

"You do not even need me for that. You managed well enough before you had a wife."

"I may not need you for that, but I want you for that. Now, we will stay here tonight, and hire a carriage to start back in the morning."

Her heart yearned to agree. Seeing him had her close to tears. "Why?"

"Because you are my wife."

She shook her head. "Due to the worst reasons."

"You were as much used as I was by your uncle's scheme."

"I was made a duchess. You were made the victim." She had to smile at his stern expression. "Why?"

He unfolded his arms. He rested them on the table. Discomfort poured off him. "It will be awkward to attend the coronation without you. You need to start preparing for that too. I have heard that the best dressmakers are already being given commissions. If you do not act fast, you will be left with the dregs."

She shook her head. "Why?"

He rose and strode to the window, looked out, then turned abruptly. "You owe me an heir, that is why. A husband has rights and a wife has duties and—"

"Did Ives tell you to say that? If so, better if you had sought advice from Gareth."

"Hell, isn't that the truth," he muttered.

He returned to his chair.

"Why?" she asked, as earnestly as she knew how.

He groaned with exasperation. "You and your infernal whys."

"I want to know if there is a good answer besides your passing pride."

"Of course there is. I don't ride for hours without a good reason."

"Actually, sometimes you do. However, I would be honored if you would share the good reason with me, because I cannot think of one that you could have."

He appeared a man undergoing an inner struggle. A torture. He reached across the table and grasped her hand. "Here is the thing. I miss you. Badly. And do not ask why again. I will tell you. Just . . . give me a moment."

She waited, savoring the hand in hers, memorizing its strength and warmth. God help her, how she loved him.

"I miss your company," he said. "And your smile. Definitely your smile . . ." He pondered some more.

"You are very green at doing this, aren't you?"

"Hell, yes. Oh, and I miss your naked body against mine. Under mine. Above mine. Begging for mine."

He said *that* easily enough. No struggle on that *why*.

Perhaps that was the only reason he was here, although surely he knew where to find better.

She did not, however.

Would it be enough to make a marriage livable? A marriage begun in such deception, and for reasons that could soon breed resentment? She did not think so. Yet he was here now, wanting her, and she did not have the fortitude to deny her heart.

She stood with his hand still on hers. "Come with me."

He followed her up the stairs. The cottage had no luxury. No dressing rooms or expensive drapes. A prosperous farmer might live in such a house, with his wife and children and maybe one servant to cook and clean.

She brought him to her bedchamber with its white coverlet and pillows. They undressed each other between kisses. First sweet and tentative, those kisses reached back to the recent past of their wedding night, when he tried to take care with her innocence so he did not shock her.

That did not last long. With each physical contact, her arousal grew. By the time the last of their garments fell to the floor, it stormed in her. Their embraces and caresses turned fevered and impatient. They fell onto the bed, entwined and grasping for more.

He tried to make it lovely and slow. He was not a soft man, however, and all his restraint could not make him one. Nor did she want that. She pulled him to her and held him close. "Now," she whispered. "Now."

Arms extended, shoulders high, he entered her slowly. So slowly that her breath caught because the feel of him awed her. For a long time, as he withdrew and entered, her love luxuriated in the most poignant pleasure.

His need strained against its bonds, then broke free. She did not mind. She wanted this part as well, this man revealing his desire and commanding hers too.

They joined in their releases. His exploded violently. Hers did not. Rather than a wave, it broke in strong ripples that went on and on, carrying pleasure and love through every part of her.

The late sunlight streamed in the window. It washed over Marianne's body.

She rested in his arms, spent and breathing hard. He pulled her closer and inhaled the scent of her.

This was right. How it should be. Surely she had to see that.

His nose pressed her head, with his mouth close to her ear. "You must come home with me. Merrywood, London, here—wherever you prefer. But with me."

Her fingertips stroked his arm absently. She did not respond.

"You keep asking why, pretty flower. This is why." He moved his hand until it covered and held her breast. "And this is why." He kissed her shoulder. "But the biggest reason is because you are mine, and I am yours, and because of what we know and share right now, in the peace afterward."

She turned her head and looked at him. Her eyes filmed. "It would have been easier, I think, all of it, including the years ahead, if I had not come to love you, Aylesbury. Can you understand that? There is a special pain in a marriage like ours if one person loves."

He kissed away a tear on her temple. "Call me Lance, please. There is no duke, and no title, when you declare your love, Marianne."

She managed a crooked smile. "Lance, then."

"I do understand, I think. However, there can be perfect happiness if *both* of them love." He kissed her, and discovered it would not be hard to say now. Not at all. "You illuminate my life, pretty flower. You have stolen my heart. You must come back, so we can love each other all our lives."

She wiped her eyes. "Yes, I must." She embraced his neck and pulled him close. "Yes." She gave a surprised, joyful laugh. "Yes."

He held her in that perfection for a long time. Finally, as twilight claimed the day, he thought of one final thing he needed to say. "Marianne."

"Yes?"

"Mr. Tewkberry must stop writing his letters. The one now on your writing table should be his last."

EPILOGUE

Marianne worried about her party more than she needed to. By the designated day she had worn out her welcome in the kitchen, and the housekeeper responded to her calls with strained forbearance.

She could not help herself. This might only be a small party for family, but it served as her debut as hostess. Nor would it be a commonplace party. Rather it served as a celebration, welcome, and farewell all at one time. To make it even more important, Nora had agreed to come, and Lance had insisted that Vincent, who was visiting town for a few days, be invited too.

The last month had passed quickly and quietly, an idyll of love and intimacy. They had been just Lance and Marianne, together. That would end soon. Duties called.

Starting soon, they would have to be duke and duchess on the world stage.

She waited for her guests in the drawing room, wearing the newest of her duchess dresses, one designed for such a dinner party, and sewn of an unusual color silk close to that of new copper. A necklace worked in gold with a single large topaz pendant set off the color. It had been a gift from Lance, a surprise last night buried deep in the bedclothes.

Nora and Mama arrived first. Nora had improved much the last few weeks. Marianne had doubted she would ever witness her cousin joining a dinner party. Yet here she was, looking ethereal in the palest green dress and her fair hair swept up and curled. She looked older this way, and no longer a frightened child.

Mama grabbed Marianne's hand and pulled her to a divan. "I must tell you before the others arrive."

"She has a beau," Nora said.

"Nora! It was for me to reveal it, not you."

Nora ignored her. "A man has been calling. A Mr. Stafford. He is the brother of someone important. I suppose that makes him important too."

"He is the cousin of a viscount, not just someone important," Mama said. "He has been very attentive, daughter. I think perhaps—well, we will see."

"We will indeed." Marianne was glad to see her marriage benefit her mother. Between that and Uncle Radley's glee at being received on a regular basis by Lady Barnell, the connection to Aylesbury was bearing the fruit hoped for by any smart family.

"That is a lovely dress, Mama. Is it new?"

"Thank you. Yes, it is."

"It looks very expensive."

"It is."

"I trust that you continue to help Uncle Horace spend Papa's inheritance, and send the bills to him."

"Of course. We all have our duties, and right now milking Sir Horace for all he is worth is mine."

"If she marries him, I will be stuck alone with Papa," Nora said, forcing the conversation back to Mama's beau. "I will just go live in the garden then. I will make him build me a little house out there. Then we might never have to see each other."

"If that happens, you will come live with me," Marianne said. "I have already spoken to Aylesbury about it."

That lightened Nora's mood. She turned her attention to the appointments in the drawing room.

Aylesbury's family arrived. Eva carried her enormous pregnancy as well as could be expected. Gareth insisted on plumping some pillows to prop her up. Padua, stunning in a dress the color of celadon pottery, laughed at something Ives said as they passed through the doorway.

Aylesbury followed them in. "Are your plans set for next week?" he asked Ives.

"Tickets bought and berths secured. We will sail into Genoa, and proceed from there."

Aylesbury cast a glance at Padua's torso. "Would it not be wiser to put this off until after that child is here?"

Ives laughed. "That would put it off a long while, Lance. We have only just learned of the blessing."

"Special care should be taken."

"You just do not want him to go," Padua said. "Why not admit it? You know the physicians in Italy are equal to any here, should such be needed." She took a few steps and kissed Lance on the cheek. "I promise to take good care of him, and let him come back. It will not be forever. Besides, Marianne has a glow about her that suggests you may have your own announcement soon."

Mama overheard that. She turned wide, questioning eyes on Marianne.

"It appears so," Marianne whispered. "I will know for certain soon."

"While he is overcome with joy at the news, be sure to ask for more jewels," Mama whispered back.

A squeal interrupted any further advice on the matter. Nora jumped up, ran, and threw her arms around a tall blond man who had just been brought to the doorway.

Tall, handsome, and dressed in his naval uniform, Vincent's gaze took in the company. Nora danced around him with happiness. Marianne rose to make introductions.

Did she imagine that Lance examined him most closely while welcoming him to the group? Was that a glint of jealousy in those dark eyes? She led the way down to dinner, rather liking the idea that it was.

A fter dinner, Ives and Gareth retreated from the dining room after a half hour of port and conversation. Lance asked Vincent to stay.

He inquired after Vincent's commission and ship, and the plans for the next voyage. He poured more wine, and took the man's measure. Vincent answered with enthusiasm. His apparent love for the naval service added its own high notes, but Lance recognized a man hoping a duke's interest would open possibilities in his career.

"Your sister is much improved," Lance finally said. "Marianne has great hope that will continue, and that Nora will return to her former self."

Vincent's interests switched from himself to Nora. "I can never thank Marianne enough. I could not be here, and without her . . ." He drank more wine.

"She has a friend. A gardener. I saw them together when we visited Marianne's mother last week."

"A gardener? That is good. She needs friends."

"To live a full life, she may also need a good man. One who understands her, and who asks for no more than she can give. I have asked and he may be such a man. I am not sure he is just a friend either. I think I witnessed a stolen kiss in the conservatory. Of course, with the glass so distorting—" He shrugged. "Would you object if she formed a tendre for this gardener? As her brother, you have some say."

Vincent frowned over the question. Lance did not blame him. Nora had not been born to marry a laborer.

Then Vincent laughed tightly, to himself mostly. He looked Lance in the eyes. "It is hypocritical of me to be particular, when my first tendre was for a gardener."

In the silence that followed, Vincent looked for a reaction. Lance gave him none. He cared not what preferences men had. Vincent would not be the first officer with these, not by far.

"Does Marianne know?"

"I doubt she is even aware of such—she does not know. I wanted to tell her, long ago and many times since."

"I expect so. Now, as to your sister, and her gardener, if affections develop, I will bring the man to Merrywood, and ensure she has a secure future. I will back him in whatever he chooses to do in life. You are not to worry about her."

"I thank you for that." Vincent glanced at the door. "Are they not missing us?"

"Probably. However, I have something for you, before we join them." Lance reached in his coat and removed a paper. He set it in front of Vincent. "The valet removed that from the bottle, and kept it. You are fortunate that he also removed and destroyed the bottle."

Vincent looked at that paper a long while. Then he picked it up, and held it to a candle's flame. It began burning.

"If he had left the bottle, nothing would have been found. I have traveled far and wide, Your Grace. There are cultures with medicines and herbs we never see here. There are shamans who concoct all kinds of potions unknown to our chemists."

Expression firm, and not the least contrite, Vincent dropped the burning remnants of the paper into his glass.

"She told me she had been raped, when I visited her in Wiltshire soon after her illness. She could hardly speak of it, and barely understood it herself, but she managed enough to damn him. I knew your brother, you see. Knew him too well. Better than I ever knew you or Lord Ywain. I would visit my mother when on school holidays, and later. I saw him with his friends, and knew what was in him. He guessed what was in me too."

"Did you confront him?"

"As soon as I could ride to Gloucestershire, I found him and called him out. He laughed. Then he described how he would break me, ruin me, if I breathed one word of my accusation. I knew he could do it. So I began to make other plans." He gestured to the ashes in his glass. "If you read the note, you saw how contrite I was. He had interfered with a promotion last year, just to make sure I had not forgotten his power. I groveled in that note, begging his forgiveness so he would cease to act against me, saying I would speak no more of the matter that estranged us. I offered the wine as a gift of appeasement. I chose one of rare quality. I convinced the château to add this other label with my letter, so he would not want to drink it in company unless it was that of his accomplices. I imagined him opening that bottle, and toasting to my humiliation."

"It was a long plot you hatched."

"One has time to think on the details while out at sea. I could not touch him any other way, Your Grace. Not through the law. Not even through gossip. He was your brother, so I do not expect you to understand or forgive, but I did my duty as I saw it."

"Do you know who those accomplices were?"

"I regret I do not. Perhaps, with time, my sister will remember."

Lance knew he should feel worse about this than he did. Angry. Even vengeful. Blood was supposed to be thick, as Mr. Payne said. Only, when he looked at Vincent, what he really saw was Nora's dead stare during that first carriage ride.

"There is no proof. More importantly, my wife holds you dear," he said, standing. "Let us join the others."

Marianne watched Lance and Vincent enter the drawing room. They had spent a good amount of time alone together. They appeared friendly as they came and joined with the company.

She made her way over to Lance. "Do you like him?" She nodded her head to where Vincent chatted with Eva.

"Very much."

"I am so glad. I hoped you might become friends."

"I do not know about friends. After all, he is competition, and I find myself jealous where you are concerned."

"You know you have no competition, and never will, Lance. With all the love in my heart for you, there is no room for even the slightest flirtation with another man."

"That is good to hear, darling. I will hold you to that, forever."

"Besides, he probably has broken hearts all over the globe."

"Undoubtedly."

She stayed close, so she felt his warmth. She looked out over her company. "I think it has gone well, don't you?"

"Magnificently, although yesterday the butler petitioned me for mercy and deliverance from your rule. You will be a grand hostess, at many more parties."

"None so important as this one. Look, they are all here. Every person who is important to me, together, in one place. My family."

He kissed her cheek. "Important to both of us, Marianne. But come with me now."

They slipped out of the chamber. Taking her hand, he led her up the stairs.

"I do not think hostesses retire before their guests leave," she said. "I am sure it is not done."

"Family will not mind. Nor are we retiring. We will return before too long."

To her surprise, he did not lead her to her chambers, or even to his. Instead he went to the door down from hers, the one that led to the duke's apartment.

She had spent the last weeks emptying these chambers of everything. Even the walls had been stripped. Nothing of Percy, or any prior duke, survived. Then she had sought the aid of an architect in rebuilding and redecorating. It had only been finished three days ago.

Aylesbury walked around, surveying the results.

She followed him, until he ended his tour in the bedchamber. "Do you like it?" she asked. "Do you think you might use it all one day?"

He looked this way and that, nodding. "I believe I will. Your taste suits me. I like the gothic touches."

"I am so glad. You were no help at all, and I thought I would do it all wrong."

"I do not think you will ever do anything all wrong, darling." He pushed on the bed's mattress, testing it. He glanced back at her. "Actually, I think I will begin using the chambers immediately."

"Now you are being naughty. It can wait a few hours." She looked down at her dinner dress, then gestured to it to remind him of the poor timing of his whim.

He pulled her into his arms. "If I ever stop being naughty, I hope you have someone shoot me." He kissed her deeply, and caressed her the ways he knew would leave her helpless soon.

She fought it, but only briefly. Their guests would not mind waiting. Most of them would probably guess what was happening. She embraced him, and let him have his way with her body, and her heart.

He managed it all without causing one lock of her hair to come undone, and without either of them undressing. When she released her hold on the bedpost and stood straight, her skirt fell into perfect folds. A stroll in the garden would have mussed her more.

He looked at the bed. "We will sleep here tonight, so the chambers and I reach a right understanding regarding who is allowed, and what ghosts are not. Also, I want my heir to grow accustomed to his home."

"Your heir?"

"I heard you talking about our child. I understand that women share such things with each other because, well, they are women. But I am wounded you did not confide in me too."

"I did not want to get your hopes up, only to disappoint you."

"You could never disappoint me, darling."

"It is only that I do not know yet."

"I know. I am certain."

She looked in his eyes. He *was* certain. She suddenly was too. She threw her arms around him. "I have been bursting to tell you all the last week. Are you happy?"

"What a question to ask me." He took her face in his hands and kissed her softly. "Even without this news I am the happiest of men, Marianne. This only makes our lives more perfect. I would say it makes me love you more, but that is not possible. However, this brings me great joy. I can picture the child already. I will raise him to be honorable, strong, and good."

She raised an eyebrow. "Good?"

He smiled and kissed her nose. "Well, maybe not *too* good. We don't want him to be boring."

She nestled against him in his embrace. She closed her eyes and savored how they shared the joy, and their love. *More perfect*, he had called their lives now. Tears formed as she thought just how perfect. She thanked fate for bringing her and the Wicked Duke together.

Keep reading for an excerpt from

THE SURRENDER
OF MISS FAIRBOURNE

by Madeline Hunter
Available now from Jove Books

"With your father's tragic passing, things are much changed, I think you will agree," Mr. Nightingale said. He stood before her in his impeccable frock coat and cravat. He always looked like this. Tall, slender, dark, and perfect. Emma imagined the hours it must take him each day to put himself together with such precision.

She had never liked him much. Mr. Nightingale was one of the many people who showed a false face to the world. Everything about him was calculated, and too smooth, too polished, and too practiced. While imitating his betters, he had assumed their worst characteristics.

They were in the large back chamber where items consigned for auction were stored for cataloguing and study. It held bins for paintings at one end, and shelves and large tables for other objects. There was also a desk where she now sat. Mr. Nightingale had positioned himself to her side, so she did not have the distance of the desktop between them, the way she would prefer.

Emma of course agreed with his assessment that things were much changed. It was one of those statements that was so true as to need no articulation. She disliked when people spoke this way, explaining the obvious to her. Men in particular had this habit, she had noticed.

She merely nodded and waited for the rest. She wished he would hurry up with it too. These preliminaries were all beside the main point, which was that he was leaving, and some plain speaking would be welcomed.

Worse, she was having difficulty even paying attention to him. Her mind was back in the exhibition hall, wondering what Southwaite was doing and whether he would still be there when she exited this room.

"You are alone now. Unprotected. Fairbourne's has lost its master, and while our patrons were kind today, they will quickly lose confidence in the sales if you think to continue them."

That got her attention. Mr. Nightingale had always struck her as a walking fashion plate. All surface and artifice. Not at all deep.

Now he had revealed unexpected capacities for insight, if he had surmised that she considered continuing the auctions at Fairbourne's.

"I am well-known to the patrons," he forged on. "Respected by them. My eye for art has been demonstrated time and again during the previews."

"It is not an eye such as my father possessed, however." Nor that she possessed, she wanted to add.

"No doubt. But it is good enough."

Good enough was not, in this situation, truly good enough, unfortunately.

"I have always admired you, Miss Fairbourne." He flashed that charming smile. He had never used it on her before. She did not find it nearly as winning when directed her way as she did when he cajoled a society matron to consider a painting that had been overlooked.

He was a very handsome man, however. Almost unnaturally so. He knew it, of course. A man could not look like this and not know just how perfect his face appeared. Too perfect, as if a portrait painter had taken a normally handsome face and prettied it up too much, to the point it lost human distinction and character.

"We have much in common," he went on. "Fairbourne's. Your father. Our births and stations are not dissimilar. I believe we would make a good match. I hope that you will look favorably on my proposal that we marry."

She just stared at him. This was not what she had expected. She found herself at a loss for how to respond.

He took a deep breath, as if fortifying himself for an unpleasant task. "You are surprised, I see. Did you think I had not noticed your beauty these last years? Perhaps I have been too subtle in communicating my interest. Credit that to my respect for both you and your father. You have quite stolen my heart, however, and I have dreamed for many months that one day you might be mine. I have always believed that you and I had a special sympathy, and under the circumstances I now am free to—"

"Mr. Nightingale, please, let us discuss this honestly if we are to discuss it at all. First, we both know that I am not beautiful. Second, you and I have held no secret sympathy. Indeed, we have rarely had informal conversation. Third, you have not been too subtle in communicating your feelings because you have entertained no such feelings to begin with. You almost choked on your words of love just now. You began making a practical proposal, and perhaps you should continue on that tack and not try to convince me of your long-secret love."

She put him off his game for a moment, no more. "You have always been a most direct female, Miss Fairbourne," he said tightly. "It is one of your more . . . *notable* qualities. If honest and practical suit you better, so be it. Your father left you a business here. It can continue, but only if it is known to be owned and managed by a man. No one will patronize Fairbourne's if a woman is the responsible authority. I propose that we marry, and that I take your father's place. You will still have the comfortable life that Fairbourne's has provided, along with continued security and protection."

She pretended to think it over, so as not to insult him too much. "How thoughtful of you to try to help me, Mr. Nightingale. Unfortunately, I do not think we will be a good match at all."

She attempted to stand. He refused to move. Mr. Nightingale no longer appeared charming as he gazed down at her. Not at all.

"Your decision is reckless, and not sensible. What is the good in inheriting Fairbourne's if you do not continue its affairs? Today's take will hardly keep you long. As for another match, one that you may consider better, I doubt such an offer will come now if it has not already."

"Perhaps one has indeed come already."

"As you demanded, let us be honest and practical. You are, by your own admission, not a great beauty. You have a manner that is hardly conducive to a man's romantic interests, what with all your plain speaking. You are headstrong and at times shrewish. In short, you are on the shelf for a reason; several, in fact. I am willing to overlook all of that. I have no great fortune but I have skills that can keep Fairbourne's a going concern. Fate throws us together, for better or for worse, Miss Fairbourne, even if love does not."

She felt her face warming. She might admit to *headstrong*, but, really, *shrewish* was going too far.

"I can hardly argue with your remarkably complete description of my lack of appeal, sir. I daresay I should be grateful that you would be willing to take me on at all. I fear, however, that your calculations are in error on one major point, and that your willingness to sacrifice yourself will be much compromised once I explain it, since it is the only point that you see in my favor. You assume that I am my father's heir. In fact I am not. My brother is, of course. If you marry me, you will not get Fairbourne's as you think. At least not for long."

He had the audacity to groan in exasperation. "A dead man cannot inherit."

"He is not dead."

"Zeus, your father harbored unrealistic hopes, but it is inconceivable that you do as well. He drowned when his ship went down. He is most certainly dead."

"His body was never found."

"That is because the damned ship went down in the middle of the damned sea." He collected himself and lowered his voice. "I have consulted with a solicitor. In such cases there is no need to wait any length of time to have a person declared dead. You need only go to the courts and—"

This conceited man had dared to investigate how she could claim the fortune he wanted to marry. He expected her to deny her own heart's certainty that Robert still lived, in order to accommodate his avarice. "No. I will not do it. If Fairbourne's is preserved at all, it is preserved for Robert when he returns."

He drew himself up tall and straight. "Then you will starve," he intoned. "Because if I do not leave here with your acceptance of my offer, I will not return to preserve this business for you, let alone for him."

He glared at her, convinced she would not pick up that gauntlet. She glared back, while she quickly calculated how much trouble his removal would create. Potentially a good deal of trouble, she had to admit.

"Obediah will calculate what you are owed. Once today's payments are made, your wages will be sent to you. Good day, Mr. Nightingale."

Mr. Nightingale turned on his heel and marched out of the chamber. Emma rested her head in her hands. One door to her future plans had opened with the success of today's auction, but another had just closed with the loss of the exhibition hall manager.

Weariness wanted to overwhelm her. So did humiliation at the bold description Mr. Nightingale gave of her faults. He had spoken as if he had even worse ones on the list, and thought limiting it to these had been an example of discretion.

You are on the shelf for a reason. That was certainly true. Mostly she was on the shelf because all of the proposals had, to one degree or another, been similar to today's. Men might as well just say, "Marriage to you does not interest me at all, but inheriting Fairbourne's will make the match easier to swallow."

She was not even supposed to mind. She probably shouldn't. Yet she did.

A tap on the door requested attention. The door opened a crack, and Obediah's head stuck in. "A visitor, Miss Fairbourne."

Before she could ask whom the visitor might be, the door swung wide. The Earl of Southwaite strode in with an invisible storm cloud hovering over his dark head.

Exit one handsome, conceited man, and enter another. Southwaite had to know that she did not want to see him. It had been a tiring and trying day, and she was in no mood to match wits with him now.

She suppressed the impulse to groan in his face. She rose and made a small curtsy. She forced a smile. She urged her voice to sound melodic instead of dull.

"Good day, Lord Southwaite. We are honored that you chose to call at Fairbourne's today."

* * *

Emma Fairbourne did not appear the least embarrassed to be greeting him, finally. She sat behind the big desk in the storage chamber and smiled brightly. She acted as if he had just tied his horse outside a few minutes ago.

"Honored, are you? I am not accustomed to being cut by someone who is honored, Miss Fairbourne."

"Do you think I cut you, sir? I apologize. If you attended the auction, I did not see you. The good wishes and condolences of the patrons absorbed my time and attention." She angled herself closer to the desk. "Yet, isn't a cut a social matter? If I had neglected to acknowledge your presence, I do not see how it could be a cut when we have no social connection."

He held up one hand, to stop her. "Whether you saw me or not does not matter. You certainly see me now."

"Most definitely, since I am not blind."

"And when last we met, I specifically informed you that I would study the future of Fairbourne's, and meet with you within the month to explain my plans for its disposition."

"I believe you may have said something to that effect. I cannot swear by it. I was a little overcome at the time."

"That was understandable." She had been most overcome. She had appeared ready to kill him, she was so irate. Her emotional state was why he had put off the reckoning. That had clearly been a mistake.

"I doubt you do understand, sir, but pray, go on. I believe you were working your way up to a lecture. Or a scold. It is hard to know which just yet."

Damnation, but she was an irritating woman. She sat there, suspiciously composed. From the way Nightingale had stormed out of this chamber, one gathered she had already enjoyed one good row with a man today and now was spoiling for another.

"Neither a lecture nor a scold will be forthcoming. I seek only to clarify that which perhaps you did not hear that day in the solicitor's chambers."

"I heard the important parts. It was a shock to learn that my father had sold you a half interest in Fairbourne's three years ago, I will admit. I have accepted it, however, so no clarification is required."

He paced back and forth in front of that desk, trying to size up where she truly was in her emotions and thoughts. A stack of paintings against a wall interfered with his path in one direction, and a table of silver plate did so in the other, so it became a short and unsatisfactory circuit. The black of her costume kept pressing itself on his sight. She was still in mourning, of course. That checked his simmering anger more than anything else.

Well, not entirely more than anything else. Ambury had been correct that, while Emma Fairbourne was no great beauty, she had a certain something to her. It had been evident in the solicitor's chambers, and now was notable here too. Her directness had a lot to do with it, he supposed. The way she eschewed all artifice created a peculiar . . . intimacy.

"You did not inform me of today's auction," he said. "I do not think that was an oversight. Yet that day I told you that I expected to be informed about any activities here."

"My apologies. When we decided not to send out invitations, due to having no grand preview, I did not think to make special arrangements for you, as one of our most illustrious patrons."

"I am not merely one of the patrons. I am one of the *owners*."

"I assumed you would not want that well-known. It so smells of trade, when you get down to it. To have made an exception and brought attention to you in that way among the staff—well, I thought you would prefer I not do that."

He had to admit that made a certain amount of sense. Damnation, but she was a fast thinker.

"In the future, please do not worry about such extreme discretion, Miss Fairbourne. Of course, there will be no cause for it, now that the final auction has been held, albeit without my permission."

She blinked twice at the word *permission*, but she did not otherwise react.

"It went well, it appeared," he said, stopping his pacing and trying to sound less severe. "It should provide enough for you to live until the business is sold, I expect. The staff did a commendable job with the catalogue. I found no obvious errors in attribution. Mr. Nightingale's contribution, I assume?"

Her expression perceptibly altered. Softened. Saddened. Her voice did as well. "Obediah's contribution, not so much Mr. Nightingale's. Obediah often helped my father with the catalogue and much, much more, and has an excellent eye. Although, to be honest, most of the catalogue had been completed before Papa's death. This auction was just sitting here, almost all prepared and ready to go."

She looked up at him directly. So directly that her gaze seemed to touch his mind. For a moment that lasted longer than time would count, his thoughts scattered under that gaze.

He found himself noticing things in detail that his perceptions had absorbed in only a fleeting way before. How the light from the window made her skin appear like matte porcelain, and how very flawless that skin actually was. How there were layers to the color of her eyes, so many that one felt as if eventually one could see right into her soul. How that black dress, so simple in design, managed with its high waist and broad ribbon under her breasts to suggest a form that was womanly in the best ways and—

"I thought it made no sense to hand all those consignments back when it was only a matter of opening the doors and letting Obediah do what he does so well," she said.

"Of course," he heard himself muttering. "That is understandable."

"I am so relieved to hear you say that, Lord Southwaite. You appeared angry when you walked in here. I was afraid that you were most displeased by something."

"No, not so much. Not angry at all. Not really."

"Oh, that is so good to know."

He exerted some effort to piece together his normal self. As his thoughts collected, he took his leave of Miss Fairbourne. "I am going out of town," he said. "When I

return, I will call on you to discuss . . . that other matter."
He had some difficulty remembering still just what that
other matter had been.

"Certainly, sir."

He returned to the exhibition hall. Ambury fell into
step beside him.

"Are we finally ready to ride?" Ambury asked. "We
will be at least an hour late meeting up with Kendale, and
you know how he can be."

"Yes, let us go." Hell, yes.

"Did you come to a right understanding with the
lady, the way you said you must?"

Darius vaguely remembered blustering something of
the sort before he barged into that storage chamber. His
mind, all his own again, sorted through what had actually happened after that.

"Of course I did, Ambury. If one is firm, right under-
standings can always be achieved, especially with women."

While he mounted his horse, however, Darius admitted the truth of it to himself. Somehow Miss Fairbourne
had turned the tables on him in there. He had roared in
like a lion and bleated out like a lamb.

He hated to say it, but that woman may have made a
fool of him today.